The Hanging of Ruben Ashford

Also by Lauren Small
Choke Creek
Wolf Constellation

The Hanging of Ruben Ashford

a novel

Lauren Small

THE HANGING OF RUBEN ASHFORD

Graphic design: Ace Kieffer

The Hanging of Ruben Ashford is a work of fiction. Names, characters, places, and incidents are the products of the author's imagination or are used fictitiously. Any resemblance to actual events, locales, or persons, living or dead, is entirely coincidental.

A version of chapter fourteen previously appeared as "Thula" in Tendon: a medical humanities creative journal.

2022

BrickHouse Books, Inc.
306 Suffolk Road
Baltimore, MD 21218

Distributor: Itasca Books, Inc.

ISBN: 978-1-938144-90-5

Printed in the United States of America

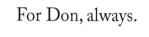

For Don, always.

One

That year they spent the entire month of August on the Cape: Adele, Calvin, Freddie, Eleanor, and Josie. It was 1917, the country was at war, and Josie considered it the height of luxury and selfishness to go away for so long when everyone was supposed to be acting so seriously, applying themselves and doing their part. But the truth was, even though they'd only entered the war in the spring, she was already exhausted by it, by the need to maintain her optimism and confidence and above all her patriotic fervor. So when Eleanor proposed the month on Cape Cod—an escape, she called it, from the dullness and drudgery that had taken over their lives—Josie was surprised and more than a little ashamed at how quickly she agreed.

Then again Josie had always known that when it came to Eleanor, it was best just to go along. The two girls had grown up together in neighboring houses in Brookline, just west of downtown Boston, where Eleanor naturally fell into the role of leader, whether organizing tea parties on her porch or games of tag on the lawn. Adele was the next to say yes to Eleanor's plans. She always seconded Eleanor's schemes, even though she was, relatively speaking, new to the group; the three girls hadn't met until college, when they spent a summer together selling ladies' shoes on Commonwealth Avenue. Eleanor's cousin Freddie was quick to agree. Of course, once Josie said yes, Freddie could hardly say no—not if he wanted her to marry him, that is. He'd proposed to her formally in June and ever since then, while he waited for her to make up her mind, had made pleasing her into his primary preoccupation. Watching him, Eleanor said with her nose turned up, was like watching a ridiculous puppy at play, and every bit as exhausting.

That left Calvin, sensible, levelheaded, dutiful Calvin, the voice of reason. Josie expected him to object, especially since he was the newest to the group and least beholden to Eleanor. Josie had introduced him to the others the previous winter after she met him in the library at Harvard where he was studying for medical exams while she researched the behavior of rats. They needed another man as ballast, she said, so that Freddie wouldn't be in danger of sinking beneath so many females. But even Calvin gave in with nothing more than a resigned smile. He had four months left in his surgical training, and when it was over would be sent overseas to operate in a hospital theater in France. If anyone deserved a break, Eleanor said—giving Josie a wicked grin in triumph because she'd won—it was Calvin.

Only Eleanor hadn't planned the escape to the Cape for Calvin. She'd planned it for Josie, so that she would finally have a full, uninterrupted month to convince her to stop her silly dilly-dallying and agree to marry Freddie. Eleanor wouldn't admit it; she rolled her eyes and affected an air of innocence whenever Josie asked. But Josie knew. Eleanor entertained the exact same opinion as Josie's mother, Cora Berenson, which was that Freddie was a perfectly suitable choice, and Josie needed to get on with it. Even Josie, in her more sensible moments, saw their point. Freddie was a dear, and that he loved her was without question. And yet, something held her back, something she couldn't understand herself or even begin to put into words. And so every morning that August on the Cape, she rose with the expectation that today would finally be the day she would do what everyone expected her to do and say yes.

Only saying yes seemed to be the one thing she was incapable of doing.

She couldn't sleep. The cottage Eleanor had rented for them was entirely unsuitable, far too small. Josie found it claustrophobic, too many people crammed into such a little space. The women shared a dormer bedroom upstairs under the eaves, while the men camped out on a screened porch downstairs. Day after day Josie woke before dawn, turning and turning in the narrow iron cot Eleanor had assigned to her—Eleanor organizing the beds, as she organized everything else, down to the last detail—just as she turned and turned things in her mind. Eventually she took to leaving the cottage as the sky lightened, creeping quietly down the stairs so as not to wake anyone, to take long walks on the beach. How she craved it: the fresh air, the wide-open sky, the view of the bay, stretching unimpeded to the horizon. One morning she would walk east along the shore, the next day west. Whenever she left the others behind, especially Freddie—dear, sweet Freddie—it felt like a betrayal, but she couldn't help it. She needed the time alone, needed the time to think.

Eleanor was right, of course, they all were: it was time to get married. Josie was twenty-seven. She could no longer say she wasn't old enough. She'd long since graduated college, long since established herself as a research assistant in the Harvard psychology department. How happy her mother would be if she married Freddie! How happy they all would be, Adele, and Calvin, and Eleanor most of all. Over and over Josie revisited the prospect of marriage in her mind, imagining herself as Freddie's wife, taking up residence in his Brookline brownstone, kissing him in the morning as he headed off to work in the men's department of his family's department store, welcoming him home in the evening, spending nights by the fire at his side reading and talking or, in the warmer months, on quiet walks through the neighborhood. In time there would be little Josies and Freddies too; that went without saying. It was all so perfect, and seamless, the scenes unfolding in her mind like acts in a play, as if she were watching her life proceed before her through curtains effortlessly opening and closing.

Only—that was exactly it. Marrying Freddie was simply too easy.

Josie would never admit it to anyone—she could hardly admit it to herself—but ever since she was a child, she'd held onto the idea that she was destined for something larger in life, something exciting and challenging and grand. It was her father's fault, no doubt; he'd spoiled her terribly and seeded her mind with these ridiculous ideas. She was an only child, and her father, who'd always wanted a boy, had gotten over his disappointment by treating her the way he would have treated a son. No ambition, no adventure, was out of reach for Josie.

Sometimes in the evening he'd take her to the laboratory of the dye factory where he worked as a chemist and run experiments just to show her how amazing science was. He'd light powders that burned with incandescent, brightly colored flames; change the color of liquids with a drop of dye; send streams of blue light arcing between terminals. Josie loved every minute of it, loved the feel of the cold, smooth laboratory benches beneath her hands, the shelves of gleaming glass beakers and graduated cylinders, the smoky smell of the Bunsen burners. Most of all she loved being with her father without her mother's interference, listening raptly to his sonorous voice as he explained the role of catalysts and reactions, even if she didn't understand every word. To Josie, science was like magic, the transformation of one thing into another, liquids into gases, solids into smoke. The world, she learned, is never what you think it is. In the blink of an eye, it can become something else entirely.

When she went to Boston University and announced her intention to study chemistry, Cora was appalled. Science, she insisted, was entirely unsuitable as a career for a young woman, whose highest calling should be as a wife and a mother. Nevertheless, Josie, with her father's support, stuck with it, even when, as the only woman in her chemistry class, she was subjected to endless teasing and cutting remarks; when her laboratory professor warned her men would never find a woman scientist attractive; and when the teacher of the materials course refused to let her enroll. The only surprise came midway through when she decided on psychology as her major instead of chemistry. On a lark she'd enrolled in the introductory psychology lectures, and they'd changed her life forever. The human mind, she realized, was even more mysterious and intriguing than the natural world, and offered endless opportunities for discovery.

She'd been delighted after graduation when she landed her job in the Harvard psychology laboratory. There she expected to indulge her curiosity and explore her interests. At first she'd found the work, which used rats to focus on learning and behavior, fascinating. Even though she was the only woman in the group, the other scientists took her seriously. That in itself was refreshing. And they valued her opinion too, consulting with her as they organized their experiments.

But lately she'd found herself growing tired of it. She was appalled at her lack of interest, which she judged self-critically as a lack of dedication. Was she really so fickle? But she couldn't help wondering if this was all life held for her: more mazes and more rats. She'd always thought the point of experimenting with animals was to extrapolate their behavior to humans. And human behavior was what interested her the most—what had drawn her to psychology from the beginning. Why did it seem so hard to make the connection?

She was lonely. Even she could see that. When she graduated college, she moved out of her parents' house and took up residence in a Cambridge boarding house for women. She was earning a salary now, and it seemed the responsible—the adult—thing to do. Maybe that had been a mistake. She had plenty of friends, but she still returned each night to an empty room and woke up each morning to the same. Freddie, if nothing else, would be good company. But then again...men's suits? Did she really want to live forever with someone preoccupied with houndstooth and tweeds?

So it went in her mind that summer, as she walked on the beach, round and round, the arguments for marriage and against it. She always walked barefoot—how anyone could go to the beach and not indulge in the pleasure of feeling the sand curl beneath their toes was beyond her—going farther and farther along the Cape Cod shoreline, until finally her mind emptied out, and she sank into the relief of thinking of nothing at all.

The beach was beautiful that summer, especially at the break of day, all but deserted. One morning she watched a fisherman in a canvas hat cast into the surf, the gossamer-thin fishing line flashing across the water full of possibility. Nearby a swimmer paralleled the shore with rhythmic strokes, filled with the purpose Josie felt she so sorely lacked. She carried a net bag with her so that if someone were to see her, they would think she was out for a reason, collecting shells. She was impossibly vain—another one of her faults her mother was quick to point out, and that came, no doubt, from her father spoiling her—and she always worried what people would think of her. And there was nothing she abhorred so much as idleness, her own most of all. But houses were few and far between and she needn't have worried. No one noticed her. She might as well have been invisible. Gulls hopped about, pecking at the scrubby grasses on the dunes, calling loudly to one another. In the distance fishing boats sailed from the port; across the bay, ferries steamed towards Nantucket. The air held the freshness of the dawn, the briny tang of the sea.

So the days passed, until life on the Cape took on a feeling of stasis, of endless return, one day spooling into the next, with Josie no closer to making up her mind about Freddie, no nearer to an answer. Then one morning, when she was far from the cottage, she stepped on a sharp shell and gashed her foot. How painful it was! She tried to walk on it, but could barely manage. The wound was too deep, and the bleeding wouldn't stop.

How ridiculous she looked. Her vanity pierced through her pain as she hobbled on her bloody foot, dressed in a bathing costume, as if she were going to swim—although she never did—with one of Freddie's coats thrown over like a wrap. Her sole nod to propriety was her perfectly proper ladies' hat, which was a nod to her mother—she of proper ladyhood—and a futile attempt to tame her hair, which was a mess of reddish-brown curls. She considered ripping the sleeve off the coat and using it to bind her foot but she wouldn't do that to Freddie. She might take—that is to say, borrow—his things, but she wouldn't dare ruin them. When she looked around, she noticed a brown-shingled house sitting nearby, at the end of a long wooden walkway, where the flat sand gave way to rising dunes. Inside a light burned, and a shadowy figure moved behind the curtains.

Well, then. At least she wouldn't be waking anyone up. She limped up the walkway to the porch and knocked on the door. "I'm sorry," she said when it opened, revealing a tall woman inside with a plain but serious face. "I don't mean to disturb you, only…" Rather pathetically, like a child, she held out her foot.

The woman in the doorway followed Josie's eyes downwards. "Oh, my." She was wearing a light blue wrapper, dark hair flecked with gray falling to her waist. "Come in." Swinging the door wide open, she stood to the side. Then, as Josie bled onto the step, she reconsidered. "No, wait here." She disappeared into the house and returned a moment later with a dishtowel. She bent down, tied it around Josie's foot, then stood and gave her an arm to lean on.

Gingerly, wincing with each step, Josie hobbled inside. The cottage was cozy in a plain but charming way, quite small, even smaller than the one she and her friends had taken. Everything here was on one floor, easily grasped in a single glance, a bedroom on one side, kitchen on the other, sitting room in the middle. It was decorated in the style Josie had always thought of as purely Cape Cod, with shells displayed on the mantelpiece and curtains printed with a sailboat theme. There was a twisted rag rug on the floor, a wooden table with benches, a pair of rattan chairs. She sank gratefully into one of those, trying not to look at her foot. Blood made her lightheaded. She'd always been a bit of a baby when it came to things like that.

Meanwhile the woman disappeared into the kitchen again, returning a few moments later with soap, a basin of warm water, and more towels. In the intervening time she had pinned up her hair and tightened the belt on her robe. She knelt down, unwrapped Josie's foot, took it between her hands, and placed it in the basin. Josie grimaced. It stung. "Sorry," the woman said. "This will hurt. Nothing I can do about that, I'm afraid."

After she had bathed the wound, she wrapped a clean towel around Josie's foot, disappeared once more, this time into the bedroom, and came back with iodine, gauze, and tape. Working studiously, with quick, practiced motions, she dressed the wound. "There." She sat back on her heels and looked up at Josie. "You should be all right now."

Josie wiggled her foot and tentatively put weight on it. It still hurt but was bearable. "Thank you. I can't tell you how sorry I am, barging in on you like this." Although truthfully she wasn't sorry at all. Already she was curious about this tall stranger with the serious face and soft brown eyes. "Forgive me," she said, recovering her manners. "I've forgotten to introduce myself. I'm Josefa Berenson. Everyone calls me Josie."

The woman smiled. "Cornelia Winters. Nell."

"I hope I haven't disturbed anyone else—" Josie said boldly, although she already suspected the answer to her question.

The smile on Nell's face remained but took on a strained quality. "There isn't anyone. Just me."

"Well, then. I won't keep you any longer." For some reason Josie had found Nell's answer surprisingly satisfying. She stood, walked carefully to the door, and waited while Nell opened it for her. With a nod she stepped through to the outside. For a moment she balanced on the porch, testing her weight on her foot. Then she spun around. "I'm here with a group of friends. We've taken a cottage on the beach, closer to the port." It was quite unnecessary to say these things, but she couldn't help it. She found herself wanting to keep talking to Nell, to draw her out. She wasn't ready to leave.

Nell nodded graciously. "That sounds charming."

"It is." Josie struggled for something more to say, but couldn't come up with anything. "I should go now," she said finally. "They'll be wondering about me."

"Of course." Nell stepped back, smiling, her hand on the door. "Good-bye, then."

"Good-bye."

Still Josie lingered. She could feel her face coloring. Thinking of it made her redden even more. Her feelings were always so transparent. It wasn't just her fair skin. She'd never learned how to hide what she thought or how she felt, even though according to her mother, dissembling was one of the most important skills a woman could acquire. In the end she just blurted it out. "Come for dinner tonight. If you can. If you don't already have plans."

Now it was Nell's turn to look away, color coming to her face. "I couldn't possibly. I wouldn't dream of intruding."

"You couldn't do anything worse than what I've done. Please. I'd like to thank you. It's the least I can do." Josie smiled and looked up into Nell's eyes. Nell was a good half-head taller than she was, all bones and angles, while Josie was what her mother, in her affectionate moments, called pleasingly plump. The plains of Nell's face were broad and generous, her eyes warm but also guarded, as if she were holding something of herself in reserve. Lines at the corners of her mouth placed her in the middle of life, a time, Josie thought with envy, when she must be settled in her life, with all the important decisions—like marriage—behind her.

But maybe not all.

Nell was still hesitating, but Josie could feel her smile infecting her, and finally she smiled in return. "All right."

"It's a cottage with blue shutters. You can't miss it. Just head towards the port." She waved a hand in the direction she had come from. "Come at sunset. We'll be on the beach, having drinks." Josie felt a sense of triumph akin to what Eleanor must have felt when she talked them all into this month at the beach: she'd won. For once she wasn't sorry about it. If not for Eleanor, Josie wouldn't be here, and wouldn't have met Nell. "We always meet on the beach for drinks as the sun goes down."

Two

Would she never come? Josie sat on the beach as the sun sank lower in the sky, shielding her eyes from the glare, anxiously looking for Nell, all the while affecting an air of not caring at all. "Just someone I met this morning," she'd said casually to the others when she returned to the cottage with her bandaged foot. "She fixed me up quite nicely, I think, after I was clumsy enough to cut myself." She held the foot out for the others to admire. "I invited her for drinks tonight. After all she did for me, I thought it only right."

But Eleanor thought it wasn't right at all. She resented this intrusion of a stranger into their close-knit group, and made her feelings abundantly plain by angrily flinging the blankets they would sit on onto the sand. Meanwhile Josie sat like a queen in a chair with her foot elevated on the stool Freddie had carried out from the cottage, a demonstration of his devotion. Josie thought it patently ridiculous and told him so, but Freddie would not be swayed. Under no circumstances must she exert herself; she must sit still and rest herself so she would properly heal.

The others bustled about, preparing the drinks and food. Calvin brought a table from the cottage, his long legs striding easily from the dunes to the sand. He was an arresting, imposing man, even in casual trousers and a collarless shirt with rolled-up sleeves. He had prematurely grey hair, a wide brow and strong chin: the kind of face even men called handsome. Josie wondered if Nell would think so too; already she was seeing everything through Nell's eyes—if only she would come.

Adele and Freddie hurried back and forth, ferrying bottles of gin and champagne, beakers of lemon juice and syrup, cheese, bread, a bowl of raspberries, and the mason jars that doubled as drinking glasses. Josie rose once from her chair in an effort to help, but Freddie scolded her and insisted she sit back down—as if, Josie thought with a sudden surge of irritation, they were already married and he was entitled to tell her what to do. He looked rather silly, dressed in a formal striped jacket, tie, and matching trousers, as if he were still at work. Beneath his straw boater, his face was flushed with the heat. But in an effort to please her, he took off his shoes and socks and rolled up his pants so he could feel the sand between his toes. "Utterly delightful," he made a point of saying, and mollified—what lengths he would go to on her behalf!—she repented for her anger and bestowed upon him an angelic smile.

Meanwhile Adele dashed back and forth across the sand, her skirts flying. Adele was like a mother hen, short and round, with freckled skin and light brown hair she wore in a bun at the top of her head like a crest. Adele thought only of others, and was constantly adjusting and settling things for their comfort, whereas Eleanor thought only of herself. Having set out the blankets—her contribution to the evening—she sat down on one with a peeved, immovable air, her chin in her hand, her pretty face set in a pout, still grumbling over Josie's invitation.

Calvin served the first round of drinks as the waves burbled lazily onto the shore and the sun sank lower and lower in the sky, sinking Josie's feelings with it. Across the water gulls called their lament; on the dunes, grasses murmured sadly in the breeze. She will never come, Josie decided at last, wondering at the depths of her disappointment. It was too much. She shouldn't have expected it. Then she spied Nell in the distance, walking towards them on the sand, and Josie's heart rose.

She couldn't help but cry out, "She's coming after all!"

A change came into the air. Around her all activity ceased. Eleanor came to her feet, as did Josie, and this time Freddie didn't even try to stop her. Josie had been wondering how Nell would be dressed; there was so much one could learn from a person's clothes. She looked endearing, wearing a fashionable, if somewhat antiquated, tailored white blouse cinched at the waist with a cloth belt, a long black skirt that ended just above her boots, and a wide-brimmed sunhat. The dark knot of her hair peeked out at the nape of her neck. Now that she was here, Josie was done seeing the others through Nell's eyes, and very much interested in seeing Nell through theirs.

Josie made the introductions.

"So you're Josie's rescuer," Adele said, taking Nell's hands in hers, greeting her warmly, drawing her into the group.

"Anyone would have done the same," Nell said graciously.

"But not so well," Eleanor said, with the frosty arch of a brow, making it clear that at least as far as she was concerned, Nell was an outsider and would always remain so. "That's quite a bandage you gave Josie. You must be a nurse."

"Doctor, actually." Nell cast down her eyes, the hint of a smile on her face. Josie felt a brief thrill as if the conversation were a game of tennis, and Nell had just scored a point.

"Then you and Calvin will have much to talk about," Eleanor said smoothly, returning the volley in her own way. She brought Nell directly to him. "Calvin is our resident surgeon."

"In training," Calvin said with a smile, as he took Nell's hand. "Do you practice in Boston, Dr. Winters?"

"Nell, please. And I'm from Baltimore."

Calvin's eyebrows raised. "You're awfully far from home."

"Yes, I suppose I am," Nell said.

"A woman with an air of mystery," Freddie said. "I like that."

Leave it to Freddie to stumble directly onto the thing no one else would say. Josie poked him in the ribs with her elbow. "Freddie, stop."

She was afraid he would ruin everything. She turned to Nell. "Don't mind him. He has no manners whatsoever but we love him anyway."

I love him, is what she meant to say, but it didn't come out that way.

"Can I offer you a cocktail?" Calvin asked. He was ever so clever at smoothing things over. "We're drinking French 75's, in honor of the war."

"And may it stay far from us," Eleanor interjected, raising her glass.

"But I can make you something simpler if you like."

"Thank you. A cocktail would be fine."

Calvin made Nell's drink then they all sat down, Eleanor on one blanket, Calvin and Nell on another, Freddie alone, and Josie in her chair—rolling her eyes so that Nell would know how silly she thought it was. Adele passed among them, refilling drinks, handing out slices of bread and cheese. For once Eleanor—who always had to be in charge—ceded her the authority.

"The bread isn't very good, I'm afraid," Josie said. "I think it's mostly potato flour. It's all we could find. But the cheese is all right and the raspberries are fresh. Adele picked them this afternoon."

Nell smiled. "It all looks wonderful."

"A doctor," Adele said admiringly to Nell, settling herself next to Eleanor. "It must be lovely to be of use. I'm not good for anything. All I do is sell ladies' hats."

"That's not true at all," Josie said firmly. "You are by far the most useful person I know. We all depend on you, and you know it."

"On the other hand I am utterly useless and wouldn't have it any other way," Eleanor said. She waited for someone to contradict her then huffed when no one did.

"Josie's a psychologist," Adele said. "Did she tell you about her work? She does research at Harvard. She's developed some fine theories. I'd explain them to you, but they're far beyond me."

Josie reddened. She might be terribly vain but one thing she

13

couldn't abide was hearing others sing her praises—especially not in front of Nell. "First of all, I'm only an assistant, and secondly, they're not my theories—"

"Nevertheless," Eleanor said, interrupting. She put a finger to her lips. "Be careful what you say around her. She might use you for one of her experiments."

"Only if you're a rat," Calvin said with a smile.

"Research?" Nell said, turning to Josie. "It sounds fascinating."

"Drudgery, mostly," Josie said. She'd never thought of it before that way, but now that she did, she feared it was only the truth. "Observations and record-keeping."

"Josie is interested in the things people do," Freddie said.

"I ought to be interested in the things *rats* do," Josie said, "given that they occupy so much of my time." She turned to Nell. "Actually it's not what people do that mystifies me, but why. I'm trying to understand the choices people make." Like why I invited you here, she thought, although she didn't say so. Or why I can't bring myself to say yes to Freddie. If Josie were honest about it, she'd begin her research with herself. Goodness knew there was enough to fathom there. "It's something I've often wondered about. Especially since so much of what people do makes no sense whatsoever." She gave Eleanor a pointed look then turned back to Nell. "Lately I've been branching out from psychology and reading up on psychiatry. I'm a great admirer of your Dr. Meyer. He's quite an archaeologist of the human mind."

"Adolf Meyer?" Nell said. "Of Baltimore? I've heard of him, of course, although I can't say I've ever met him."

"Meyer's the chief of the Phipps Psychiatric Clinic at the Johns Hopkins Hospital," Josie explained to the others. "He's quite at the forefront in the psychiatric world. He's developed a theory he calls psychobiology, a grand attempt to unify our understanding of the whole person. She turned to Nell. "Are you familiar with his work?"

Nell shook her head. "I'm afraid I don't know much about psychiatry. I never studied it in medical school." She smiled. "It's all I can do to figure out what's wrong with my patients' bodies, let alone their minds."

"But that's where you're wrong," Josie said. "There's nothing more influential on the body than the mind. If nothing else Sigmund Freud has shown—"

Eleanor rolled her eyes. "Josie, please, you'll bore our guest."

"Not at all," Nell said.

"Don't encourage her," Eleanor said sternly. "She'll most certainly bore me." She stood up. "Another cocktail, Calvin, if you please." As Calvin fixed her drink, she turned to the sea. "Ladies and gentlemen, I believe the sunset is at its peak."

They all stood and fell silent, watching as the sun finished its descent, leaving streaks of crimson in its wake. The air softened and a hush fell over the dunes, broken only by the hiss of the waves across the sand. How beautiful it was, Josie thought, with a shiver of pleasure, and glanced at Nell, to see how she was taking it. Nell had become guarded again, lost in her own thoughts, a veil across her dark eyes. Her skin reflected the last of the sun, giving it the color Josie had seen that morning at her cottage when she asked her to come for drinks. Her eyes lingered on the knot of hair at the nape of Nell's neck, and she found herself thinking of the way it had looked that morning when she first met her, and it fell to her waist.

Nell must have realized she was being watched. She met Josie's eyes, smiled, and for a moment the veil dropped. Josie smiled back, feeling as if they'd created a private bond between them, as if they were the only ones there and had forged a quiet language of their own.

"Is this your first time on the Cape?" Calvin said finally, speaking with the air of a person realizing someone must say something, as if to break a spell.

"Yes."

"We've been coming here for ages," Eleanor said, restoring Nell purposely to her role as outsider. "Freddie and Josie and I. Freddie's family used to have a house in Falmouth but his father sold it after his mother died."

"I'm sorry," Nell said, turning to Freddie, "about your mother, I mean."

"Oh, it's all right," Freddie said. He took off his hat and batted at the air, waving off a sand fly. "It was a long time ago."

"And we'll come again next year," Eleanor said firmly to Nell, "when the war's over and Calvin comes back." Like a general, she was amplifying her fortifications. She might as well have said: without you.

"Will you be leaving soon?" Nell asked Calvin.

"I've a few more months yet."

"The war has changed everything, hasn't it?" Nell said. "You see men everywhere in Baltimore, lining up for the draft." She shook her head. "It's a terrible business."

"It's the same in Boston," Josie said. "Everyone we know is going."

"Only not Freddie," Eleanor said brightly. "His father has pots and pots of money. Everyone says money has nothing to do with it but it always does, doesn't it? Freddie never has to do anything he doesn't want to."

"That's not true," Adele said pointedly to Eleanor. "Freddie always does exactly what Josie wants him to."

Poor Freddie. He looked so pained. He turned away, his face reddening.

"I think," Calvin said, rescuing them all, "what Adele means to say is that it's time for dinner." Ever the gentleman, he gave Nell his arm. "Shall we go in?"

Dinner was roast chicken, canned peas, boiled potatoes, beach plums poached in brandy. Eleanor arranged their seats, putting Josie next to Freddie with Nell at Calvin's side. As cocktails gave way to wine, Josie fell silent, letting the conversation flow around her. She was tired, her foot throbbing, and she was more than a little angry at Eleanor for the things she'd said about Freddie. Freddie didn't say anything about it, but Josie knew Eleanor's words had stung. She put her hand on his arm. She was sorry now she had invited Nell to dinner. She questioned the wisdom of inserting a stranger into such a close-knit group. Eleanor was right. All of their faults seemed suddenly glaringly on view, Josie's most of all.

Why did Freddie always seem to bear the brunt of her impulses? She shook her head. That was a line of thought that bore consideration, but she had no energy to pursue it just now. Instead one of her father's chemistry demonstrations came into her mind. With a stone and a piece of iron, he'd created a spark, and from the spark came fire. "You see," he'd said, grinning at her with a showman's flair, as flames leapt into the air, "from two things entirely inert can come a completely different form of life."

Calvin gallantly kept the conversation going, steering them away from medicine and war to books they'd read, plays they'd seen in the theater, and moving picture shows. As the lanterns burned down, and the room darkened, Josie found herself watching Nell again, the gleam of her skin in the shadowy light. Her hands were surprisingly pale and fine-boned, her voice melodious with a husky current underneath. Throughout the dinner she remained bright and smiling, but the veil was back. Beneath it Josie sensed a deep reserve, a well of sadness. Just as Freddie had said, Nell was a woman of mystery. While she easily kept up her side of the conversation, she gave little of herself away.

After dinner they went outside to look at the stars. The wind had risen, chasing the last of the clouds from the sky, stirring the waves, which slid easily across the sand. Calvin cleared his throat and made an attempt at conversation again, but by now they were all tired and no one answered. Finally Nell broke the silence by thanking them for the evening. Then she excused herself, saying she'd be heading back home now. Calvin offered to walk with her, but Josie was secretly glad when Nell said no, that wouldn't be necessary, she'd be all right on her own.

She headed down the beach into the wind, her hand on her hat. All at once Josie darted after her. When she caught up to her, she put her hand on her arm. Nell turned to her with an air of surprise. "It's my turn to go into the village tomorrow for supplies," Josie whispered in a rush, feeling a bit breathless. "Meet me on the dock at noon."

When she came back, Eleanor eyed her suspiciously. "What was that all about?"

"Nothing," Josie said airily. "I thought she'd forgotten something but she hadn't." There was no reason to lie and she had no idea why she did, but it seemed utterly necessary. Feeling rather guilty, and a touch ashamed, she touched Freddie on the shoulder in atonement. She left her hand there for a moment, waiting for a spark to come, and when it didn't, she let go of him and went inside.

Three

The next day Nell was already on the dock when Josie rode up on the bike she'd borrowed from the cottage. In a basket were the provisions she'd obtained from the village market: heads of lettuce and spinach, a bottle of vinegar, a bag of shiny black mussels, fresh eggs wrapped in a cloth. "I'm starving," she said, winded from the ride. "Let's eat." She led Nell to a cook shack, a ramshackle shed with a grill behind, that sat at the end of the long wooden sailing pier. "It doesn't look like much, but the food's heavenly. Shall I order for you?"

"Yes, please."

"Fish and potatoes," Josie said to the cook. "For two." The food came in paper cones, which they took along with two bottles of beer that Josie fished out of a tub of ice. Then they walked to the dunes and sat down to eat in the shade of a pitch pine.

The dock sat in the heart of the port, a small village of painted wooden cottages strewn along the shore, a squat lighthouse rising in the middle. The sand here was scrubby, strewn with overturned rowboats, bordered by ragged beach grasses and the stunted pines. Here the ferry steamed to Nantucket and fishing boats sailed forth. It was quiet now at midday, in the height of the summer's heat, the fishermen still out. Even the houses clustered on the shore seemed to slumber. A pony tied to a fence dozed, harnessed to a wagon, its tail slapping at flies. A woman strolled by with a basket of melons on her hip while a truck, piled high with crates of chickens, rumbled down the dirt road. Nearby a fisherman sat on a bench, mending nets, and in the harbor a naval frigate rode at anchor.

"Oh," Nell said, as she dug into her lunch. "Delicious." She smiled then used her beer to point at Josie's foot. "How is it?"

"Better. Calvin fixed the bandage for me this morning. I'm just able to get it in my shoe." Josie held her foot out for Nell to see. "He said it's healing well." She laughed. "I think he's disappointed he won't get to amputate."

Nell smiled. "I'm glad."

Nell was right, the fish was delicious, hot and salty, the beer a welcome coolness in the heat of the sun. Josie watched as a group of sailors in naval uniforms came chatting to the cook shack. They must be on leave from the frigate. They took their food to the dock and sat easily on the wide planks, swinging their feet over the water, while they ate.

"I'm sorry about last night," Josie said. Maybe it was the sight of the sailors—the reminder of the war—but she had grown suddenly serious. "I know we didn't put our best foot forward. But they're a good group—even Eleanor."

"They seem awfully fond of you."

"Yes. I suppose they are."

"Especially Freddie."

Josie didn't realize Nell was so perceptive. She had surprised her. What else had she noticed? "We've known each other for years. We grew up together. Eleanor and Freddie are cousins. Their families own department stores up and down New England."

"Ah," said Nell. "Ladies hats."

"Yes, that's right. Where Adele works. And Freddie too. He manages an entire department by himself—men's clothing. He's one of the youngest ever to be a manager like that." It was something Josie was supposed to be proud of and usually was, but just now it seemed impossibly dull. She didn't want to talk about Freddie. She wanted to talk about Nell. She was enjoying this time with her, enjoying having her to herself, and didn't want to spoil it. She leaned forward, feeling once again a connection forming between them, like the magical blue light her father used to set arcing between points in his laboratory. "Tell me about Baltimore. I've never been there. Tell me everything."

"Everything? That's a tall order." Nell rested her chin in her hands, steepling her long fingers. "I suppose I should start by saying I love it there, although I can't say I have much to compare it with. This trip—to the Cape—is the farthest I've ever been from home."

The woman of mystery. She still hadn't explained why she had decided to come so far north.

"Did you do your medical training there?" Josie asked.

"Yes. At Johns Hopkins."

"Isn't that a school for men?"

"Just the university. Not the medical school. Mary Garrett saw to that. I don't suppose you've heard of her?"

Josie shook her head.

"The Baltimore & Ohio railroad heiress. She was a remarkable woman. I met her once. I confess I was a bit intimidated by her. When the university trustees needed money to start a medical school, Miss Garrett said she'd donate it—but only if they agreed to admit both sexes equally." Nell laughed. "She didn't give them much of a choice."

"That was clever of her."

"And fortunate for me. I was in one of the first classes. I owe a lot to Mary Garrett. She inspired me. She lived a life of service. But tell me about you. About the work you do." She lowered her voice. "I think we can safely talk about it now that Eleanor isn't around."

"I'm afraid Eleanor is right, and I will bore you," Josie said. "I work in a psychology laboratory. It's just like Calvin said—most of my research is with rats. We run them through mazes, stimulate them, observe their responses. We're trying to develop models of learning and behavior."

"It sounds fascinating."

"It is," Josie said. "I mean, it ought to be. Only lately—well, lately I've been wondering. I chose to study psychology because of how curious I am about people, about what they think and feel—what goes on behind the veil." She lowered her eyes, hoping Nell wouldn't realize she was thinking of her, too. "My mother says it's an entirely inappropriate avocation for a lady. Far too nosy." She laughed. "By my mother's standards I'm afraid I'm not much of a lady at all. I'm far too interested in science and have virtually no interest in dresses."

Josie took a sip of her beer and put the bottle down on the grass. "Here's what I want to know: why is it that so much of what we do makes no sense?" She gestured towards the sailors on the dock. "Like those men. Why go to war when you know very well you might lose your life? Why not protest or run away? And yet look at them. Off they go in droves, and cheerfully too."

Nell nodded. "I can imagine it would take a lifetime to answer a question like that—if then."

"Yes," Josie said, with a rush of the pleasure that came from feeling understood. "I've spent so much of my time observing rats, but lately it seems to me that all I've gotten is a better understanding of—well, rodents. What's the good, really, of watching them run after bits of food in a maze? What can that really tell us? People are far more complicated—and fascinating. That's why I started reading the psychiatrists, like Dr. Meyer. And Sigmund Freud, the Viennese analyst. He has the most intriguing theory about the unconscious mind."

The ferry was coming in, and Josie fell silent for a moment, watching it. "Freud says that much of the time we have no idea at all why we do the things we do," she said finally. "We're driven by conflicts hidden deeply in our minds. There's no proof for his theories, at least not in terms of the laboratory, but he's had surprising results treating people suffering from mental diseases. I can't help thinking we're at the beginning of a revolution in our understanding of the human mind, if such a thing is ever to be. But no one knows anything definitively—yet."

She laughed. It was easy, she found, to laugh when Nell was around. "Truthfully, it's a mess. People are just too unpredictable."

"That," Nell said, "is something I can definitely agree with."

Was she referring to herself? "Lately I've been wondering if I might have made a mistake in my career," Josie said, growing serious again. "I've always been such a believer in science. I was sure the truth was out there to be captured, proven and pinned down. I thought what I needed was to focus on my laboratory work. Now I wonder if I was wrong about that." She sighed. "Maybe my mother was right and I'm not fit for work in science at all."

"I hardly think that's so," Nell said. Briefly she reached out and rested her hand on Josie's.

Josie looked down at their two hands together, Nell's long tapering fingers resting easily on her own rosy skin. Something was stirring in her, but she couldn't put a name to it, and then Nell's hand was gone.

"But now I'm afraid I am boring you," Josie said. "And what I want to hear is more about you. Do you practice at the Hopkins Hospital?"

"Talk about boring." Nell laughed, a rich, trilling sound that warmed Josie's heart. "No, I see my patients in my house—the same house I grew up in, if you can believe it. I live a few miles from Hopkins, on the west side of town. Mostly I take care of whoever walks through my door. I love my patients, but…" Her smile faded. "Things have gotten harder lately. The neighborhood is changing."

"Changing, how?"

"Becoming poorer. People used to get along with each other. They don't so much anymore. A lot of the older families have moved out." Her eyes took on a sad cast. "Including my parents. They live on the north side of Baltimore now."

"And you? Will you move too?"

"Never," Nell said firmly. "I wouldn't dream of leaving my patients."

The sailors were leaving the dock. As they walked by, Josie felt their eyes on her, evaluating, judging, as if she were an item for sale in a market. Men. How they irritated her sometimes. "I'm supposed to marry Freddie," she said suddenly.

Nell turned to her in surprise. "Supposed?"

"Everyone expects it. His father, my parents, Eleanor. They've practically planned the wedding. Even Calvin thinks it makes sense. All I have to do is say yes."

"And will you?"

"Yes, of course, I will." She dropped her eyes. Just saying it so made it real. Then she was angry. "That is, I don't know what to say. I told Freddie I needed time to decide. It sounds so selfish when I say it like that, doesn't it? He's wanted me to marry him for years, although he only just proposed a few months ago. For a long time, I put him off. First I said I had my studies, then there was my work and getting settled in my research, but now I'm afraid I've run out of reasons." Josie crumpled the paper from the fish in her fist, still feeling irritated—mostly with herself. "I'm in such a muddle. I want to marry Freddie, of course I do. He can be so ridiculous at times, but I'm used to that. And he adores me. There's something special about having someone who cherishes you most of all, isn't there?"

Nell turned her head away and didn't answer.

"We have the chance to make a life together. That's what everybody says." Josie wondered if she should risk the question. The woman of mystery. "Have you ever been—are you—married?"

Nell looked back. "To my work, I suppose."

Josie felt a quickening in her blood, the passion she'd missed ever since she'd come to the Cape—the passion she'd been missing, she realized now, for ages. "I don't want to say marriage is a mistake. My mother would never forgive me if I did." She gave Nell a small smile. "But I've always wanted more. Freddie—it's what I'm afraid of—he says he supports my work, and I believe he does, but once we're married, everything is bound to change. There are so many expectations that come with being a wife. No one says so, but everyone knows it's true. Freddie makes it sound so simple—our being together, I mean. And it's true, we do get along well. We always have. Marrying him—it feels like the easiest thing in the world, like sinking into a soft pillow, so comfortable and secure. Only sometimes—"

"Yes?"

Sometimes it felt like drowning.

They walked together down the road, saying goodbye at the point where their paths diverged. Josie watched Nell walk away, the tall figure in hat and boots, the familiar knot of hair at the nape of her neck. Then she climbed onto the bike and rode back to the cottage. As she pedaled, she found herself growing angry with herself again. Why on earth had she confessed everything about Freddie? It would only give Nell the wrong impression, making her seem childish and indecisive. She interrogated her own feelings, deciding finally she had just needed someone to talk to, someone who wasn't in the group, who could listen with an objective ear. What other reason could there be?

When she got back to the cottage, the others had set up a game of badminton on the sand, but she didn't feel like playing. She spent the rest of the afternoon inside, reading some psychology journals she'd brought with her to the Cape, trying to recapture her sense of purpose. But even inside the shadowy cottage it felt too hot, her clothes tight and binding, and she was restless. She turned the pages, forcing herself to concentrate, chiding herself when her thoughts wandered. All of the articles circled around the same question: How could behavior be predicted and controlled? But what was the point of that, she thought traitorously. Was that really all one wanted out of life? An army of automatons, trained and conditioned, like the sailors on the dock, doing exactly what they were told? She threw the journals aside. Eleanor was right. Suddenly everything about her work did seem boring, even to her.

For a while she slept. She dreamed she was working with a recalcitrant rat, trying to get it to push open a door. When she woke it was evening, and she felt disoriented, caught in the twilight between sleep and wakefulness, a moment of transformation like in her father's experiments, becoming and un-becoming all at once. Finally she roused herself and joined the others on the beach for drinks. The breeze had picked up with the setting of the sun, and she turned her face to it, a welcome breath of coolness, taking off her hat so that the wind played through her hair. She hadn't told anyone about her lunch with Nell, and wondered again about her need to hide the truth. As the darkness deepened, the naval frigate sailed from the port, lights winking from its tall smokestack, and slowly vanished out to sea.

That night Josie slept fitfully. The burden of deciding about Freddie weighed on her, making the room feel stuffy and oppressive. Long before dawn she went outside into the cool air where the sound of the waves, washing onto the beach, sounded only one note in her mind: Nell, Nell, Nell.

Two days later Josie was at Nell's door, knocking frantically. The sun had dazzled her eyes and when the door opened, it took her a moment to find her in the darkness of the cottage. She threw herself, distraught, into her arms. "The most awful thing has happened. It's Freddie. He enlisted. He just told me. He did it before we left for the Cape. Now he will have to report for duty. He *volunteered*. Can you believe it? Such a stupid, stupid thing to do. And it's all my fault. Because I wouldn't say yes to marrying him. He was ashamed of himself for not being drafted—he thinks he has to be brave for me. He thinks he has to *earn* my love. So now he's going off to get himself killed. And he will, you know, get killed. He's not at all suited for it—guns and the rest. He'll never survive. But he thinks he will. Only he isn't thinking at all. He's got such idiotically romantic notions about what war is. He says he wants me to wait for him, and when he comes back—"

"Shh." Nell put a finger to Josie's lips, quieting her. "It's not your fault. You can't possibly know how things will turn out." She took Josie's hands. "Before I came here, I made a terrible mistake. I did something foolish. I gave my heart to someone I shouldn't have. He was married. It ended the way—well, it ended the way I should have known it would from the beginning. He stayed with his wife and I—"

Tears came to her eyes. "I fell apart. I had to get away and this was the farthest place I could think of."

"At least you had a heart to give." Josie reached up and brushed a tear from Nell's cheek. "There's something you should know about me. I'm an awful person. No one knows my faults as well as I do. I'm vain and greedy and selfish, and I always think I'm right. Once I put my mind to something, I never give up. In the end I drive everyone who knows me crazy." She laughed. "It's amazing Freddie wants to marry me at all."

Nell smiled. "It's not too late. You can go back to Freddie and say yes. You can still have an ordinary life."

Josie tipped up her face. Just like that she knew. No, more than knew: she *chose*. "An ordinary life? It's the one thing I never wanted." She cupped Nell's face in her hands. Just touching her, she felt the light arcing, the sparks flying, igniting into flame. She rose up on tiptoe, pulled the pins from Nell's hair, watched it fall to her waist, then kissed her.

Four

Miss Josefa Berenson
1534 McCulloh Street
Baltimore, Maryland

June 17, 1918

Dearest Josie,

There is no easy way to say this so I will just have to plunge ahead and do it. Freddie has been killed. He was at the battle of Cantigny. His commanding officer has sent a letter, saying he acted courageously and with honor, always putting the needs of others above himself. So we can hold onto that and try to take some comfort in it.

Eleanor asked me to write to you about it—she's too upset to do it herself. She's beside herself with grief and furious with Freddie for enlisting when he didn't have to. I would be lying if I said she wasn't angry with you, too. She still holds you responsible for not marrying him. But you mustn't blame yourself. Freddie volunteered before we even left for the Cape. Even if you had said yes, he would still be gone. He made his choice and there was nothing any of us could do about it.

I wonder if you have heard from Calvin? As far as I know, he's still working in the hospital at Boulogne sur Mer with the Harvard group. He wrote to me a few months ago and said he was doing well. I suppose he means as well as one can, given the situation. Amputations and operations—I can't imagine and frankly don't even want to try. It's too awful to contemplate. When I think back to last summer and our weeks on the Cape, it all seems so distant to me now. Sometimes it feels completely unreal, the peacefulness we all felt—our moment of happiness. The lucky moment when you met Nell. How any of us will survive this war unchanged is beyond me.

I want to share with you some good news. I am to be married. My betrothed is a widower with two young boys, so I will soon be in the happy midst of a family of my own. Don't be angry with me, Josie. You know it's what I've always wanted. I'm not like you. I am not so brave in life. And I don't have any other aspirations. As a wife and mother, I hope to finally find the fulfillment in life I have always longed for.

Please give my best to Nell. I hope this letter finds you both well. If you are ever in Boston, and I hope you will be soon, please come by. You will find me as Mrs. Charles Forester on Beacon Street.

Until then I remain affectionately,

Your Adele

Five

Nell woke in the middle of the night to a knock on her bedroom door. She sat up in bed and slid her feet to the floor. "Esme?" She opened the door to find her cook on the other side. "What is it?"

"Mr. Wright," Esme said. "He just came to the kitchen door. He says it's time."

"Tell him to wait for me. I'll be right there."

Nell closed the door, pinned up her hair, then pulled a skirt and blouse out of the wardrobe, an apron with a bib. No, not that one, it was clean and freshly ironed. The one out of the hamper from yesterday. It was bound to get soiled again. It was mid-September but the weather was still beastly hot, oppressive and stultifying. Would fall never come? When they went to bed, Josie had left the windows open to the night air, the shutters thrown wide, hoping for a breeze, but nothing stirred.

Nell dressed by the light of the streetlamps, a sulfurous glow, feeling the excitement tempered by anxiety that moments like this always brought. She moved quietly, trying not to wake Josie, but she woke anyway. She turned in bed, murmuring sleepily, "Is everything all right?"

"Yes. It's fine. It's just Mrs. Wright. She's gone into labor." Nell pulled on her boots then reached down, brushing the wild curls that Josie despaired of, but that Nell loved, from her face, and gave her a light kiss. "Go back to sleep."

It had been over six months since Josie had secured her position as a research assistant to Dr. Adolf Meyer at the Phipps Psychiatric Clinic and moved to Baltimore, taking her place at Nell's side. Still Nell couldn't help feeling a bit surprised every time she saw Josie there, as if she were somehow the result of a magical trick, as if Nell had conjured her up. At the Cape, Adele had called her Josie's rescuer, but the truth was Josie had rescued her. She'd been lost, with no idea of how to go forward, when Josie opened up to her an entirely new, and unexpected, world. Now she couldn't imagine living any other way. She cast an affectionate glance at her beloved, whose light snores announced she'd fallen back into sleep, then still fumbling with her hat, slipped out the door.

Esme had already gone downstairs. She was nothing but efficient, Esme Dubois, the West Indian cook who'd been in Nell's family since Nell was a child. Esme had been young, a childless widow, when she came to work for the Winters. She took on the intimate, domestic activities Nell's mother had so little interest in, forever securing Nell's affection. Letitia Winters enjoyed theater, concerts, card games, and dinner parties—all aspects of life played out on a larger social stage— exactly the kind of activities Nell's father, Mercer, who'd spent his life in contentment working quietly in a bank, eschewed. Esme never remarried, although Nell suspected the cook had her share of suitors; she was as fiercely private as she was independent and kept such things to herself. To Nell's great relief, when Mercer retired and her parents moved out of the city, leaving their house to Nell—her sister had long since married and decamped to Chicago, where she happily raised two boys—Esme declared she had no interest in going and stayed put, making theirs a cozy household of two, until Josie arrived, growing the household to three.

Nell followed Esme quickly past the third-floor office that once had belonged to her father, and that Josie had comfortably settled into for work at home, then down the broad front staircase to the second floor, walking, walking, the voice of her medical school preceptor sounding in her mind: *Walk, gentlemen—and ladies. A doctor walks and never runs.* Then down the long corridor past the bedrooms that had once belonged to herself and her sister, and that she'd fashioned into a parlor and dining room when she set up her practice on the first floor: waiting room, examination room, dispensary, and office. Only Esme's room had survived unchanged, and was still exactly where she wanted it to be: near the narrow, winding back stairs that led to the kitchen. There Nell found Jonah Wright waiting for her, his hat in his hands, shifting on his feet. It didn't matter how many times she told him to come to the front door and ring the bell; he was a patient just like everyone else. But he was also a colored man and as a colored man insisted on knocking at the back door. It was no use asking him to sit either. Esme, warming coffee on the stove, gave Nell a look that said as much. But he would drink, Nell could make sure of that, thrusting a mug of hot coffee into his hands while she took one of her own. "We'll both be needing it."

She went to her office and grabbed the medical bag that stood ready on the shelf for times like these. Quickly she double-checked her supplies: scissors, hypodermic syringe, Lysol, two sterile umbilical ties—in case of twins—Argyrol tablets, artery clamps, sutures, silver nitrate drops for the baby's eyes. Then walking—always walking—she returned to the kitchen. At the last minute she slipped two candles from the pantry into her pocket. "All right," she said to Mr. Wright. Then to Esme, "Try to go back to sleep," although she knew she likely wouldn't; Esme was famous in the household for her insomnia. Nell smiled and put a hand on Esme's arm as she swept past, whispering, "Thanks." Then she took Mr. Wright to the front door and stepped back as he left the house, letting him lead the way.

The Wrights lived near North Avenue and Mount Street, a twenty-minute walk away. This was the fourth child Nell had delivered at their home, and she well knew the way there, but she also knew Mr. Wright would feel better taking her there, maintaining some measure of control. He was a worrier, always imagining the worst, although he would never admit it. She sensed his anxiety in the tenseness of his shoulders, the quick, jabbing strides of his walk. Anything she could do to bolster his spirits would be a good thing.

She followed him up McCulloh Street, with its tall, genteel, three-story row houses on either side, the street quiet and empty at this time of night. The wind was stirring now, swirling dust on the street into dancing dervishes, bringing the familiar sour smell of sewage and rotting garbage from the inner basin of the harbor, a mile to the south. Lightning crackled in the distance with a low rumble of thunder.

Now and then they passed a motorcar parked on the road. The cars were still a bit of a novelty to Nell, although they had become increasingly common in the city in a way she found maddening, barreling down the downtown arteries, the noise and speed of them unnerving. She much preferred horse-drawn carriages, although the smell of manure rankled—the mayor had yet to accomplish the street cleaning he had promised—and was particularly pungent tonight in the heat.

Mr. Wright didn't speak and neither did she. She had learned not to try to strike up a conversation with him, nor expect anything more from him than the terse "Yes, Ma'am" and "No, Ma'am" that characterized his answers to her questions. He had been born in Baltimore; this Nell knew from his wife, who in contrast to her husband was quite chatty. His parents had been enslaved in Virginia, and had made their way to Baltimore at the end of the Civil War where they found work in a factory on the east side. Wright's move to the west side represented progress of a sort, a change from manual labor to a life in service. He worked for a wealthy family in Bolton Hill where he doubled—or rather tripled—as butler, carriage driver, and jack-of-all-trades. His wife, on the other hand, had lived on the west side her entire life. She came from a long line of free black Baltimoreans, going back for generations. She was confident and sunnily optimistic, a balance to her husband's gloom. These were good qualities to have, Nell thought, when you approached the birth of your fourth child.

Nell had delivered them all: two girls and the youngest, a boy. He would be two now, coming on three. As Nell recalled, he looked much like his father, with wide, anxious eyes and ears that stuck out in an affectionately comical way.

Strictly speaking this wasn't Mrs. Wright's fourth delivery; it was her fifth. Nell had attended the first one a dozen years ago, just after she'd finished her medical training and opened her practice. She'd lost that baby and had never quite gotten over it, although she knew she ought not blame herself. The baby had emerged with the cord wrapped tightly around his neck, lifeless and still, and there was nothing she could do about it. To her great relief the Wrights hadn't held it against her, coming to her for subsequent births, when they might have relied on any of a number of unlicensed midwives, both white and colored, who plied their trade throughout Baltimore. Or the faith healers who set up shop in churches and halls throughout the city, practicing their own brand of medicine, often doing as much harm as good. But Mrs. Wright was adamantly progressive, insisting on a "real" doctor—even if that doctor, Nell thought with a smile, was a woman.

Mr. Wright turned off McCulloh into one of the narrow west-side alleyways where the colored folk lived. Here the houses were smaller and more cramped, huddled in the darkness. The street was unpaved, thick with grit and dust, with planks of wood across the worst spots where mud collected when it rained. Despite the late hour, the neighborhood was lively and awake, people sitting outside on their front stoops, hoping to catch a cool breeze. They passed women gathered in groups, laughing easily, calling out to children or rocking babies in their arms. Several nodded or murmured greetings as they went by. Someone had made a fire in a tin drum and was grilling sausages, spilling spicy smoke into the air. Chickens roosted in a box beneath a tree. Men, hunched over a card game, lifted their caps to the lady doctor. In the gutter a feral pig rooted in a pile of trash—another scourge the mayor had promised, and failed, to eliminate. He might leave the pigs alone, since at least they kept the garbage under control and for many families provided an important source of food.

The Baltimore divide. Nell had learned the term as a schoolgirl in geography class. The teacher stood in front of the classroom pointing with a long wooden stick at a map of their hometown. A *divide*, she intoned, was a line of high ground forming the division between two river valleys, in their case the Gwynns Falls to the west and the Jones Falls to the east. To the south was the harbor, to the north the green stretches of Druid Hill Park, and in between, their neighborhood: West Baltimore.

Even as a child Nell knew the term had another meaning, harder to pin down but far more telling: the divide that ran through her neighborhood, separating the airy north-south avenues where the white people lived from the cramped east-west colored alleyways. The Baltimore she knew was not one city but two, or rather any number of cities, filled with people conducting their lives in close, overlapping proximity to one another while at the same time remaining infinitely far apart. The racial divide determined everything in her hometown: which streetcar you rode on, where you walked and where you shopped, where you ate, with whom you spoke, where you worked, where you worshiped. If you were unlucky enough to be sent to war, the divide determined which regiment you served in, and if you died, it dictated where you were buried.

When Nell became a doctor, she'd determined to treat colored and white equally. People were people, illness was illness, suffering was suffering, no matter the color of your skin. Over the years she'd learned that the diseases her patients suffered from depended largely on where they lived. There were the colored streets the doctors called "lung alleys" for their markedly high rates of tuberculosis, and where typhoid fever peaked every summer. The malaria that came every autumn, the smallpox that cropped up in the winter—all hit black Baltimore the hardest. The divide even determined where her patients were treated when they were hospitalized, the colored sent to the segregated wards at Johns Hopkins or to Provident Hospital.

Politics, class, money, religion: all these things played a role in the scissoring of her city into its maze of neighborhoods. But mostly race. Always race. Nell was never so much aware of that fact as on nights like these, when she followed Mr. Wright to his home. No matter how much she knew *of* the Wrights, she never really felt as if she *knew* them. They lived less than a mile away from each other but they might as well be on different planets. As long as they came in through the back door of her house, and she used the front, there would be a distance between them. That to her was the final meaning of the Baltimore divide: how deeply it ran through the human heart.

Just as they reached the Wrights' house, the rain broke with a great peal of thunder, and a flash of lightning split the purple night sky. Nell dashed inside, shaking the rain from her hat, calling, "Mrs. Wright? It's Dr. Winters. I'm here."

"Goodness," Nell heard a cheerful voice calling from the upstairs, followed by a groan. "Where have you been? My husband taking his time?"

Jonah Wright shook his head, and then he led Nell to the room where his wife was waiting and stepped aside as she went in.

Six

Later that morning Josie was in the dining room, eating breakfast, when Nell came home.

"It's a girl," Nell said. "Another girl. Can you imagine?" She looked giddy and exhausted. "That makes three for the Wrights, and only one boy. They're doing well, baby and mother. Delivered by candlelight." Then she frowned. "Still no electricity in the house, or running water. I'll have to write again to the *Baltimore Sun*. They—"

Josie stood up and greeted her with a kiss. "The letter can wait." She took Nell's hands and led her to the table. Nell, Josie had learned, never thought of herself where her patients were concerned—or rather only thought of herself last. "Now sit down and eat. And don't even try to tell me you don't have time." She rang a bell and Margaret Sanders, the young colored woman who came in daily to help with the housework, appeared with a tray of hot coffee, rolls, butter and marmalade.

"Thank you, Margaret," Josie said. "Now, there, good," she added, as Nell sank into a chair. Margaret exited with her eyes downcast, a shy smile on her face. Despite the fact that Josie had been living in the McCulloh Street house since the spring, she had the feeling Margaret had never gotten used to her. Neither, Josie suspected, had Esme. They never said a word about it, but secretly Josie thought they both found her "arrangement" with Nell to be comical. More than once she'd caught them exchanging meaningful glances, as if to say: why take a woman into your bed when you could have a perfectly good man?

Josie leafed through the morning mail while Nell perused the newspaper. It was a lovely day. The night's rain had finally put an end to the heat, bringing the coolness of fall into the air. The window overlooking the garden was open, letting in the sound of birds singing. On the mantel a clock companionably ticked. Josie found the dining room, which still held traces from the days when it had been Nell's bedroom—books she'd read as a child, watercolors she'd painted in her young, "artistic" days—charming. Nell kept telling her to make any changes to the house she wanted—to put her stamp on it—but Josie insisted she wouldn't change a thing.

"The Ladies' Auxiliary is holding another rally for women's suffrage," Nell said, shaking the paper out. "This one's tonight at six, outside City Hall. Maybe that will finally get the mayor's attention." She smiled and rolled her eyes. "Hope springs eternal. I'll go by after I finish with my last patient. Meet me there, won't you?"

"Of course."

Nell turned the page. "Hutzler's is having a sale on ladies' boots. I just might have to look into that." Then she frowned. "How strange."

Josie looked up from the letter she was reading. "What is it?"

"It says here that Ruben Ashford's been arrested for murder."

"Who?"

"Ruben Ashford." Nell's frown deepened. "I know him. That is, I know his family. I treated his mother once for typhoid fever. They live on Lemmon Street. It's not far from here. That was a long time ago, at least ten years, I think. Ruben was just a child. His father was a blacksmith. I remember that. His mother worked as a domestic. They're a colored family, entirely ordinary as far as I could tell, better off than some." She studied the newspaper. "It says here that he was working at Rosewood. He killed a teacher there—a white woman."

"Rosewood?" Josie said.

"It's an asylum for feeble-minded children. It's in the county. I've never seen it, but I've heard of it. I referred a child to it once years ago. Poor thing just wasn't developing." Nell lifted her coffee cup then put it back down. "I still remember Ruben when his mother was sick. He stood at the back of the room while I tended to her. He couldn't have been older than eight at the time, maybe nine. He looked absolutely terrified. He must have been awfully attached to her. But he never said a word. I had the feeling he was painfully shy." She put the cup down. "How could someone like that become a murderer?"

"Of all the choices a person could make," Josie said, toying with her own coffee cup. "To kill someone—it's so extreme, isn't it? It makes you wonder." She grew thoughtful. "There's a psychological question for you. Maybe it wasn't a choice at all, at least not consciously so. Maybe it was just impulse. But even impulses have to come from somewhere. Dr. Freud would say—" She saw the look on Nell's face and broke off. "Sorry. I'm going on and on when you're so upset." She took Nell's hand. "How awful to think you knew him."

"I don't know what to think. But it must be true. It says here that he confessed."

Nell shivered, as if shaking off the news. Then she turned back to the newspaper, and Josie returned to the mail. Another letter from her father had come today, but still nothing from her mother. Cora Berenson hadn't written once since Josie moved to Baltimore. She'd been furious when Josie announced her refusal to marry Freddie, and her anger had only hardened when Josie had announced she would be leaving Boston for Baltimore. Cora had no compunction about letting her feelings be known. Josie had hoped in time she would change her mind, or at least soften. Apparently, she learned as she read through her father's letter, not yet.

She put the letter down. She'd write back later. One way or another, she'd have to write to her mother, too. She sighed. No easy solution to that problem. Her mother was right about one thing; Josie still felt guilty for Freddie's death, even though she knew she wasn't responsible. She still couldn't think of him without pain and regret.

Freddie hadn't been right for her for reasons she understood now, even if she hadn't understood them at the time. But he would have been right for someone else. Freddie would have made a wonderful husband. The world was poorer without him.

"There's more news today from Dr. Blake today," Nell said after a time. "He says there's still no flu in Baltimore."

"That's a relief," Josie said. The city's health commissioner had been consistently reassuring all summer long about the Spanish influenza. It was nothing to worry about, he said, just the ordinary grippe they'd seen before. Common sense measures—plenty of fresh air and rest—was all that was needed to keep it at bay.

"I suppose so," Nell said, although she sounded distinctly doubtful. But she didn't say anything more about it, and Josie let it go.

Nell returned to the newspaper. "My good friends the Haberstams have returned from their California tour," she said as she turned the page. "I will have to take you to meet them sometime. And the Elks are holding another Liberty bond rally." She stabbed a finger at the paper. "Oh, and Mrs. Winston Bryce of Roland Park—do I know the Bryces?" Nell thought for a minute then shook her head. "No, I think not, although they must live near my parents. In any case it says that Mrs. Bryce has gone to Richmond to stay with her sister during her confinement."

"Bryce? Richmond? Are you sure?" Josie frowned. "That's odd."

"Odd?" Nell said. "Why?"

Before Josie could answer, James Horne stuck his head into the room. "Sorry to interrupt, Dr. Winters, but the waiting room is full." He turned to Josie. "Morning, Miss Berenson."

"Good morning, James," Josie said with a smile. James, Nell's assistant, was a wonder, a graduate of the Colored High School, who was spending a year working for Nell while he prepared to go to pharmacy school. He kept Nell on schedule, managed her dispensary, and—according to Nell—no one could better coax a smile from a child frightened by the doctor than James. Having gangly limbs and an appealing face with warm brown eyes didn't hurt. Much in his favor, as far as Josie was concerned, was that James took her presence in the household in stride.

Nell stood. "Sorry," she said to Josie.

"Go." Josie made a shooing motion with her hands. "Off with you."

It was time for her to leave for work, too. She fastened her hat as she went downstairs. Quickly she walked past Nell's office and examination room, then with a wave to James, who was in the dispensary, and a nod to the patients in the waiting room, she left the house. She was glad about the Wrights—a bit of good news to temper Nell's worries about Ruben Ashford. But mostly Josie was curious about Mrs. Winston Bryce, who Josie knew very well was nowhere near Richmond, but was firmly established as a patient on the Johns Hopkins surgical ward. And that, she decided, was something that very much needed looking into.

Seven

Winston Bryce's wife, Evangeline, had arrived at the Johns Hopkins Hospital three days earlier, suffering from an ingestion of lye. The surgeons had operated on the young woman immediately to stabilize her throat, which was badly burned. The incident, her husband said, was the result of a terrible accident, but he refused to say anything more about it, even when closely questioned by the doctors.

The surgeons had called in Dr. Meyer to consult. Mr. Bryce stuck to his story, even when closely questioned by the chief psychiatrist. Meanwhile Mrs. Bryce was too ill to speak for herself. No one doubted Mr. Bryce's sincerity; he was clearly distraught, loved his wife deeply, and had yet to leave her side. But if the lye were as innocent as he claimed, why cover it up with a story in the newspaper?

That was exactly the question Josie put to Dr. Meyer when she arrived at the clinic that morning. She found him in his laboratory, studying a slide under a microscope.

"Winston Bryce is lying, of course," she said. "The question is why."

"Hmm," Meyer said. And then, apropos to nothing, "Cerebellum. Fascinating." Finally he tore himself away from his microscope to give Josie his full attention. "Gone to Richmond? Is that what he said? In the *Sun*?"

"Yes. I thought you ought to know."

Meyer was a small man, small enough for Josie to meet eye to eye. It was a feeling she found quite disconcerting. Meyer was famous in psychiatric circles, both for the advanced, modern care he gave to his patients in the Phipps Psychiatric Clinic and for his theory of psychobiology, which purported to understand people as whole organisms, uniting body and mind. But Meyer's interests ranged widely, and whenever Josie went to see him in his laboratory, she was just as likely to find him examining the brains of an exotic animal, reptile, or bird as writing in a patient's record. She wondered what he was looking at under his microscope now. Parrot? Ferret? Anything was possible.

Her position as Meyer's assistant required her to be available to him for whatever he needed. That encompassed everything from writing summaries of patients' treatments to ferrying brain tissue in jars of formaldehyde from his laboratory to the storage vaults in the basement, a task she still hadn't managed to get used to; the brains, floating in the liquid, wiggled back and forth in a spooky fashion like squiggly worms as she walked. She helped him run his experiments—thankfully never on rats—and was gratified when he allowed her to pursue her own research interests on the psychology of choice, most often recruiting hapless medical students as her subjects.

She loved assisting him with his patients. Mental illness, she'd learned from Meyer, was a tricky business, and it was often premature to speak of cures. But every patient who landed in the Phipps Clinic, Meyer insisted, had a history, and the more one knew about it, the better one could be at fashioning effective treatments. He and his staff subjected each patient to a thorough examination on admission, both physical and mental, including a detailed accounting of their background. No detail was unimportant, Meyer said; although once Josie heard one of his resident psychiatrists complain that Meyer expected him to know everything about his patient, from the color of his eyes to the color of the paint on his bedroom walls.

Often Meyer called in a patient's family to give their perspective on their sick relative, thereby gaining important information on symptoms, duration of the illness, and the like. But sometimes he still wanted to know more, especially when he suspected that something in a patient's record was missing—or hidden. At times like these he sent Josie out into the community to visit a patient's home or place of employment, speaking to family, associates, and friends, gathering information. She'd developed a kind of fearlessness in these interviews, and had a style of her own—one she suspected Meyer might not always approve of. But she often was able to get results that no one else could find. She typed up her findings into carefully written reports that she turned over to the psychiatrist, to be shared with the rest of the staff as he saw fit. She was gratified at the trust he showed in her, and more than once had the satisfaction of seeing her work influence a patient's treatment—for the better.

Most of all what she loved was leaving the world of rats behind for the messy unpredictability of human life. Her work at Phipps was ever challenging, but also surprising and satisfying. That, coupled with her relationship with Nell in their McCulloh home, left her eminently satisfied with her Baltimore life.

Now she waited for Meyer to decide what was to be done with Evangeline Bryce. She felt the great psychiatrist's eyes on her as he reflected. Officially Meyer might be known as the dean of American psychiatry but unofficially, in the halls of Phipps, he was known as the Mind Reader. All Josie could hope was that he couldn't read hers.

"That is most concerning," Meyer said finally, his hand stroking his beard. He was an imposing man, but also charming, although somewhat stiff in appearance and formal in an Old World way, his Swiss upbringing betraying itself in his rigidly correct manners and German-accented English. His hand had a slight tremor—the reason, Josie had once heard, he had abandoned his original ambition of surgery for psychiatry—which he often concealed by tucking it into his jacket pocket. He put it there now as he answered her. "Most concerning, indeed. I suppose we'd better find out more about the situation. Look into it, Miss Berenson, won't you please?"

"Yes, Dr. Meyer, of course." Josie hid a smile as she left the laboratory, having achieved exactly the outcome she'd hoped for.

An hour later she was in the back seat of a motorcar, being driven by Meyer's own chauffeur to the Bryces' home. Good that the rain had stopped. The windows on the car were open, and as the driver took her out of the city, the breeze rushed in, filled with a delightful crispness. Josie shivered pleasantly and held onto her hat. Autumn seemed finally to have arrived, and although most of the leaves had yet to turn, a few early achievers, tinged russet and gold, glinted in the sunlight and gathered in windblown clumps on the roads. Crushed under the wheels of the car, they released a heady scent.

She'd never quite gotten over the advent of motorcars, never expected to love them the way she did. To the long list of her faults that her mother was ever eager to enumerate—vain, greedy, and selfish—she added one more: reckless. Speed exhilarated her. Faster, faster, she wanted to shout to the driver. But he was a professional and guided the car with caution. She couldn't wait to learn how to drive one of these contraptions herself.

The Bryces lived in Roland Park, a leafy suburban neighborhood a few miles north of Baltimore, with winding roads and a country feel. Josie had been there twice before, both times on visits with Nell to her parents. The Winters's reception of her had been frosty, with Letitia Winters directing her remarks pointedly to Nell while Mercer said little at all. Josie had the feeling nothing would make the Winters happier than if she were to decamp for Boston and leave their daughter behind. Neither had yet to publicly acknowledge the truth of her relationship with Nell. How clever, Josie had heard they said to others, for our daughter to take on a boarder, to share expenses.

Nell declined to press them on it, preferring to keep the peace. Josie could hardly blame her. She'd never been brave enough to tell her parents the truth about the reason she'd moved to Baltimore: because she'd fallen in love with the person she wanted to spend her life with.

Instead she'd made vague comments about work opportunities at
Phipps. Her father, she suspected, knew the truth, and her mother
probably did too, although she would never say so. Speaking of such
things, to Cora, was simply unseemly, and a betrayal of her ideal of a
woman as wife and mother. The closest she'd come was in her parting
words to Josie: You'll be doomed, she'd warned darkly, to a life without
marriage—or children.

The remark had stung. Josie cared little about marriage, but she
hadn't closed her mind to the idea of having children. Perhaps she
would want to be a mother one day. How she was to reconcile the two
things, she had no idea. If children were the price she had to pay for
fulfillment in love and work, so be it. She considered her feelings on
the subject too contradictory and messy to share with anyone, even
Nell. Nell had never broached the subject with her. Josie assumed that,
at thirty-eight, Nell was simply too old to be thinking of children.

The driver steered carefully to the side to avoid a carriage—the
horse lifted its head to gawk at the roaring machine but didn't spook—
and turned onto a street lined with well-appointed houses of stone or
brick, surrounded by lush gardens. The road was still damp from the
night's rain, water droplets glistening on hedges and trees. The Bryces'
home was covered in grey stucco, half-hidden by boxwoods. The driver
pulled to a stop in front.

"Thank you," Josie said. "Please wait for me here."

She walked up to the porch and rang the bell. A moment later the
door opened, revealing a young woman in a maid's uniform, a blond
braid tucked beneath her white cap. "Yes?"

"Josefa Berenson from the Johns Hopkins Hospital." Josie handed
the maid her card. "I'm here about Mrs. Bryce."

"Mrs. Bryce is in Richmond, attending to her sister," the maid
said automatically, studying the card. Then her face reddened, and she
clapped a hand over her mouth. "That's what I'm to say if anyone asks."

"Of course," Josie said with a smile. "Is there anyone else I might
speak with?"

"There isn't anyone else. Just Mr. and Mrs. Bryce, and they're…"

"In Richmond?"

The maid mutely nodded.

"I see." Josie fell silent for a moment. "Then I guess it will just be you and me." She pushed purposely past the maid into the house.

"Oh," the maid said, then again, "Oh." She scurried after Josie. "Miss, please, I don't think, that is, Mr. Bryce is most insistent that no one come in when he's not here."

Josie was already halfway down the front hall. "You know as well as I do that neither Mr. or Mrs. Bryce is in Richmond. She is in the hospital, and he is at her side." She frowned at the maid. "I believe what you want to say is that Mr. Bryce is most insistent his wife have a full recovery, isn't that so?"

"Yes, miss." The maid swallowed hard. She was wringing her hands, turning Josie's card into a twisted mess.

"Good. Then I expect you will cooperate with me, just as Mr. Bryce would want."

The maid averted her eyes but didn't say anything. Josie turned from the hall into the parlor, a room large enough to run the length of the house. It had several seating areas, a grand piano, a stone hearth, and windows overlooking the garden. It was tastefully decorated, with a plush carpet on polished wood floors, flowered curtains on the windows, chairs upholstered in leather or silk. But it had an empty, unused feel; no magazines or books left open on the tables, no sign of tea cups or reading glasses, no throw rugs left casually about for chilly evenings. Josie chose one of the chairs and sat down. "Now then, Miss…?"

"Harmon," the maid said. "Sally." She had followed Josie into the room, and stood nervously watching her, with a stricken air.

"A pleasure to meet you, Miss Harmon," Josie said with a reassuring smile. "Won't you please sit down?"

Sally hesitated then, with the air of someone who had no choice, perched on the edge of a sofa.

"Thank you," Josie said. She beamed at her. Then she grew serious. "I want to say how sorry we are about your mistress." She lowered her voice. "We know about the lye. I'm just here to try to understand how it happened."

"It was a mistake," she said automatically as before. "An accident. Mr. Bryce told me so. I wasn't here when it happened. It was on a Thursday afternoon." She looked expectantly at Josie, and when Josie didn't say anything, added, "I have Thursday afternoons off."

Josie nodded.

"Mr. Bryce said it was the cook's fault. She mixed up Mrs. Bryce's medicines. She's gone now. Mr. Bryce fired her."

"I see." Josie pursed her lips, thinking. Then she tried a different tack. "Tell me about your mistress. Is she kind?"

"Oh, yes, miss, most kind." The maid spoke gratefully, apparently relieved at the safer course this conversation had taken.

"I'm glad to hear it," Josie said. On the table next to her was a needlework basket. She lifted the top casually and peeked inside. "Does she like to do needlework?"

Sally hesitated. "Yes, miss."

The insides of the basket were a mess. Several unfinished pieces had been crushed into a ball. The thread was a tangle of knots. There were no needles or scissors. Josie put the basket down. "But perhaps not recently?"

Sally averted her eyes and didn't answer.

"And the piano? Does Mrs. Bryce play?" The piano was closed, with no music out, as if it hadn't been touched for a long time.

"Yes, miss." Sally's face reddened. "That is, she used to."

Josie walked to the window, pushed aside a drape, and looked outside. "Perhaps Mrs. Bryce likes to garden when the weather is nice." The garden looked as if it might have been lovely at one time, but was badly in need of tending now. The flowerbeds were overgrown, thick with weeds, and the roses needed pruning.

Sally didn't say anything.

Josie turned to her directly. "How does your mistress spend her time?"

Sally bit down hard on her lip. "Mrs. Bryce has delicate nerves. Mr. Bryce says she tires easily. Most days I'm to leave her to rest and not disturb her."

"Then perhaps you will show me where Mrs. Bryce rests when she is at home."

"I don't think—" The maid stood up, clearly distraught.

"Shall I go look for myself?"

Sally led Josie up the stairs, her eyes downcast. She opened one of the doors on the second floor and stood aside as Josie walked in. It was a lovely bedroom, bright and airy, with a large, four-poster bed, delicate fabrics, a window overlooking the street. But it had the same empty, unlived-in feeling. The mirror above the dressing table had been removed, and the knitting basket held only yarn, no needles. There were no perfume bottles on the table, nothing sharp or breakable in sight. She stepped closer to the window. It had been nailed shut. This, Josie thought with sadness, was the room of a woman who was very much cherished and loved. A woman who was also very ill, and that someone had been trying very, very hard, against all odds, to fix. She stepped back into the hallway. On the outside of the door was a sturdy lock, the kind meant to keep someone in.

"I think," she said softly to Sally, "you had best show me now where you keep your lye."

Sally had the miserable look of someone who had realized it's no use anymore trying to pretend. Defeated, she dumbly led Josie downstairs to the kitchen. She pointed to a brown bottle on a shelf above the sink. "Mrs. Bryce's tonic. She takes it several times a day."

Josie examined the bottle. It was for nerves, one of those "patent" medicines Dr. Meyer railed against. Most of them were worthless. Some did real harm. She put the bottle back. "And the lye? The bottle the cook confused for Mrs. Bryce's tonic?"

Sally led her to a room with a pair of slate laundry tubs. She opened a cupboard above one of the tubs and pointed to a can of lye with a prominent red and white label. Josie looked at the can then left it where it stood. There was nothing more to be said. She closed the cupboard door. "Thank you, Miss Harmon. You've been most helpful." Moving quickly now, she walked back to the front door.

"Please, miss." The maid hurried after her. "What shall I say to Mr. Bryce?"

"Don't worry about that," Josie said grimly as she let herself out. "We'll be in touch with him. I can promise you that."

An accident, Josie thought. Gone to Richmond. A mistake. One lie after another. She shook her head. She was back in her office at the clinic, preparing her report. The cook's fault. The *keeper's* fault more likely, the one Bryce had hired to look after his wife while he was away at work, and who had failed in his job, leaving Evangeline Bryce alone just long enough for her to escape to the laundry room and swallow the lye. A suicide attempt, plain and simple. Josie drummed her fingers on her desktop. Meyer would have to speak to Winston Bryce about that.

Josie's office was small, but to her mind, perfectly satisfactory. It sat down the hall not far from Dr. Meyer's. She had a desk, a chair, room for a cabinet and a set of bookshelves. Her window overlooked the main hospital building; by looking up she could see the iconic dome that hovered over the top. Wards radiated out beneath the dome like spokes on a wheel, so as the doctors visited their patients, they were said to be making their "rounds."

Her anger softened as she thought of the young husband, stricken and terrified, who'd been hovering at his wife's bedside for days, begging the doctors to save her life. Clearly Evangeline Bryce had been seriously ill for a long time, and her husband had been trying to cope with her on his own, holding out hope against hope that somehow she would get better. If only he had brought his wife to the clinic when she first began to manifest symptoms. The tragedy might have been averted. Now, most likely, she would need extended care at Phipps after she recovered from the surgery to correct the damage from the lye. *If* she recovered. It was all so terribly sad. They were both so young, with so much time ahead of them. Josie wondered what kind of future awaited them now.

She sat for a moment in her chair, reflecting on Winston Bryce's lies. On the one hand, they were easy to understand. He wouldn't want anyone to know the truth about his wife's condition, given the way people felt about mental illness. But on a deeper level, they still represented a choice. Somehow, sometime, Winston Bryce had made a decision to lie about his wife's illness. How had that choice been made?

Her fingers strayed to a folder containing the results of an experiment she'd run recently at the clinic. She'd presented a group of medical students with a hypothetical choice with a moral component: Would you turn in a classmate if you knew they'd cheated on an exam? The students were forced to make a choice between two moral values: class loyalty and the ethic of honesty. It had been fascinating to watch them struggle with their decisions. In the end, she'd been happy to see, most had decided to report the student's dishonest behavior. It boded well for their future as doctors.

Choice, Josie had come to believe, always depended on some kind of value, no matter how fluid and shifting that might be. In the case of Evangeline Bryce, Winston would have had to weigh the value of her reputation against the value of seeking care for her. Add in the complication that he was no doubt uncomfortable lying—as even Sally was—and you had a quite complicated situation. But not without repercussions. Unless Meyer knew the truth about Evangeline's condition, he wouldn't be able to treat her properly.

There was another component to Evangeline's suicide attempt that bothered Josie, although she wasn't sure how, or if, she should include it in her report: the fact that Evangeline was a woman—and a wife. To what extent had her choices in life been constrained by expectations society imposed on her? Was her beautiful bedroom nothing more than a gilded cage? It made Josie feel ever more strongly about attending the upcoming rally for women's suffrage with Nell. *Choice*: now there was something women might very well benefit from, beginning with their vote.

She turned back to her report, and was just in the process of finishing it up, when a knock came to the door and Nicholas Sweeny, Meyer's secretary, stuck in his head.

"Good day, Miss Berenson. If you don't mind, Dr. Meyer is in his office, and he would like to see you now."

Eight

Adolf Meyer's office was as intimidating as the man himself, a grand space with bookcases that stretched to the ceiling, windows overlooking the courtyard where patients took their walks, a wall of mahogany filing cabinets, and a sprawling seminar table for meetings of the psychiatric faculty. Meyer rose from his desk as Josie entered the room, tucking his hand into his jacket pocket.

"The Bryce report," Josie said, rushing to him with the typewritten pages in hand. "I have it right here." It was, she assumed, the reason he'd called for her. "I think you will find it most interesting—"

Meyer held up his hand. "Miss Berenson," he said gravely. "May I present Norbert Richards."

In her hurry she had neglected to notice another person in the room, a tall black man who stood by the windows with his back to her. He turned and eyed her gravely.

"Mr. Richards," Meyer said, completing the introduction. "This is Josefa Berenson. Miss Berenson is the research assistant I spoke to you about—the one I believe can help you with your inquiries."

Richards seemed surprised to hear it. "*Miss* Berenson? Not a doctor?"

Meyer smiled. "I assure you Miss Berenson has my greatest confidence. In the time she's been working at Phipps, she's demonstrated herself to be an excellent researcher and interviewer, and a good judge of human psychology."

Josie colored. Such words were well appreciated—and also quite embarrassing. She tucked the report under her arm, hurried to Mr. Richards, and shook his hand. He was a daunting man, dressed formally in a suit, with penetrating eyes and a severe, brooding face. "How do you do, sir."

"Miss Berenson," Richards said with a small bow. He took a seat in one of the two chairs fronting Meyer's desk, leaving Josie hovering between the two men, unsure of what was expected of her.

"Please," Meyer said. "Do sit down." He waved her to the other chair.

Josie sat down, her hands crossed, the report balanced on her knees.

"Mr. Richards is a lawyer," Meyer said, settling himself in his own chair. The tremor had quieted, at least for the moment, and his hands rested easily on the desk. "He requires our assistance with a client."

Josie nodded, hoping to keep her surprise from showing. Meyer had never called her in on a legal case before. She appreciated his confidence in her, but she knew little about the law, certainly as far as mental illness was concerned.

"His name," Richards said, "is Ruben Ashford."

"Ashford?" The papers on Josie's lap rattled and nearly fell to the floor. She scrambled to contain them.

Richards eyed her curiously. "Do you know him?"

"No, I, that is—" She stumbled in her efforts to explain herself. Should she tell the two men that Nell knew Ruben Ashford's family? She'd yet to tell Dr. Meyer about Nell—that is, about the truth of their relationship. Now was hardly the time. "There was an article about him in the paper this morning."

"Then you know he's confessed to murder," Richards said.

"Yes," Josie said. Richards's face was set in a scowl, so deep, Josie found herself wondering if he ever smiled. She turned to Meyer. "Is it a question of insanity then?"

Meyer shook his head. "Two psychiatrists have examined Mr. Ashford. Both found him to be eminently sane." He smiled. "The findings of one of them, at least, we can be sure of."

Ah. He meant himself. She turned to Richards. "If it's not a question of insanity, then, is it possible that he was innocent and his confession was false?"

"I'm afraid not. There were two eyewitnesses to the murder."

"I see. Then how can I help?"

"It might be useful to review the facts in the case." Richards settled back in his chair. Meyer too settled in to listen, tucking his hand in his pocket. "Ruben Ashford was a bookkeeper, working at the Rosewood School. Do you know it?"

"It's an asylum for feeble-minded children. So I've heard. I've never seen it."

Richards nodded. "Rosewood is a state facility, near the village of Owings Mills, about twenty miles north of the city. Mr. Ashford was hired there in the spring. A few weeks ago he was found in a stable on the property, standing over the body of Miss Constance Prentiss, one of the teachers at the school. She had been bludgeoned to death. He was holding a hammer with blood on it. He also had blood on his shirt."

Josie swallowed hard. It was horrible to think about—horrible even to hear. Had these details been reported in the newspaper? If so, no wonder Nell had looked so distressed that morning.

Richards must have noticed her discomfort. "Shall I go on?"

Josie pulled herself together. "Yes, please."

"Ashford was immediately apprehended and taken to the jail in Towson, the Baltimore County seat, where he confessed. The eyewitnesses to the crime submitted statements at the Towson courthouse. A few days later he was removed to the Baltimore City jail, where the warden informed me of his presence. I consulted with Mr. Ashford there."

"And when will his trial be?"

"There will be no trial. Given the fact that he has pled guilty, he will simply go before a judge for sentencing, where he will be condemned to death by hanging."

Josie fell silent. The lawyer fell quiet too. He seemed to be waiting for her to say something. She felt like a bug pinned under glass—and had as little idea of how to respond. "Is a sentence of death always the result in these kinds of cases?" she said finally.

"Always?" Richards gave her a grim smile—or at least what Josie assumed passed for a smile. "*Always* is a word I prefer to avoid when it comes to the law, but when the accused is a black man and the victim is a white woman, then yes, I would say always."

"I don't understand. If he confessed—if he's guilty and will be sentenced—" Josie turned to Meyer. "If there's no question of insanity—then I don't see what you need from me."

Richards looked to Meyer who offered a peremptory wave of his hand: go on. "What I need, Miss Berenson," the lawyer said, "is for you to help me save Ruben Ashford's life."

This was beyond imagining. Save a murderer's life? Richards's face was set in its scowl again, as inscrutable as ever. Even Meyer had become unreadable. No rescue was forthcoming; both men were simply waiting again for her to speak. "I don't—" she said, then stopped and started again. She didn't want to disappoint, but she had to be honest. "I'm sorry, but I don't see how I could possibly do that."

Slowly, as if the effort exhausted him, Richards maneuvered his bulk to his feet. He walked again to the window, giving her his back. "You're not from Baltimore, are you, Miss Berenson?"

Josie found herself coloring, although she didn't know why. "No, sir. Boston. But I've lived in Baltimore for over six months now."

"Ah," Richards said, as if that explained a great deal. He turned and studied her. "Things might be different in Boston, Miss Berenson, but Baltimore is not Boston. Baltimore," he paused, searching for the right word, "is a *border* town. Northern in some ways, Southern in others. When it comes to color, very southern indeed. Someone who

56

has lived here for such a short time could be forgiven for not knowing that." Again he gave her the ghost of a smile. "As you might recall, I said that after some time in the county jail, Mr. Ashford was removed to the city. Did it ever occur to you to wonder why?"

"No, sir."

"When Mr. Ashford was first apprehended, every effort was made to keep his arrest a secret. Aubrey Foyle, the superintendent of the Rosewood School, wanted time to inform the victim's family before the news got out. He also needed to prepare his students and his staff. As you can imagine, they were all quite shaken, the children most of all. The county jailer had his own reasons for wanting Ashford's arrest to remain hidden."

"Why would that be?"

"A few years ago, a black man was lynched outside the Towson jail for the alleged rape of a white woman. I say alleged, because there was no investigation. No trial. No due process. A mob simply broke him out of jail, hauled him to the nearest tree, and hanged him. Meanwhile the sheriff stood by and watched, as did any number of people, including women and children. A train, passing by, slowed down so that the passengers could get a good look. Afterwards the rope was cut into pieces and handed out as souvenirs. The sheriff claimed not to recognize a single person in the mob. They must have come, he said, from out of town. No one was charged with the crime."

Richards lowered himself again in his seat. "That event is hardly unique. Hardly a week goes by without something similar happening in some southern jurisdiction. No one has ever been held accountable for one of those crimes." He wiped a hand over his face. "Eventually the county jailer thought it best to transfer Mr. Ashford to the city for his safety. Once there, word got out."

Hence the story in today's newspaper. Richards was right. Josie knew nothing of these things. Growing up in Brookline, she'd heard of lynchings, but they'd always seemed so far away, deep southern affairs, from places like Mississippi and Alabama. Boston was hardly a paragon when it came to race relations, but nothing like that had ever happened there. It had never occurred to her that Baltimore might be any different. Baltimore was Nell's hometown. It was modern, cosmopolitan. Or so Josie had always thought. Had she been wrong about that? The thought chilled her.

She turned to the lawyer. "Isn't it simply a matter of letting justice take its course?"

"Ah, yes, justice. It always comes down to justice, doesn't it?" Richards closed his eyes, swaying lightly in his chair. "'Let justice flow down like waters and righteousness like an ever-flowing stream.' Amos 5:24." He paused, savoring the words. "What is justice, if not a story, a simplified version of what might otherwise be deeply troubling or complicated events?" Then he looked back at her. "There is much about Mr. Ashford's case that troubles me, above all, the fact that he appears to have had no reason for killing Constance Prentiss."

Meyer cleared his throat. "It's highly unusual. While Ruben Ashford insists he is guilty of the crime—that he killed Constance Prentiss in cold blood—he is unable to say why. When I interviewed him, I expressly questioned him on this point. Was the crime driven by passion, by hatred, jealousy, fear, or some other overpowering emotion? Was it premeditated or the result of an uncontrollable impulse? He couldn't say. At some point—in some way—Ruben Ashford made a choice to kill." He looked at her significantly. "I thought it might interest you to find out why."

Yes, indeed, it very well might. Already Josie found herself intrigued by the question. At the same time, she wondered if she would be up to an investigation of this kind—despite Dr. Meyer's endorsement. She'd never dealt with a murderer before. The case could very well take her to unknown—and daunting—places. She paused, considering. Once again she shifted the papers on her lap, straightening and organizing them, more purposefully now. Then she turned to Richards. "If I understand you correctly, it's not a question of guilt or innocence. The facts are known. It's a question of motive. You want to know *why* Ruben Ashford killed Constance Prentiss."

Richards smiled at her, more openly this time. "Yes, Miss Berenson, that's exactly what I want to know."

"And if you did know, you believe you might be able to change his sentence? You could even save his life?"

The smile faded. "There are no guarantees. But if there is some kind of extenuating circumstance behind the crime—perhaps it would give me the basis for filing an appeal. It's the only chance Ruben Ashford has." Richards stood and crossed the room to a shelf holding one of Meyer's collections—a group of skulls. He picked one up and studied it, turning it in his hands. Lizard? Fox? Josie had no idea. Richards put the skull back.

Then he tipped up his face, speaking with his eyes upraised, as if in prayer. "My parents were enslaved in Georgia. After the war— after they were *freed*—they moved north, as did so many others like them. They thought to find a better life for themselves here—to find the fulfillment of promises that had been made to them at the war's end, and to their children and their children's children. Promises of freedom. Promises made by the law. I was born in Baltimore. I am one of those children. I know what happens to a people when promises aren't kept—when the law is left unfulfilled." He turned to Josie. "What do you know of the law, Miss Berenson?"

Josie colored again. "Not much, I'm afraid."

"I assume you've heard of the Fourteenth Amendment?"

"It grants—" All at once she wasn't sure. "It grants citizenship and…"

"And equal protection under the law. To everyone, no matter their color. Would it surprise you to hear Maryland has yet to ratify the Fourteenth Amendment?"

Josie didn't know what to say. Baltimore was beginning to seem very different to her from Boston indeed.

"No matter," Richards said. "It's the law of the land, and as the law it must be obeyed." For a moment the lawyer fell silent, trailing his fingers again among the skulls. "There are many things I don't believe in, Miss Berenson, but the law is not one of them. It may be imperfect, it may fail us, but we have no choice but to turn to it. We must make its perfection our project. Through it will come our remedy. Maybe not today, maybe not tomorrow, but someday."

He grew meditative. "Today all too often the law serves the cause of injustice. Just last year in Annapolis a black man was hung—lawfully this time—for murdering a white woman. Her husband was found at work the day she died with red stains on his shirt—what he said was ink. At the trial we learned she had a lover. Meanwhile the black man was seen outside their house by an eyewitness. He was an ice-seller, and there wasn't a single house in the neighborhood he didn't visit on his rounds. The judge said it was the most perfect case of circumstantial evidence he had ever seen. But the ice-seller had no reason for killing that woman. And he went to his death proclaiming his innocence."

Richards returned to his seat. "I'm saying the law needs to fulfill its promise to be applied equally to all, black or white. I'm saying justice needs to mean more than simply finding the closest black man and rounding him up. I believe before we watch Ruben Ashford hang, we must—the law must—know why he killed Constance Prentiss."

Save Ruben Ashford? It seemed like an impossible request—a fool's errand—like Don Quixote tilting at windmills. If Josie were sensible, she would turn the lawyer down. But being sensible had never been her strong suit. So her mother always said; add that to her list of faults.

She turned to Meyer. "The case would take me away from my usual clinic duties."

"No doubt. And yet—" Meyer's hand was trembling again. Discreetly he tucked it in his pocket. "It's not just a question of assisting Ruben Ashford. Mr. Richards believes his case might make a useful precedent, one that could lead to real legal reform. That is something all of us who care for justice can surely support."

Josie nodded. "I would need to see his confession." She stopped, then started again, her thoughts gathering speed. "And any other evidence you might have. Interview transcripts, testimony of the eyewitnesses, and the like. Mr. Ashford. I would want to speak to him and to his family." She looked at Richards. "If that's possible."

"I will see what I can arrange."

"Medical records, place of employment, school records." She ticked them off on her fingers. "I can't promise anything." Already she felt the weight of the responsibility she was taking on.

Richards nodded. "None of us can."

"I think you might find, Mr. Richards, that even in difficult cases like these, surprising things can happen," Meyer said. "We must hold out hope."

Richards stood and handed Josie his card. "I will be in touch."

The burden she felt was nothing compared to the one he carried, and had been carrying, his entire life. This she knew. Automatically she stood as he left the office.

When she turned around, Meyer was smiling at her. "And now, Miss Berenson, if you don't mind, I believe you have some information for me about Evangeline Bryce?"

Nine

Dinner that night was late because of the rally. Afterwards Nell and Josie sat in the second-floor parlor, playing whist. Light from the electric lamp pooled on the table, leaving the rest of the room to fade into darkness, so that the armchairs by the hearth took on the shadowy shapes of slumbering animals. A fire smoldered in the grate. It was Nell's turn to play. She studied the cards in her hand, considering—cautiously, ever cautiously, just as she always did in her ministrations to her patients—then lay down a jack of spades. Josie picked it up then, changing her mind, put it back down, and cocked her head at Nell mischievously. "An experiment, if you please."

"Very well." Nell put down her cards and sat back with a smile. She was used to Josie's little experiments, which sometimes took the form of long, hypothetical conversations—what Josie called "thought experiments"—and sometimes required Nell's more active participation. "What is it this time?"

Josie smiled but didn't say. She moved the jack aside and placed a king and queen, side by side, in its place. "Now," she said, pointing to the two playing cards. "Choose."

"One of those cards? The king or queen?"

"Yes."

"Based on what?"

"Ah," Josie said, her smile widening. "That's the question, isn't it?"

"Hmm." Nell considered. Then she poked her finger at the king. "There. That one."

Josie pursed her lips. "The king. Very good. Now what made you choose him?"

Why had she chosen him? Nell had to think. "He's worth more than the queen, so I picked him."

"A sensible choice, from my sensible girl." Josie gave Nell's hand an affectionate pat. "Now, what if I told you that the king on the card was Henry the Eighth, who famously beheaded or divorced most of his wives?"

Nell shuddered. "Well, I certainly wouldn't want to have anything to do with *him*." She stabbed a finger at the queen. "I'd pick her."

"Of course, you would," Josie said, pleased. "Now you've changed the basis of your choice from a question of power and influence to one of justice and fairness. Completely understandable—and admirable. But what if I told you I'd give you a kiss if you chose the king?"

Nell laughed and immediately picked up the king.

Josie leaned over and kissed her heartily. "A thoroughly selfish choice, putting your own pleasure first."

"That's not fair," Nell said, pouting. "It's only a playing card."

"True," Josie said. "But choices have consequences, don't they? At least in life, they do."

Josie sat back, and a troubled look came into her eyes. Nell felt a change in the air. She reached over and took Josie's hand. "What is it?" she said softly.

"I took on a new case at the clinic today."

"The Bryces?"

"No, I mean, yes. I did take on Mrs. Bryce's case. But this is something different. It's Ruben Ashford."

"The murderer?" Nell was shocked to hear it. "But how—why—?" She withdrew her hand. "Have they called in Dr. Meyer? Is Ashford claiming insanity?"

"Actually it appears that he's quite sane. The question is motive.

He owns up to the murder and even gave a full confession, just as the newspaper reported. But he can't say *why* he did it."

"That's strange. Is it possible he's innocent? I can't imagine the little boy I met so many years ago becoming a murderer. He was so shy." Nell ran a finger along her chin. "Although, of course, that was a long time ago, and I suppose anything is possible."

"I wondered the same thing. But it's not just that he confessed. He was found next to the victim with the murder weapon in his hand, and there were two eyewitnesses to the crime."

"Oh," Nell said. "Still, I don't understand. If that's the case, then why does his motive even matter?"

"Norbert Richards—his lawyer; Dr. Meyer introduced me to him today—believes that if he understood Ashford's motive, he might be able to make an appeal. It could even save his life."

"I see," Nell said slowly. "If Ashford's life could be saved…" Her voice trailed off. "Believe me, no one would like to see that more than me. I know his parents. They're good people. They don't deserve to suffer through something like this. But if he did commit murder…" She frowned. "Are you sure you want to be involved with something like that?"

Josie cast down her eyes. "I've been asking myself the very same question." She toyed with the cards on the table. "Honestly, I don't know if I'm even up to it, although Dr. Meyer seems to think I am." She picked up the king and smoothed it with her fingers. Then she raised her eyes. "But I've decided to try. Ashford's lawyer seems to think his case might be a useful precedent for other black men. He didn't expressly say so, but he seems to think race played a role in the murder." She put the king down on the table. "Anyway, I've never believed in capital punishment, as you know. I can't see taking one life for another. If I can help save Ruben Ashford, I think I owe it to him to try."

Nell fell silent. She didn't believe in the death penalty either. And as she well knew, in Baltimore it hit black men the hardest. She'd never discussed it with Josie—she didn't want her to gain the wrong impression of the city—but Nell had long despaired of the black men who were put to death each year in the courtyard of the city jail. The hangings were such a common occurrence, the *Sun* had stopped covering them. Still, Ashford's case was complicated. It was bound to engage people's emotions. Indeed, as she well knew, it already had.

Just that morning, Edith Moskowitz, one of her patients, who'd come in to consult on heart palpitations, had confessed to being disturbed by news of the murder. "And to think Ruben Ashford lived on Lemmon Street! It's practically around the corner," she'd said as Nell laid fingers on her wrist to take her pulse. Not surprisingly, it was racing. Edith was quite well off, and employed a colored butler as well as chauffeur. "How can a white woman feel safe in her own home anymore?"

Nell hadn't had an answer to that. Then Maxwell Donauer, a haberdasher, who was suffering from gout, and who was normally quite sensible, had shocked Nell by saying he hoped Ashford would be hanged soon. "If he's not, it will tear this city apart," Maxwell said grimly. "Mark my words."

Nell hadn't answered Maxwell either. It was her duty to treat her patients, she believed, not to argue with them. But she had to admit his remarks had upset her, mostly because—if she were to be honest about it—she sympathized with them, more than just a little. She didn't think Ashford should hang for his crime, but she shared Maxwell's concerns about what might happen to the city if he didn't. Ashford's case hit close to home—too close. But how could Nell explain all this to Josie? Josie was from Boston. She didn't understand Baltimore the way Nell did.

As if to prove her point, Josie said, "Did you know there was a lynching in Towson a few years ago?"

"In Towson? Impossible." But even as Nell denied it, she knew it was true. She remembered seeing a story about it in the *Sun*. She'd completely forgotten about it. Isn't that what one did with news like that, too horrible to contemplate? Put it aside? What else was she to do?

"Tell me about your parents," Josie said. Where, Nell wondered, did *that* come from? "Why did they move out of the city? You never explained."

Nell colored deeply. "I didn't agree with them," she said. "I didn't want them to leave. It's just that…" To her chagrin, she found herself telling Josie how a few years earlier a black man had moved into a house on McCulloh Street—the first person to break through the color line that delineated West Baltimore's black alleyways from its white avenues. "He was perfectly respectable," Nell added hastily, "a Yale lawyer." Nevertheless white residents on McCulloh had panicked. They had begun putting their houses up for sale, selling at a discount in their rush to flee. Nell's parents had been among the first. Real estate speculators bought the houses and resold them at inflated prices to black families. Soon fear swept through all of West Baltimore, changing the nature of the neighborhood.

"It wasn't all bad," Nell said, surprised at how defensive she sounded—at how defensive she felt. "Colored families benefited from the change. They'd long been overcrowded and needed the space." Still she knew how sordid it all sounded. "I never left," she pointed out, unnecessarily. "I don't care about the color of my neighbor's skin."

"Of course not," Josie said soothingly. She took Nell's hand. "And no one works harder for the black families of Baltimore. I know that. I've seen it. But some things…"

Nell nodded, but she dropped her eyes. She felt ashamed.

Josie rose and walked to the window, looking out into the darkness. Her voice dropped. "I'd heard of Jim Crow before I came here," she said, speaking with her back turned, "but I didn't really understand what it meant. I had no idea how deeply it affected people's lives. I blame myself for that, for how blind I was." She turned and gave Nell a sad smile. "It's as if the decision to take on Ruben Ashford's case has broken me open, exposing me to new ways of thinking."

Josie sat back down and picked up the playing cards, shuffling and reshuffling them idly in her hands. But Nell had no wish to resume their game, and Josie seemed to have lost interest too. A chill seemed to have come over the room.

"Every choice we make has consequences, as I've always said," Josie said finally. "We would be foolish to think otherwise." She dealt two cards out randomly, an eight of spades and a ten of diamonds. "Ruben Ashford made the most consequential choice a person can make: he committed murder. The consequences for his victim were—do I even have to say it?—catastrophic. But they were catastrophic for Ashford, too. He may very well end up paying with his life. If I'm to understand why—if I'm to plumb the reasons for the murder—I'll have to consider its context, like I do every time I study a choice that has been made." She picked up the ten and pushed the eight aside. "That means beginning with Baltimore, the place he comes from."

Nell nodded. She had nothing to say to that, although she wished she did. Her home town was a wonderful city, but it had a sinister underbelly. No one knew that better than she did. And Josie was a northerner, through and through. As the saying went, north was north and south was south and never the twain should meet. Josie didn't have the deep roots in the city that Nell did; she didn't know how to love it despite its many faults. Already Josie's view of Baltimore was changing. Nell could see that. She wanted to believe in Josie's quest to save Ruben Ashford's life, but she knew how Baltimore treated men like Ashford. What would Josie think if her efforts failed—as they most likely would—and he ended up on the gallows?

Josie might spend her days studying how people made choices, but she was surprisingly opaque to her own. So often she was reckless and driven by impulse. Nell learned that the day on the Cape when Josie suddenly abandoned all thought of marrying Freddie and reached up and kissed her. Nell couldn't help believing that Josie's decision to involve herself in Ruben Ashford's case was impulsive, too. Impulse, like the wind, had driven her to Baltimore. Could it just as easily drive her back to Boston? Nell believed in Josie, and wanted to believe in the constancy of her love, too. But she worried about it. She couldn't imagine returning to the lonely existence she'd led before they met. Like Josie, she'd learned that the person she was meant to live her life with was not a man but a woman. They were only six months into the grand experiment of their communal life, but already what Nell feared most was losing her.

Ten

Early the next morning a courier arrived with a package for Josie, containing documents in the Ruben Ashford case. That night Josie closed herself in her third-floor office, and long after Nell had gone to bed, stayed up late reading. The next morning, when Nell asked her what she had learned, Josie was uncharacteristically circumspect, saying only it was "too soon to know." The next night, and the night after, Josie stayed up late in her office, reading and taking notes, while Nell went to bed alone. But Josie said little about the case, and eventually Nell stopped asking. All she knew was that Josie was troubled. As the days went by, she looked increasingly worried, pale and drawn.

Meanwhile news of the murder continued to ripple through West Baltimore. On Sunday, when Esme came home from church, she reported to Nell that Ruben Ashford's mother, who had worked for years as a domestic for a Hollins Street banker, had been fired, and his father had seen a distinct falling off in his blacksmith trade. Most of his white customers had stopped coming by, and some of his black customers too. The family was worried about having enough money to hold onto their house, and the congregation had taken up a collection on their behalf.

The Ashford case was on Margaret's mind too. Nell overheard her tell James she was sure Ruben's arrest must be a mistake. One of her cousins had gone to the Colored High School with Ruben and insisted he'd never been in any trouble before. No one had ever had a bad word to say about him. It just wasn't possible he would commit murder. One of Nell's colored patients, a seamstress who'd come in about her arthritis, echoed Margaret's view. "I know Violet Ashford," she said, her mouth set in a thin line. "I know George too. No way they would have raised a boy who would do something like that." She shook her head. "This is going to destroy that family. No way they survive it."

Everyone, it seemed, had an opinion about Ruben Ashford, on his guilt or innocence, and everyone came down on one side or the other. Worst of all, they all wanted to know what Nell thought. But she kept her thoughts to herself. Josie's involvement in the case had put Nell in an impossible situation, and she just didn't see where she could say anything about it. But it was more than that. As a doctor, she'd been trained to put her personal feelings aside. She remembered working one night in the emergency room at the Hopkins hospital when she was still a medical student. A man came in with a stab wound, and she assisted the surgeon who saved his life. Afterwards the police came and arrested the patient who, it turned out, was wanted for robbery and assault. "You could have saved yourself the time," the officer said to the surgeon as he hauled the patient away with a ghoulish laugh. "Could have saved us all a lot of time, if you'd just let him go." The surgeon hadn't responded. None of that mattered to him, Nell understood. He'd abided by his oath.

Nell had taken that lesson to heart. She treated every patient who crossed her doorstep the same—whether they came in the front door or back. Ruben Ashford wasn't about to change that. Still, she'd never felt so caught in the middle before. She feared some of the people she encountered assumed she sided with Ashford because she treated colored folk, while others assumed she was against him because she was white. When two of her patients—one colored and one white—unexpectedly canceled their appointments, Nell found herself wondering if it was because of Ruben Ashford. At least, she thought with a sour sense of irony, she was being boycotted equally by both sides.

Then a week after news of the murder had broken, just as they sat down to breakfast, Josie told Nell she was going to the Baltimore City Jail to interview Ruben Ashford. "I wrote to the warden about it. He's granted my request."

Nell was dumbfounded. "Are you sure you want to do that? Is it even safe?"

Josie seemed taken aback by the question. "You can't expect me to form an opinion of the man without meeting him," she said, bristling.

The city jail was a grim, forbidding-looking place. Nell never went past it without a sense of foreboding. The very idea of Josie going there—let alone sitting down with a murderer—frightened her. But Josie looked determined, and Nell knew better than to argue. All she could do was let it go.

Then something happened that drove Ruben Ashford completely from her mind. Later that same morning, as she was in her office preparing for her first patient of the day, Esme came to the door.

"It's Delia Mitchell," Esme said. "She's in the kitchen. Her mother sent her and told her to wait until you came."

Something in Esme's voice made Nell realize she'd better hurry. She told James to hold her patients in the waiting room and followed Esme to the kitchen, where Delia, a nine-year-old girl with cornrow braids, was waiting for her. The last time Nell had seen her, she'd had the measles. That was in the spring. What could it be now?

Delia seemed perfectly fine, at least on first view. Only she looked worried, terribly worried. She bit her lip, her eyes downcast, hardly daring to look Nell in the eye.

"What's wrong?" Nell said. She dropped down on her knee to speak to the girl face to face.

"Mama says to come," Delia whispered.

"It is your mother?"

Delia shook her head.

"Your father?"

"No. It's Theo."

Theo was Delia's older brother. As Nell recalled, Theo had enlisted in the army well over a year ago and had been sent almost immediately overseas. She straightened up. "Did something happen to him? Is he—"

"He's home now," Delia said.

Nell gave the girl a smile. "That's good then, isn't it?"

Another shake of the head.

"Is he wounded?"

"Not wounded. Sick."

"Sick—how?"

Delia was done talking. She was clearly terrified. She raised her head and looked Nell firmly in the eye. "Mama says hurry."

A few minutes later Nell was struggling to keep up with Delia as the girl led her on a run through the West Baltimore alleyways. They passed the backs of houses, chicken coops, pig sties, and stables. Nell, who thought she knew every nook and cranny of her neighborhood, found herself getting lost. Delia said Theo was sick. What did she mean by that? Nell's thoughts tumbled to stories she'd heard about soldiers returning from the war blinded by gas, disfigured, suffering from shell shock. Could Theo have lost his mind? Her anxiety quickened, and her grip tightened on her medical bag.

As Nell recalled, the Mitchells lived in a spacious brick home just north of Franklin Street. She had been there several times over the years, the first time after Delia was born. Delia's mother, Ada, had birthed the child on her own but had grown worried when the baby's color took on a yellow cast. Nell had diagnosed a mild case of jaundice and recommended a solid dose of sunbaths. The baby had quickly recovered, and Ada was forever grateful. Nell remembered Theo as a happy-go-lucky young man who was always up to some kind of mischief. But he'd grown serious when war broke out. He'd decided to enlist, he told Nell, because he wanted to prove himself, to demonstrate his loyalty and usefulness. He didn't say so, but she suspected he hoped white Baltimore would sit up and take notice too, and that when he came back, his lot would improve. Nell knew a lot of young black men like Theo who had gone to war for the same reason. She could only hope they were right, and their sacrifice would not be in vain.

The Mitchells were no longer on Franklin. To Nell's surprise, Delia passed by their old house and took Nell to a warren of alleys on a hill near City Hall—one of the most downtrodden and congested parts of the city. Houses here leaned haphazardly against one another, hardly more than shacks, with tin or tar-paper roofs and windows covered in paper as often as glass. The family had come down in the world. When Nell saw Delia's father, Eber, she understood why. He used to work in a foundry. Now, as he stood outside their front door, anxiously awaiting the arrival of the doctor, he cradled his arm, which had been amputated below the elbow. He must have lost his hand in one of the many accidents Nell knew were all too frequent in the city's factories.

Nell followed him inside, while Delia hung back, lingering by the door. The house was close and gloomy, overly warm, tinged with the sharp smell of steam and scorch. The ground floor consisted of a single room in the front and a kitchen in the back, where Ada was at work, stooped over a laundry tub. Beyond her a door opened to a courtyard, where sheets hung on a line. She must have taken in washing to make ends meet. Boarders too. Beside her a ladder led to a second-floor loft. Voices of a man and woman talking drifted down, while a baby cried.

"Dr. Winters," Ada said, coming forward to take Nell's hands. "Thank the Lord."

It took Nell a moment to see Theo, who was lying on a pallet at the back of the room. She knew she ought to hurry to him, but something held her back.

Still holding Nell's hands, Ada led Nell to the bedside. "Theo." She swept aside a curtain, and light fell in. "My boy."

As light fell on Theo's face, he groaned and threw up his arm like a shield. His lips were a dusky blue as was the skin near his eyes.

The Blue Death. Later Nell would hear the illness called that and would call it that herself. She would never forget it. Theo was cyanotic, literally suffocating, drowning in his own secretions. She didn't need her stethoscope to know this; she could hear it in his ragged, rasping breaths, the straining in his face and back and neck as he struggled to force air into his lungs.

She knelt down, opened her bag, and got to work.

One touch to Theo's skin told her he was consumed by fever. His pulse was surprisingly slow given his condition, just slightly above normal, but his blood pressure was markedly low. The fever had brought on chills; his body shuddered and shook. He must have been vomiting; standing by the bed was a bucket with a thick yellowish liquid collected at the bottom. His eyes were reddened, weeping, and swollen. His tongue was coated, the cheeks and gums marked by crimson spots, the throat bright red. His face was discolored with a reddish-plum rash, which had extended to his chest, midsection, legs and arms. She put her hands on his belly. The abdomen at least felt normal, the spleen not enlarged. She put her stethoscope to his chest, hearing what she knew she would, crackles and rales. She closed his shirt and covered him. Meanwhile he struggled to breathe, his body jerking with racking coughs. A thin line of blood trickled from his nose.

"Bring me water," Nell said. "Bring me water, and a glass, and a rag." Delia darted out of the house with a basin, returning a few moments later with it brimming full. Nell took an aspirin powder from her bag, dipped a glass into the basin, and swirled in the powder. Then she lifted Theo's head, elevating him, bringing the glass to his lips. But he grimaced and pushed the glass away.

She put the glass down, wet the rag, and pressed it to his temples. "How long has he been like this?"

"Two days," Ada said, her voice barely above a whisper.

"We heard last month he was coming back from the war," Eber said. "They sent him to Camp Meade. He came home after that. Two days ago, like Ada said. He was feeling poorly—he said he had the grippe. Said a lot of the boys got it on the ship. But he was fine. He was *fine!*" Eber said the word in a way that turned it into a demand, insisting it was true, insisting it *be* true. "Then yesterday he fell down and couldn't get up again. We put him to bed, and when we got up this morning—" He turned away, covering his eyes.

Twenty-four—forty-eight hours—from an ordinary case of the grippe to this? Nell could hardly believe it. Theo was fit, muscled, army strong. No one—certainly not someone at the peak of his manhood—should succumb to an illness like this. The questions raced through her mind. What could it possibly be? She'd never seen anything like it. "He needs to go to the hospital," she said.

Ada avoided Nell's eye. "We can't afford hospitals."

"Doesn't matter. We'll worry about that later."

Nell sent Delia to find someone, anyone, with a wagon, a cart, any means of conveyance. Meanwhile she bathed Theo with the cool water. Soon two men appeared and carried him to a mule-drawn cart outside. "Take him to Johns Hopkins," Nell said. She wouldn't send him to Provident, the colored hospital. Whatever this was—they needed to see it at Hopkins. Especially if more sick soldiers were on the way. "I will check on him later," she said to Ada. "I'll let you know."

Outside a crowd had gathered in the alleyway. Nell pushed her way through and hurried back home. Just that morning there had been another report in the *Sun* from the city's health commissioner on the Spanish influenza. Dr. Blake was still insisting it was nothing to worry about; it just laid a person low for a day or two like an ordinary grippe. His words were reassuring—but were they overly so? Was Blake hiding the truth, knowing the panic that would ensue once it came out?

Could Theo have the flu? If so, it was like no flu Nell had ever seen. She thought of how the people of Baltimore had cheered when the flu infected the Kaiser's troops over the summer. All across the city, preachers took to their pulpits to declare the illness a modern-day plague, a sign from God that the wicked would not escape and evil would be punished. What would they say if the plague descended on their own houses? God help them if what she saw in Theo Mitchell was the Spanish influenza. God help the people of the alleyways. God help them all.

Eleven

Letter from Dr. Aubrey Foyle, Superintendent
The Rosewood State Training School
Owings Mills, Maryland
September 4, 1918

Since May twenty-seven of this year, Ruben Ashford has been in my employ as bookkeeper at the Rosewood School. He works in the Great Hall, the building where the administrative work of the asylum is done, in an office down the hall from my own. In exchange he is given a salary, and room and board in a cabin on the grounds.

Mr. Ashford is a pleasant young man, nineteen years old, from Baltimore. His father is a blacksmith and his mother, I believe, works as a domestic. Initially Mr. Ashford trained to be a blacksmith, too, but when he graduated from the Colored High School, one of his teachers recommended him to me for his intelligence and mathematical ability. Thinking he would be grateful for the opportunity to engage in a more elevated occupation, I hired him to work at Rosewood. At no time during his three months here did he cause any trouble. He always reported for work promptly and successfully completed all tasks required of him. I was quite satisfied with his performance. He had a congenial demeanor and was extremely compliant. My only complaint—if such a thing can be called a complaint—is that he tended to be overly quiet and hold himself apart. I assumed he was shy, given his age and the newness of his position. I thought in time he would come out of himself.

I can give no explanation for his attack on Constance Prentiss and even now find myself at a loss to understand it. Miss Prentiss, who was twenty-two at the time of her death, came to us as a teacher in the summer of 1917 from a small town near Albany, New York. She was well liked, of good ability, and at no time were any complaints lodged against her. She resided in the teacher's dormitory. For more information, please apply to Mrs. Ida Crofter, head matron. As far as I know, Miss Prentiss and Mr. Ashford hardly knew one another. The murder comes to all of us here at Rosewood as a blow, and I fear the reputation of the school may never recover.

(Signed) Dr. Aubrey Foyle

Report of Frank Hopper, Sheriff
Owings Mills, Maryland
September 2, 1918

The call came to the Owings Mills Station at 2:20 in the afternoon on Saturday, the thirty-first of August. A teacher had been murdered at Rosewood and the murderer, a colored man, was being detained in the Great Hall. As Deputy Abner Ridgely had taken the station's motorcar to the Waldman farm where a horse had been reported stolen, I hitched the horses to the buggy and headed to the asylum, leaving word with Micah Creedwell, manager of the general store, that Ridgely should follow as soon as he was able.

I arrived at the asylum and proceeded to the Great Hall, where I was met by Dr. Aubrey Foyle, the superintendent. He informed me that his bookkeeper, Ruben Ashford, had murdered one of the school's teachers, a Miss Constance Prentiss. Ashford was being detained in his office down the hall. I proceeded to the office where I found the door locked and Abram Sledge, a field hand, standing guard outside it. Sledge told me he had been on his way to the stable when he witnessed the murder, which took place inside. Ashford had attacked Miss Prentiss and bludgeoned her to death.

I entered the office and found Ashford pacing back and forth, apparently overcome, wringing his hands and wiping his eyes. "Oh, Lord. Oh, Lord," he said over and over again. "What have I done?"

Ashford is a young man of middling height with regular Negroid features and medium dark skin. He appeared to be fit with unusually powerful arms and wrists. He was dressed in casual clothing, dark blue cotton pants, shirt, and boots. There were visible bloodstains on the front of his shirt.

I introduced myself and told Ashford I had come to "see about things." I spoke to him kindly, as was my wont in these kinds of situations. I didn't want to alarm him, or provoke him to more violence.

My tone of voice seemed to calm him. He stopped pacing and looked at me anxiously. "What will happen to me now?" he said.

"You had best wait here until we can straighten it all out."

I was relieved when he nodded and sat down.

I left the room, locking it securely behind me. In the meantime, Deputy Ridgely had arrived. Since he was well armed and Ashford appeared at the moment to present no immediate danger, I directed Ridgely to remain at the Great House guarding him while Sledge took me to the site of the murder.

The asylum occupies a large tract of land that spreads over many acres of woods and fields. Much of it is given over to farming. The school buildings are situated at the top of a hill, while the stable, along with a barn and other outbuildings, sit in a farmyard below. I followed Sledge as quickly as I could down the hill to the stable, which is a long building with a low ceiling and narrow windows. Sledge waited for me outside while I went in. The sun was strong, and it was so dark inside, it took my eyes a few minutes to adjust. Once I could see, I spied a woman in much distress, kneeling midway down the long aisle that runs through the center of the building, with stalls on either side. I ran to her, and as I helped her to her feet, she introduced herself to me as Mrs. Ida Crofter, head matron. She stated that she had also witnessed Ruben Ashford slay Miss Prentiss.

The victim was lying on the floor beside Mrs. Crofter. Miss Prentiss was on her back and the blows of the hammer were visible on her forehead, which was crushed in. Blood pooled on the ground around her and onto a hammer that lay on the floor beside her. I collected the murder weapon and took Mrs. Crofter, who was in shock and in danger of collapse, out of the stable. Then I directed Sledge to remain there, ensuring that no one else disturbed the murder scene, while I escorted Mrs. Crofter to the Great House.

At the Great House, Mrs. Crofter was met by several teachers who gathered around her to offer comfort. The asylum is a close-knit community, and news of Miss Prentiss's death had already traveled through it. Once Mrs. Crofter had calmed down somewhat, I asked her if she had any idea why Ruben Ashford would kill Miss Prentiss. Mrs. Crofter said she had no idea whatsoever, as she was sure the two didn't even know each other. In any case, she added, it would hardly be tolerated at the school for a white woman to associate with a colored man.

As there is no coroner in Owings Mills, I telephoned the Baltimore County courthouse and requested that the coroner be sent immediately to the asylum. I asked Dr. Foyle to instruct both Sledge and Mrs. Crofter to report to the courthouse in Towson on Monday to make statements. Deputy Ridgely and I then secured the prisoner and transported him by motorcar to the county jail. By the time we returned to the asylum to fetch the buggy, it was quite dark. Dr. Foyle informed me that in my absence the coroner had come to remove Miss Prentiss's body. As there being no other tasks required of us, Deputy Ridgely drove the motorcar back to Owings Mills, and I followed in the buggy.

(Signed) Frank Hopper

Report of Joseph Milner, Baltimore County Coroner
Towson, Maryland
September 2, 1918

The victim is a young woman of twenty-two years of age, Constance Prentiss by name, of Fullers, New York, near Albany, lately of the Rosewood School in Owings Mills where she was employed as a teacher. On Saturday, the thirty-first of August, she suffered a devastating blow to the frontal bone of her cranium, directly above the nasal bone, in the center of her forehead as it were. The blow crushed the bone, driving fragments into the frontal lobe of her brain, leading to violent hemorrhaging and death. Examination revealed the blow to be the result of a blunt instrument. Frank Hopper, the Owings Mills sheriff, who was in attendance, produced a hammer, which I identified immediately as the murder weapon. Bloodstains were visible on both the head and handle. In all other respects Miss Prentiss appeared to be of good health, and therefore I have ruled the death a homicide.

(Signed) Joseph Milner

Statement of Abram Sledge, field hand
The Rosewood State Training School
Owings Mills, Maryland
September 2, 1918

I was on my way to fetch a horse from the stable when I saw Ruben Ashford inside, attacking Miss Prentiss with a hammer. When she fell to the ground, he dropped to his knees to see that she was dead. I was on him before he could stand up. For a moment light flickered in Miss Prentiss's eyes, and then it went out and she was gone. Meanwhile the murderer began to wail and moan. "Oh, Lord. Oh, Lord," he said. "What have I done? Oh, no, no, no." Clearly he was terrified at having been found out. He must have thought that by luring Miss Prentiss to the stable, where no one was about, he would be able to kill her without being found out. He hadn't counted on me coming by. I feared he might turn on me next, although I know how to hold my own in a fight, and would have made a good accounting of myself if he did. But he knew the game was up and let me lead him quietly to the Great House, where Dr. Foyle summoned the sheriff by telephone to arrest him.

(Signed with his mark) Abram Sledge

Note: as the witness is unable to write, this statement was transcribed at the Baltimore County Courthouse by Alfred Sloane, Clerk of the Baltimore County Court.

Statement of Mrs. Ida Crofter, Head Matron
The Rosewood State Training School
Owings Mills, Maryland
September 2, 1918

On Saturday afternoon last I was walking to the stable when I heard a commotion inside. Fearing the worst, I hurried ahead and had just reached the door when a field hand ran past me into the building. I looked in and saw Ruben Ashford on his knees next to Constance Prentiss, a teacher at the school. As I watched, the hammer dropped from his hand. At the sight of Miss Prentiss slain on the ground, I was struck as if by a blow myself. It felt as if my heart had stopped and my legs turned to lead. The field hand took Ashford by the arm and led him away. Once the murderer was gone, I summoned my courage and ran to Miss Prentiss's side. The sight of her head, bashed in, with blood all around, terrified me, and I am sure I will never recover from it. I've never seen such evil before. Nevertheless I remained at Miss Prentiss's side until the sheriff arrived and took me away. It was my Christian duty.

(Signed) Mrs. Ida Crofter

Statement of Dr. Adolf Meyer, Chief
The Phipps Psychiatric Clinic
The Johns Hopkins Hospital
Baltimore, Maryland
September 12, 1918

I have examined Ruben Ashford, murderer of Miss Constance Prentiss, and find him to be eminently sane.

Mr. Ashford is a Negro male of nineteen years of age. Other than a scar on his right wrist, obtained in his years assisting his father in his blacksmith trade, he has no distinguishing marks. He is of average stature with unremarkable features. I examined him in his cell in the Baltimore City Jail. The prisoner presented a clean, neatly groomed, orderly appearance, and was calm and of cooperative nature. At no time did he show any sign of agitation or other dysregulated emotion. At my prompting, he willingly described his assault on Constance Prentiss, saying how he used a hammer to strike the woman dead. Asked why he committed the crime, Mr. Ashford fell silent, finally admitting he didn't know; he was sure he must have had some reason, but he couldn't say what it was. "Did you know Miss Prentiss?" I asked. Mr. Ashford shook his head, saying, "She was a teacher at the school. I wasn't supposed to have business with any of the teachers. Mrs. Crofter told me so directly when I was hired. She's the head matron. She said it would cost me my job." "Nevertheless," I asked, persisting, "Did you have some reason to dislike her?" Again the prisoner shook his head, saying, "Miss Prentiss was always kind to me." "Were you," I asked, "driven in the moment by an extreme emotion such as anger or fear?" Again the prisoner shook his head. "Did you know that your actions would likely result in the death of the victim?" Mr. Ashford assented. "And did you understand that murder is both morally wrong and a crime?" He hung his head and said most assuredly so. "Had you ever acted in violence towards anyone or anything before?" Again he shook his head. "When you attacked Constance Prentiss, did you feel as if someone else, or some other force, was directing your actions? Were you under the influence of alcohol or any other kind of drug? Did you feel strange in your body or your mind, as if you were blacking out, or unable to control your limbs?" All of these questions were answered in the negative. As I finished the interview and prepared to leave, the prisoner said he had only one request: that I would please tell everyone how sorry he was. He was willing to take responsibility for his crime and suffer the consequences.

In my opinion, Ruben Ashford was well aware of his actions and their implications, and is appropriately contrite. While it is highly unusual for a criminal to be unable to provide a motive for his crime, that in itself is not a sign of insanity. In conclusion, I declare the accused shows no evidence of mental disorder or distress, either organic or functional, and is most assuredly sane.

(Signed) Dr. Adolf Meyer

Statement of Dr. Rawlings Carpenter
Central State Hospital
Petersburg, Virginia
September 13, 1918

I am chief staff psychiatrist at the Central State Hospital in Petersburg, Virginia, formerly known as the Central Lunatic Asylum. Central is the oldest hospital in the country for colored persons of unsound mind. And so I am well versed in dealing with Negro lunatics.

On Wednesday of this week I travelled to the City Jail in Baltimore, Maryland to conduct an examination of Ruben Ashford. Ashford is a dark-complected male of around twenty years of age with a menacing appearance. He has a low forehead, narrowed eyes, a heavy cranium, and in every respect exudes an air of animalistic danger. In late August, Ashford murdered a white woman, which he readily admitted to me. At no time was he able to provide a motive for his crime. I find this not at all difficult to explain. It is well known that people of color are far more excitable and subject to acting on impulse than the white race. Their intellectual and reasoning capabilities, as has been documented, are only poorly developed. Therefore, in my expert opinion, it is of no surprise that the prisoner would be capable of killing Constance Prentiss and having no motive for it. All of this is the result of innate traits of the darker races. In conclusion, Ashford's actions have nothing to do with insanity, and the murderer is most decidedly sane.

(Signed) Rawlings Carpenter, MD

Confession of Ruben Ashford

I give this confession willingly and under no duress. Since my arrest five days ago, I have been treated fairly in every respect and no one has wished me harm.

I am a bookkeeper at the Rosewood State Training School in Owings Mills, Maryland. On last Saturday afternoon around one I was in the stable shoeing a mare for Dr. Foyle. It was exceedingly hot that day. I had set up a small coal fire in a bin to heat the iron horseshoes. I also had with me an anvil and a box of tools. From time to time as I worked, I wiped the sweat from my brow with my shirtsleeve. A horsefly was buzzing around the mare, making her skittish and hard to work with. She kept bobbing her head up and down, swishing her tail, and stamping her hooves. Because she wouldn't settle, I tied her to both sides of the aisle with chains that we keep there for that purpose. Once the fly bit her, and she reared up, rattling the chains of the cross-ties. It took me some time after that to calm her down.

I had just finished nailing the third shoe when Miss Constance Prentiss came into the stable. She is a teacher at the school. She asked me to hitch up the buggy and drive her to the train station, as she was going into Baltimore that afternoon. I said I would, but asked if she wouldn't mind waiting until I finished with the mare. I told her I had only one shoe left and it wouldn't take long. She said that would be fine. I then took my hammer and smashed her in the forehead with all of my might. I remembered quite well how the hammer felt in my hand, the weight of the iron head as it swung, the smoothness of the wooden handle in my palm. The air was smoky from the fire and smelled from the burned hoof trimmings.

As Miss Prentiss fell to the ground, I dropped to my knees beside her. Just then Mr. Sledge, a field hand, came into the stable and saw me there. I dropped the hammer and let him lead me away. On our way out, Mrs. Crofter ran past us inside. I have no idea what happened next to Constance Prentiss. I didn't look back to see. Sledge took me to the Great House where the sheriff was called by telephone. A little while later he came and arrested me. I have nothing else to add. I know what I have done and am willing to accept the consequences.

(Signed) Ruben Ashford

Note: This confession was written at 11 o'clock in the morning on Thursday the 5th of September at the Baltimore County Jail under the supervision of Alfred Sloane, Clerk of the Baltimore County Court.

Twelve

Josie hurried up McCulloh Street on her way to the Baltimore City Jail to interview Ruben Ashford. At North Avenue, she stopped and waited for a streetcar to take her to the east side of the city. A crowd had gathered on the platform, white people standing on one side, black on the other. The first car that came along was for colored passengers, and the white people stood patiently aside while the colored people boarded. It was a process, like a dance, that Josie had witnessed countless times since she'd moved to Baltimore. It had never bothered her before. She'd hardly even noticed it. It was just the way things were, and she'd followed along unthinking. But today it rankled. Ever since she met Norbert Richards, nothing about Baltimore looked the same.

It wasn't just Ruben Ashford. It was the stories he'd told her about the lynching in Towson and the Annapolis ice seller who'd been railroaded to the gallows. Josie knew that when she left Boston to move to Baltimore, she was going south. But she hadn't really thought through what that meant. She'd had a naïve view of Baltimore—an idealized view. She'd let her love for Nell color her vision of the city. It was the place where her beloved had been born, the place where she grew up, and set down roots. Nell was wonderful and so by extension Baltimore must be wonderful too.

Besides, it wasn't like Boston was so perfect. Boston neighborhoods were segregated too. There were deep divisions between black and white in the city, and everyone knew what they were, even if they didn't talk about it. As a child Josie knew very well which of the streets in her Brookline neighborhood to play on, which ones to visit, and which ones to avoid. It wasn't something anyone explicitly said, you just absorbed it like you did water or sunshine. She never questioned the fact that her mother's gardening club and bridge club were entirely white, as were all of her father's colleagues at the dye factory, and everyone in her own social circle, too. It wouldn't have even occurred to her to think about it, let alone question the rightness of it or the implications.

Later, when she went to Boston University, and enlarged her world to take in the whole city, she'd become aware of the differences between the neighborhoods, black and white, rich and poor. But even then poverty remained an abstract concept to her, an injustice that, of course, every thinking, feeling person opposed, and needed to fight against. But it seemed as if simply holding that opinion and registering it in conversations with other likeminded people in lecture halls or late at night in coffee houses was sufficient. One wasn't exactly required to do anything about it. Josie was quite happy to hold her liberal ideas and ignore them at the same time, while she busily immersed herself in her studies and her social life.

But now apparently the impetus to do something had been thrust upon her, and in a compelling way. She had to acknowledge the truth, that Baltimore wasn't Boston. In Baltimore, the separation of the races was taken to a whole new level. In Boston, at least, black and white could ride in the same streetcars, shop in the same stores, study together, even work together side by side. In the department stores that Freddie and Eleanor owned, while few black people could aspire to managerial positions, many worked as clerks or salespeople. Here everything was segregated, from the streetcars to the churches, the schools, and the stores. And people's feelings about the racial codes ran deep. She hadn't been surprised to learn that Nell's parents had fled

McCulloh Street when its racial barrier was broken, leaving the city behind for the lily-white suburbs of Roland Park. The thought angered Josie, and she found her anger spilling over onto Nell, too. She took a deep breath. That wasn't fair. Nell hadn't left when her neighborhood changed. She'd stayed. She treated black and white patients equally in her practice. No one, Josie knew, worked harder on behalf of black people than Nell.

Another colored streetcar came—and went—and as Josie waited, she bit her lip, trying to control her irritation. According to Norbert Richards, race played a role in Ruben Ashford's case. Josie was quite willing to believe it. But how? Ashford wasn't like the ice seller; he hadn't been taken to the gallows insisting on his innocence. He'd confessed. And he wasn't like the man lynched in Towson either. Instead, he'd been brought to the Baltimore City Jail precisely for his safety. Besides, the question facing her was one of motive: why Ashford had killed Constance Prentiss. Even Dr. Meyer said he didn't know. What could race possibly have to do with motive?

At last a white streetcar came, and Josie boarded. It was crowded inside, and a man in a grey suit stood to give her his seat. She settled herself between an elderly woman with a cane and a young woman in a lavender coat. She was wearing a dark woolen suit which she had chosen for its professional air. Outside it had been pleasantly cool, a few clouds riding in the autumn sky, but inside the car it was overly warm, and she was beginning to perspire. She loosened her jacket.

As the streetcar rattled eastwards, she reviewed in her mind what she had learned so far in Ruben Ashford's case. Over the last few nights, she'd studied the documents Norbert Richards had sent her, but they'd only raised more questions than they answered. She hoped her interview with Ashford today would provide some clarity. She certainly hadn't gotten any from the reports she'd read, including his confession.

Ashford claimed to be in the stable, shoeing one of Dr. Foyle's horses, when Prentiss came in, but how, Josie wondered, could that be?

What business did a bookkeeper have shoeing horses? Surely there were regular blacksmiths at the asylum to take care of such duties. Neither Abram Sledge nor Ida Crofter mentioned seeing a horse in the stable, although Sledge had a clear enough view of Ruben Ashford to see him attack Prentiss with the hammer, and Mrs. Crofter saw the hammer fall from his hands. Could Ashford be lying about the horse? Nothing, Josie knew, was so common as people who lied. Winston Bryce lied about his wife's illness in the hope of sparing her reputation. His maid, Sally Harmon, lied simply to save her job. But if Ruben Ashford was lying, what was he trying to accomplish? What value could there be in lying about the horse? It hardly furthered his cause.

He said Constance Prentiss came to see him because she wanted him to drive her in the buggy to the Owings Mills station. Was he lying about that too? He wasn't employed at the school as a driver. According to Mrs. Crofter—as reported by Sheriff Hopper—associating with any of the teachers could cost him his job. Surely Ashford knew that. Could Abram Sledge be right, and Ashford lured Prentiss into the stable under false pretenses?

One fact was consistent throughout all of the reports: Ruben Ashford hardly knew his victim. Even Dr. Meyer was satisfied on that account. But if Ashford didn't know her, why did he kill her—and in such a vicious manner?

Then there was the odd way in which the confession was written. Ashford spent a great deal of time describing the shoeing of Dr. Foyle's horse: the fire, the heat, the smell, the horsefly tormenting the mare. He spoke directly about striking Prentiss dead. He even recounted how the hammer felt in his hand. And yet the entire confession was made without emotion. Surely he must have felt something when he killed her. He said he didn't know why he did it. Was that another lie? Could his motive be buried so deeply in his mind as to be completely hidden? Sigmund Freud might very well think so. As Josie well knew from her reading of Dr. Freud, the unconscious mind had the power to influence people's behavior in ways they couldn't begin to understand.

According to some people, the racial laws maintained order. All you had to do was read the *Baltimore Sun* to hear that opinion expressed. Josie hardly believed that—it seemed an awfully insidious rationale for oppression—but it made her wonder. Could Ashford have killed Prentiss because of a *breakdown* in racial codes? After all, he was black and she was white, as Richards had so aptly pointed out. But if so, where was the evidence? As much as Josie wanted to believe that Norbert Richards was right, and race had played a role in the murder of Constance Prentiss, she had to entertain the possibility that he was wrong, and his racial theory was simply a dead-end.

The streetcar traveled farther along the avenue, with more people boarding at each stop, making it feel even more stuffy and warm. The young woman beside Josie in the lavender coat dug into her handbag, pulled out a handkerchief, and mopped her brow. All at once, as they crossed the Jones Falls River, the handkerchief fell to the floor. With a smile, Josie bent to retrieve it, but just as she was about to hand it back, the woman moaned and fell to the floor. Josie leapt to her feet and knelt beside her. Poor thing. She must have fainted from the heat. She was gasping for breath.

As Josie loosened the buttons of the woman's dress, the man in the grey suit hollered for the streetcar to stop. The conductor jumped off and flagged a passing motorcar. Then two men carried her to the motorcar, laid her down inside, and the motorcar took off—going, Josie assumed, to a hospital. She hoped the woman would be all right. There had been something so unnerving about the way she looked when she collapsed. She had been so unearthly pale, so limp, with a faint bluish tinge to her lips, her eyes fixed in the distance as if she saw something no one else could.

Josie was relieved when the streetcar finally arrived at Greenmount Avenue, and she could disembark into the fresh air. Instead of waiting for a transfer, she decided to walk the rest of the way to the jail, a mile or so to the south. It would help clear her mind. The east side of the city was poorer than the west, and more crowded, crammed with small rowhouses, most of which had shops on the ground floor and living quarters on top. Greenmount was busy, chockablock with trucks and horse-drawn carts, the air sooty from manufacturing enterprises and factories. As Josie walked down the street, she dodged peddlers who pushed carts, hawking their wares. She passed a bakery, a tinsmith's workshop, and then a store for hats. The hats made her think of Adele, and thinking of Adele lightened her mood. Working as a salesgirl was far behind Adele now, who was happily ensconced on Beacon Street as a wife and mother. Josie smiled. What would Adele think if she knew Josie was on her way to the Baltimore City Jail to speak to a murderer? Everything about Josie's life in Boston—her rats and mazes—suddenly seemed very innocent, and very far away.

In time the jail loomed before her, an ominous-looking structure, built of black stone, surrounded like a medieval fortress by a towering wall. Most people seemed to avoid it, and the streets around it were all but deserted. But a half dozen white men lingered nearby, their eyes downcast, their shoulders hunched. Workmen, from the looks of them, with thick, soiled jackets and heavy boots. Something about them unsettled her. Josie walked quickly past.

The letter she'd received from the warden directed her to present herself at a door on Madison Street. There was the door, made of an iron grille, but it was securely locked. Josie tried peering through, but no one was in sight, just a long corridor disappearing into darkness. She rapped, but that only created a dull thud which echoed emptily. Then she saw a doorbell on the side. She pressed it, and distantly a buzzer sounded.

Her presence seemed to have irritated the workmen. They shifted, shouldering one another, coming closer. Josie felt a stab of fear in her throat. She pressed the bell again, and at last, to her relief, a man appeared in the distance, walking towards her with a heavy tread. He was a tall white man, with a thick neck and wrists, dressed in a dark blue uniform with dull brass buttons. At his midriff, a belt held a truncheon and a ring of keys.

"Josefa Berenson," Josie said. She slipped one of her cards to him through the grille. "From the Phipps Psychiatric Clinic."

The jailer took the card and studied it.

Josie glanced at the workmen. They were close enough now that she could feel the heat of their bodies and smell their sour sweat. Would he never open the door? "The warden is expecting me."

"Very well." The jailer slipped the card back to her without expression, then sorted through the keys at his belt and opened the door. Suddenly the workmen charged forward, thrusting Josie through the doorway in the melee. But the jailer was too quick for them, and by wielding his truncheon, shoved them back and slammed the door shut. Locked outside, they erupted in fury. "Give him to us," they howled. "We'll take the nigger. We know what to do with him." They rattled the grille. "Hang the bastard. Do it now or we'll do it for you."

Josie stumbled back, her heart pounding, her hand at her throat. The jailer eyed the men through the grille, shaking his truncheon at them. One of them had a bloodied nose, another a welt on his forehead. "Try that, will you?" the jailer said with a ghoulish grin, as if taking satisfaction in his handiwork. He shook his head. "They never learn."

Josie took deep breaths, steadying herself. She had never thought it could feel safer inside a jail than outside. But in Baltimore... She shuddered as she thought again about the Towson lynching, and the decision to move Ruben Ashford here. She took a last look behind her at the sturdy iron door, the high prison walls, the men still gathered in an angry mob outside. All she could do was hope he stayed safe here.

The jailer returned the truncheon to his belt and, with no further comment, his face once again devoid of expression, turned to Josie. "This way, miss."

Entering the jail felt like walking into a cave. Water dripped down the walls and puddled on the floor; the air was dank and smelled of sewage. Now and then a narrow-slotted window gave forth a view of the Jones Falls River, flowing just outside. Nell had told her that the river doubled as an open sewer for much of the city, especially the poorer neighborhoods, creating all kinds of health hazards. Residents complained constantly about it, and Nell wrote letter after letter to the newspaper, but nothing was done.

They came to another door, which the jailer opened with his ring of keys, then locked behind them. This led to a hallway with a dozen or so cells on either side, each holding a lone male prisoner. Most paid Josie no heed, swallowed in attitudes of indifference or despair, but a few looked up in idle curiosity as she passed by. Almost all of them were black. Was one of these men Ruben Ashford? The jailer didn't say and she had no way of knowing. She'd never seen a photograph of him, and the descriptions she'd read had been far from precise.

At the end of the cellblock, the jailer unlocked yet another door, this time leading her into an open courtyard. Josie blinked at the sudden influx of sun and sky. If this was where prisoners were brought for their exercise, they weren't here now. A broken chair sat in the center of the empty courtyard, next to a pile of lumber.

The next corridor had a bureaucratic air, solid wooden doors on either side with nameplates identifying each one: *Procurements, Accounts, Service.* From one door came the muffled sound of voices. Somewhere someone was typing. A telephone rang. The last door was labeled *Warden.* The jailer rapped on it. "Wait here." With a touch to his cap, he walked away.

As Josie waited for the warden, a door down the hall opened, and a man emerged, glanced at her, then disappeared without comment into a room on the other side. Minutes passed. Just as she was wondering if she should knock again, the door opened, revealing an elegant white man with hooded eyes, dressed like a banker in an expensive-looking suit. "Yes?"

"Josefa Berenson." She handed him her card. "I wrote to you earlier. I'm here to speak with Ruben Ashford."

"Miss Berenson. Of course. Please, forgive me. I've been occupied with other things and forgot you were coming today." He smiled at her with good cheer. "Allow me to introduce myself. Everett Crane."

He laughed. "But, of course, you know that. Do come in." Ever the gentleman, he stood to the side, and ushered her in.

Inside was a room as surprising as the warden, neither of which she would have imagined finding in a jail. It was furnished with a simple elegance, exuding a feeling of calm. The floor was of black stone like the rest of the building, but the walls had been covered in white stucco, with small oil paintings hung here and there. Bookshelves held a smattering of Greek and Roman philosophy, poetry, religious treatises, and some of the more popular contemporary novels. The air had a faint smoky scent like incense in a church. In the center sat a mahogany desk fronted by a pair of comfortable looking chairs. It could have been the study of a medieval scholar or monk.

Crane smiled as he directed her to one of the chairs. "I know. It's not what you expect from a warden." Sitting down behind his desk, he gestured to the books, the paintings. "We have such an unfortunate reputation. Heartless and all that." He beamed at her. "So, today we have a visitor from the Phipps Clinic. And a member of the fairer sex at that. A rare delight. How is Dr. Meyer?"

"Quite well," Josie said. The comment about the "fairer sex" rankled and she found it belittling, but she held herself in check and made no response.

"I'm glad to hear it." He grew meditative. "Psychiatry. Such fascinating work. At one time I, myself…" His voice trailed off. "Never mind. Mine was a different path. But perhaps one day you and your colleagues will unlock the secrets of the mind, making my work, making all of this" —he gestured with elegant, tapering fingers at the jail around them— "entirely unnecessary. Until then…" He lifted a teapot from his desk. "Tea? I believe it's still hot."

"Thank you." She was still trying to make sense of this unusual man and didn't know what else to say.

He poured her a cup then one for himself. "Ah," he said, sipping gently. "Better."

They drank for a moment in silence. At last Crane reached over and delicately took her empty cup. "So," he said. "You've come to see Ruben Ashford."

"Yes," she said, glad finally to address the business at hand. "I met his lawyer at the clinic. He spoke to both Dr. Meyer and me. He's most anxious for our help in Ashford's case."

"Norbert Richards. Yes." Crane nodded. "A good man. We've had many interesting conversations over the years. Always a pleasure." He picked up a pipe, gestured towards her. "Do you mind?" She shook her head. With an air of immense satisfaction he packed the pipe with tobacco, lit it, taking his time, enjoying every moment of the ritual. Smoke puffed out—the incense smell she had noticed before. He leaned back, smoking contentedly.

"I'm been asked to look into Mr. Ashford's motive for murdering Constance Prentiss—the psychology behind the crime," Josie said.

The warden puffed contentedly on his pipe. "I see."

"I don't suppose you have any idea? Perhaps Mr. Ashford has given some indication since he's been in jail here?"

"No, I'm afraid not." He fell silent. "And you believe this information could be helpful?"

"Mr. Richards thinks it might furnish him with the basis for filing an appeal. It could even save Mr. Ashford's life."

"I see." The warden tamped down his pipe. When he spoke again his countenance had changed. Gone was the good cheer, and he regarded her with regret. "I will grant you your interview with Ruben Ashford, if that's what you truly desire. But I ask you to think for a moment—to hear me out."

He stood and walked to a bookshelf, retrieved a book, studied it for a moment, then put it back. "Norbert and I have discussed Mr. Ashford's situation at length. It may be hard for you to imagine that a defense lawyer—the man who wants more than anything to get his client out of jail—and the client's jailer—the man whose duty it is to keep him in—would meet with one another, would speak to one another, indeed could be friends." He inclined his head. "But it's true."

He returned to his desk, occupying himself again with his pipe. When it was glowing again in a satisfactory manner, he continued. "Norbert and I share many things in common. One of them is our vision for the world—for the ideal world, that is to say, one based on civility, on justice, on dignity. On the fulfillment of the law. I know what Norbert hopes to accomplish with Ruben Ashford. I, perhaps more than anyone else, sincerely wish that he succeeds. He thinks through Ruben Ashford he can effect judicial reform. *Racial* reform."

A note of weariness entered the warden's voice. "Norbert is like a general. He has long-term, strategic goals. To Norbert, Ruben Ashford is simply a foot soldier, to be utilized—perhaps even to be sacrificed. That I simply can't countenance. I've tried to make Norbert see my point, but I couldn't persuade him. When I received your letter, I told him I would grant you your interview with Mr. Ashford. For the sake of our friendship. Because Norbert so strongly desired it. But I ask you to consider this—this—help you are so determined to give."

Josie frowned. Nothing the warden had said made sense to her. Norbert as a general? Ashford as a foot soldier? "I don't see what you mean."

The pipe had gone out again, and this time the warden put it down, letting it grow cold. "Ruben Ashford has been with us for several weeks now. In that time, I've gotten to know him. As long as he's here, he's under my protection. It's a responsibility"—he put a hand to his heart— "I take seriously."

That, at least, she could well understand. She nodded, thinking again of the mob at the door.

"He's a most remarkable man. When—if—you meet him, you will see that. As I said, Norbert believes through Mr. Ashford he can advance his mission. But Norbert, I fear, is blinded by the vision he holds of the future, the shining possibility of what might be. I admire him for it—for this ability to live for the future. Sadly I'm confined to the present, the here and now. I'm unable to indulge in such consolations. And you, Miss Berenson, do you share Norbert's vision of the future? Are you, too, blinded by hope?"

Blinded by hope? The warden made it sound like a liability. She'd never thought of it that way before. She'd always held out hope for a better society, for a more just world for all, whether man or woman, black or white. Those were the values she'd held dear her entire life, even if she'd never acted on them before. But now she was willing to step up and take responsibility for what she believed in. How could working for justice be wrong? How could believing in *hope* be a liability? "No, Mr. Crane, I don't think I am."

"If you were, I wouldn't hold it against you." He picked up the pipe again, then thought better of it and put it down. "You do know your chances of succeeding with Ruben Ashford—of giving him the help you desire—are exceedingly small. The facts are arranged against him. He has confessed to the crime. And, we're in Baltimore, and Baltimore has a certain way of dealing with black men like Ruben Ashford. Soon he will be sentenced. I assume Norbert Richards has told you what that sentence will be."

She nodded but said nothing.

"I told you Ruben Ashford was a remarkable man. One of the most remarkable things about him is how fully he has reconciled himself to his fate. By that I mean his death. He is at peace with it. If by helping him you mean raising false hopes—" Crane passed his hand over his eyes. "I ask you to consider how that might affect him. How it might even bring him pain."

Josie had begun to grow tired of this man with his pompous, condescending ways. Perhaps he was right, and her chances of succeeding were small. Even she had thought that was likely to be true. But that didn't mean she shouldn't try. Did Everett Crane truly believe Ruben Ashford would be better off if she just walked away and left him to die?

"Mr. Crane." She stood up, her back straight, drawing herself to her full height. "You said I might speak to Ruben Ashford. I ask you to follow through on what you have promised."

Crane lifted his hands with an air of defeat. "Of course, Miss Berenson. I'm here to oblige." He stood up, returning once again to the solicitous gentleman who had welcomed her into his office. "I will have you taken to him now." The charming smile returned. "And if there's ever anything else I can do to be of service to you or Dr. Meyer, please don't hesitate to let me know."

Thirteen

The jailer with the truncheon returned and once again led Josie through the jail, this time to the interview room, a small space austerely furnished to the point of emptiness, nothing but a scarred wooden table flanked by two chairs. The floor and walls were of stone; the air soured by the familiar smell of river sewage; there were bars on the window and on the door, which was of solid iron and bore a sturdy lock. The jailer deposited her inside and then, as expressionless as ever, excused himself to fetch the prisoner.

As she waited, she paced the room, too anxious to sit. She'd bristled that morning when Nell suggested she cancel the interview, but the truth was, she wasn't at all sure she was up to it. None of the work she'd done so far at the Phipps Clinic had prepared her for a task like this. She'd tried to prepare herself by reading up on psychiatric legal cases, but they all focused on insanity pleas; no one ever asked psychiatrists to consult on the sane. She'd gone to Meyer for advice, but he'd had little to offer. The prisoner, he'd said, had been quite cooperative when he examined him. He was sure she would have no trouble. But Meyer was a man, filled with the gravitas of his position—two qualities she most sorely lacked.

Despite all of her efforts, she'd been unable to come up with a strategy for the interview. It was a failure of the imagination. She simply couldn't imagine what Ruben Ashford was like and therefore couldn't imagine how to approach him. As she paced back and forth in the oppressive, claustrophobic room, words appended to him in the documents she'd read floated into her mind. *Evil. Menacing. Impulsive. Animalistic.* The first had belonged to Ida Crofter, one of the eyewitnesses to the murder, the others to the Virginia psychiatrist who'd examined Ashford. Even if they were biased—as, in the case of the psychiatrist, she was sure they were—they were chilling. On the other hand, Aubrey Foyle, the superintendent of the Rosewood asylum, had called Ashford *congenial* and *compliant*, and Everett Crane, who knew him well, had called him remarkable. What was the real Ruben Ashford like?

She would soon know. From outside the room came the distant sound of footsteps. Steadily it grew closer. Then the door opened, and the jailer walked in, bringing her Ruben Ashford. He was dressed in prison clothing, a loose pair of rough grey cotton pants and jacket, with shackles at the wrists and ankles. He was of average height, with regular features, a smooth forehead and deep, dark eyes. He looked timid and withdrawn, uncomfortable in his own skin, as if he would sink into the floor and disappear if only he could. In every other way he seemed entirely ordinary. In a crowd Josie never would have picked him out. She could well imagine him as a blacksmith or a bookkeeper—both of which he'd been. He was the last person she would have taken for a murderer.

Ashford kept his eyes trained on the ground as he came forward, avoiding her eye. The jailer showed him to his seat, then returned to the door, where he stood on guard, his hand resting lightly on his truncheon. As Ashford sat down, he rested his hands on the table and the heavy shackles clattered. Josie caught her breath. She couldn't take her eyes off the iron chains, couldn't stop thinking how with one move he could lift them and strike her dead. He might appear innocuous, but once he'd killed a white woman just like her, acting out of some kind of unknown impulse. What if he were similarly seized by impulse and attacked her now? She was grateful for the jailer, for the shadow of intimidation he threw across the room.

As she studied him, she realized that, while she might be afraid of him, he was absolutely terrified of her. He was trembling, trying with difficulty to keep himself under control. He must be wondering what she wanted from him, why she had come here. And he was terrified of the guard, too. He kept glancing timidly in his direction, then averting his eyes. The guard seemed to be quite pleased with his ability to intimidate Ashford. He lifted his truncheon and swung it with pleasure by his side.

Then Josie remembered: intimidating Ashford was the last thing she wanted. If she wanted him to open up to her, to speak to her freely and truthfully, she would have to find a way to set him at ease. She pulled herself up, addressing the jailer directly. "Please wait outside." He stared at her in surprise. So did Ashford, who raised his eyes to hers for the first time. "I will speak to the prisoner alone." Still the jailer didn't move, and she didn't either, pinning him with her eyes. Finally he shook his head, muttering something that sounded like "women" under his breath, then shrugged and left the room, clanging the door shut behind him. Josie waited for a moment for the sound to die down. Then she walked to the table, sat down, looked at Ashford, and smiled.

"Mr. Ashford." Her heart was beating in her throat, and she took a deep breath, steadying herself. "I'm sorry if I've startled you. My name is Josefa Berenson. I heard about you from your lawyer, Norbert Richards. I met him at the Johns Hopkins Hospital. I work there, with Dr. Meyer. I believe you met with him previously."

Ashford didn't answer. He had dropped his eyes again, avoiding her. He slouched in his chair, making himself as small as possible. Once again she had the feeling he would disappear if only he could. He was still trembling.

"Mr. Richards asked me to assist in your case. Both he and Dr. Meyer believe I may be able to help you. They've asked me to look into the circumstances surrounding Miss Prentiss's'"—she hesitated—

"Miss Prentiss's death. I've read your confession, but I still have some questions, and thought it might be helpful if you told me what happened in your own words."

Still Ashford said nothing. Other than the slight trembling, he might have been carved of wood. She almost wondered if she'd been understood.

"I thought we might start with the Rosewood School. Did you like it there?"

Again there was no response.

"Perhaps..." Josie said. She fell silent. She didn't know what to say. Already she was despairing of this interview, of her ability to encourage Ashford to speak to her. Nell had said that as a boy, he had been painfully shy. Perhaps that quality was affecting him now. She tried a different tack. "I know your mother. That is to say, I know someone who does. Dr. Winters. She took care of her when she was sick."

"Dr. Winters?" Ashford raised his eyes.

"She's a close friend of mine," Josie said, smiling. "She met you as a child."

"Yes. I remember her."

"Dr. Winters speaks highly of you. She said you were very attached to your mother. I imagine you still are."

Ashford didn't answer, but he at least he was listening and the trembling had stopped.

"Your father is a blacksmith. Is that right?"

He nodded.

"I heard you were apprenticed to him."

Ashford shifted in his chair. "Did you say Mr. Richards sent you?"

"Yes."

"And will you see him again after I talk to you?"

Josie nodded.

Ashford considered this. Then he slumped in his chair, as if he'd been waging a war with himself and had just lost. "Okay. I'll talk to you. I'll answer your questions."

"Thank you." Once again Josie gave him a smile, and while he didn't return it, he at least seemed a bit more easy in her presence. "I was just asking about the years when you were growing up. I heard you worked as a blacksmith with your father."

Ashford nodded. "I was going to be a blacksmith too. It was all I ever wanted. I always liked working with horses."

"I can understand why. I've always liked horses too." Josie rested her hands easily on the table. "How did you come to work at Rosewood?"

Ashford shrugged. "I'm good with numbers."

"Numbers?"

"I see them in my mind. I always have. They line up for me, form patterns. When I have a problem to solve, I look at them for the answer, and see it there."

"Like twenty-seven times forty-eight?"

"One thousand two-hundred and ninety-six." He gave the answer effortlessly. "I didn't realize other people couldn't see them the same way. Mr. Sorenson—"

"Sorenson?" Josie said.

"My mother worked for him. He was a banker. It was a game we'd play. Ever since I was a little boy. He'd recite a list of numbers and I'd give him the sum. Or subtract, or multiply. Whatever he wanted. It amused him. He'd call people in to watch. He liked showing me off. Once he took me into the bank with him and had the tellers gather round. He laughed, telling them how smart I was. Told them they needed to watch out for their jobs. But that was just a joke." His voice trailed off.

A joke. Of course. Black men didn't work as tellers. Even Josie knew that. Certainly not in Baltimore. They might clean floors or toilets, but they would never stand behind the counter and count out white people's money, no matter how smart they were. Had Ashford resented Sorenson's mockery of him? Is this what Richards meant when he said race played a role in the murder? Had Ashford built up a resentment of white people after a lifetime of living under Jim Crow—a resentment that ultimately snapped into violence against his white victim? If so, he didn't say. He just continued with his story.

"When I got old enough, Mr. Sorenson told my mother I should go to the Colored High School. She wanted to send me, but my father didn't see the point. What did a blacksmith need with school? He said I was plenty old enough to start working. All he could talk about were the wages I would lose, day after day, wasting my time in school. So Mr. Sorenson agreed to pay."

"For school?"

"My father. He paid my father so that I could go to school."

He must have felt ashamed. Josie knew she would, if she were in his place. But Ashford didn't elaborate. Instead he fell silent, studying his hands. In the light from the window, the shackles on his wrists gleamed. A certain heaviness had come into his body. More than anything else, he seemed resigned to his situation, as if he'd long ago given up hope of expecting anything different, not just in this conversation with Josie, but in all of his interactions with white people. "One of the teachers at the high school used to work at Rosewood. After graduation she wrote a letter to Dr. Foyle—the superintendent—about me. She told him I was good at mathematics."

"And he hired you?"

Ashford didn't answer. There was no need to.

"And then?"

"I went to work at the asylum. I was Dr. Foyle's bookkeeper." He raised his eyes. "But I expect you know that."

"Your father accepted that?"

An indifferent shrug. "Even a colored bookkeeper earns more than a blacksmith. And I always sent my wages home. Every penny."

"Did you like working there?"

"Dr. Foyle was fair. I'll give him that."

"How do you mean?"

He hesitated. "He always paid me on time."

"That was all?"

"He told me I should be proud of myself. He said I was doing important work. Whenever official visitors came to the asylum—members of the Ladies' Auxiliary, or the board, or the state—he'd make sure they met me. He told them how he'd hired me, giving a poor colored boy from the city a chance. He always finished by saying that he, himself, was blind to color, that he treated everyone alike, black or white, but sadly such was not the state of the world."

"And was he blind to color as you say?"

Again the hesitation. "Dr. Foyle said I should consider myself fortunate to work at Rosewood. He said I was the first colored man to have a job in the Great House—where the administrative work of the asylum is done. He said I had the chance to better myself, do my Christian duty, and be a credit to my race."

A credit to his race. Josie took a moment to think about that. It cut both ways, as if colored people who didn't rise to positions like Ruben Ashford's—people like his mother the maid and his father the blacksmith—were a disgrace. Had Ashford resented that too? Had Dr. Foyle's "color blind" judgments increased his shame? If so, he showed no sign of it. He just sat quietly in his chair, his face impassive, waiting for her to speak.

"Tell me about Rosewood," she said. "I've never seen it."

"I hadn't either before I started working for Dr. Foyle. It's far away, out in the country. I think they put it there on purpose. It's like…"—his voice trailed off—"a place that's been forgotten. That's meant to be forgotten."

"I've been told they care for feeble-minded children."

He nodded.

"What are they like?"

"The children?" Ashford fell silent for a moment, considering. "It's hard to say. I never did understand what feeble-minded was supposed to mean. Dr. Foyle has lots of categories for the children: simpleton, idiot, imbecile, and so on. He keeps track of them in a book. I had to mark down which group each one belonged to. But I never could tell them apart. Most seemed all right to me. Sometimes you could tell there was something different about them, in the way they walked, or talked, or looked at you. But most had a sweetness to them. They would smile when they saw me."

The smiles seemed to have meant a lot to him. His face brightened as he thought of them.

"The youngest are five or six. They can stay until they turn eighteen, then they have to go. They live on the property and work there, too. They even have their own school. The teachers teach them how to read. That's a big goal. Some of them can, but some never learn. But all of the children are supposed to improve at Rosewood. That's what Dr. Foyle says. They're to improve themselves so that they can live productive lives and be good citizens."

"Did you spend a lot of time with them?"

The smile faded, and he shook his head with an air of regret. "I wasn't allowed to—I wasn't supposed to have anything to do with them. They're white and I'm…" Again his voice trailed off. She was struck with how reconciled he seemed to the things he was describing. She would have found them infuriating. For the first time she was realizing how infuriating it must be to be on the other side of the black-white equation. "The teachers are white too. Dr. Foyle says it wouldn't do to have white children taught by someone who was colored."

"Are all of the children white?"

"Colored children don't go to Rosewood. They go to Crownsville. It's near Annapolis. I've never been there myself. From what I hear, I wouldn't want to. It's supposed to be a terrible place. Naked children left unattended in locked wards."

"But Rosewood—Rosewood isn't like that?"

"No." This was spoken fiercely, with an air of pride. "I give Dr. Foyle credit for that. The children are well kept. They're clean. They have uniforms to wear. Plenty to eat." He fell silent for a moment. "You asked me before if I liked it at Rosewood. I suppose I did. I'd never been in the country before. It's quiet there, green and pretty. There are fields and woods and meadows with a little stream that runs through the middle."

Ashford turned away, and Josie caught him looking out the window, where the branches of a tree were visible, the leaves shivering lightly in the wind. He looked at them with longing. The tree was only a few feet away, but it might as well have been on a different planet. If she didn't succeed in helping him, he might never touch a leaf again, smell its earthy scent, feel its silky softness in his hand. It made her heart turn.

"Did you ever go home?" Josie asked softly.

He pulled his gaze away from the window to answer her. "I did at first, but Rosewood's far from Baltimore. You have to take the train. Tickets are expensive, and the station's over two miles away. After a while I just stayed at the asylum. My mother said she would come see me, but she never did. It was hard for her to get time off work. She wrote me letters. My father—well, I don't think he ever wanted to see Rosewood. He was against me working there from the start. He said nothing good would ever come of it."

"What did he mean by that?"

Ashford didn't say.

"You said the children work at the asylum. What do you mean by that?"

"Most of the property is set out for farming. The boys do the labor on it. They run the plows, plant the crops, hoe the fields, help with the animals. A few colored men work there, too, as hired hands. They do blacksmithing, masonry, roofing, fencing, things like that. The hired hands live in a bunkhouse. Martin Rutledge—he's the farm manager—oversees them. He's a white man." Ashford shrugged as if to say, what else would she expect? "They grow corn, vegetables, wheat, and hay. They've got cows for milk and hogs for meat. Anything that doesn't get eaten gets sold. Rosewood's supposed to be self-supporting, but it isn't. I saw that in the ledger books well enough. We were always running behind. I heard Dr. Foyle arguing more than once with members of the board about that. He said we needed more money, that what we got from the state wasn't enough. Over three hundred children at the school and another hundred on the waiting list. He said it broke his heart to turn them away."

"And the girls? Do they work on the farm, too?"

"No. They learn housekeeping. Sewing and cooking and cleaning. When they leave the school, they go to work as maids for wealthy families in the city." His voice dropped. "It doesn't always work out."

"What do you mean?"

"I heard some of them can't do what's expected of them. They're let go. Only there's no place for them after that, and they end up on the street."

How quiet he was when he spoke of these things, seemingly without emotion. Did they mean nothing to him? Or had he long ago decided they were out of his hands, and there was no use caring about them? She couldn't tell and didn't know how to ask. "Did you live in the bunkhouse with the other colored men?"

This elicited a sad smile. "Dr. Foyle wouldn't allow that. I wasn't supposed to associate with the field hands. Dr. Foyle said I was above them, and I was to work on improving myself. He gave me my own place."

"Where was that?"

"I had a cabin in the woods near the front gate."

"But if you weren't allowed to associate with the children, and you weren't allowed to talk to the field hands—who did you associate with?"

Ashford didn't answer.

"With the teachers?"

He looked at her as if the question didn't even merit a response.

"What about the other people in the Great House?"

"They wouldn't have anything to do with me." A hint of bitterness surfaced in his voice then was gone. "There was one woman…"

"Yes?"

"I met her at church. I went on Sundays. It's a small place, just down the road from the asylum. The pastor lets colored folk in, as long as we sit in the back. I didn't mind. I was just glad to be there. It reminded me of church at home. This woman—she worked at Rosewood too. She was a seamstress. Plenty of colored women work at the asylum, cleaning, cooking, doing the laundry. I started talking to her, and even walked out with her once or twice. But then Mrs. Crofter found out about it."

"The head matron?"

He nodded. "She said she couldn't have things like that going on at the school. She said it was immoral." Once again he let this remark pass without further comment, and Josie couldn't think of what to say. "She let the seamstress go. Mrs. Crofter wanted me to go too, but that was up to Dr. Foyle, and he wouldn't agree."

A picture was beginning to form in Josie's mind of Ashford's situation—a picture that could easily lead to his motive for killing Constance Prentiss. Ruben Ashford would have had more than enough reason to be consumed by resentment for white people—even hate. They'd thwarted his every attempt to satisfy his desires in life, from blacksmithing to courting. Constance Prentiss may very well have paid the price for that. Above all, Ashford had faced isolation at Rosewood. Every effort he'd made to reach out had been denied. He'd been a man apart, belonging to neither the black world nor white. But everyone needs companionship, someone to talk to, to touch. He must have suffered from a deep and abiding loneliness. It must have been unbearable.

"Why did you stay?"

He seemed surprised by the question. "A lot of people wanted me to work at Rosewood. My mother, Mr. Sorenson, my high school teacher, Dr. Foyle. I didn't want to disappoint them."

They had been sitting a long time. Josie stood and stretched and walked to the window, looking out at the lone tree.

"Something you said in your confession puzzles me," she said at last, returning to her seat. "You told me they had blacksmiths on the farm. And yet on the day Constance Prentiss died, you wrote that you were shoeing one of Dr. Foyle's horses."

Ashford dropped his eyes and spoke with a guarded air. "The mare was Dr. Foyle's special mount. He liked to ride her around the property on Sunday afternoons. She was a good horse, fine, but with sensitive feet. They bruised easily. Shortly before I arrived, the farm blacksmith botched her shoes, leaving her lame. Dr. Foyle was furious. He knew I'd been trained as a blacksmith and asked me to tend to her. I gave her new shoes, and after that she was sound. Dr. Foyle let it be known that no one was to touch her feet again except for me."

"But surely blacksmithing wasn't your job."

"I didn't mind. Like I said, I always liked working with horses."

"But no one else saw you working with a horse that day."

He had no answer to that.

His diffidence was beginning to annoy her. It was all very well to have a theory about motive, but she needed more than that. She needed some kind of proof. "Mr. Ashford." She looked at him directly. "You do know there are two eyewitnesses in your case."

"Yes. The sheriff told me."

"Neither of them reported seeing you with a horse. How do you explain that?"

Again he gave no answer.

"On the day—on the day Constance Prentiss died, you said she came looking for a ride to the train station."

"Yes."

"But driving the buggy wasn't part of your job either, was it?"

"They all asked me for rides to the station. Dr. Foyle and Mrs. Crofter and Martin Rutledge, too. That was the only time most of them would talk to me. When they had something they wanted from me."

"And you drove them?"

For the first time she thought she saw a hint of resentment come into his face, but again he gave no answer.

"And Constance Prentiss? Did you drive her to the station too?"

"Yes." He spoke so softly, Josie could hardly hear him.

"But you said you didn't know her. Everyone said that was so."

"Did I know Miss Prentiss?" Ashford raised his eyes. "No, I can't say I did."

Josie was beginning to become irritated with this man, with his impenetrability, his lack of emotion, the way he answered her questions without answering them at all. Something had made him murder Constance Prentiss, most likely shame or resentment or loneliness, or a combination of all three. But she was having trouble sorting it out.

"Miss Prentiss was always kind to me," he said, as if he could read her thoughts. "I had nothing against her."

Then why, Josie wanted to say, why on earth did you kill her? Could her murder really be the result of a symbolic lashing out at the white race? It hardly seemed likely. Why pick her? And in any case, she was beginning to have trouble imagining this passive, shy, diffident man lashing out at anyone in any circumstance. He seemed primed to go along with what anyone asked of him, black or white.

Once more she took herself to the window. The wind had died down and the limbs of the tree hung limply. As she watched, a leaf came loose and fell towards the ground. "Tell me," she said, keeping her back to him, "about what happened, about the day you killed Constance Prentiss."

"I—" he said. "I can still—" For a long time there was silence, then he began to speak. His voice sounded strange, otherworldly. When she turned around, his eyes were focused elsewhere, gazing into the distance, as if he were in a dream. "I can still see it. The hammer, the horse, the anvil, everything. I think about it all the time. I see Miss Prentiss, I hear her ask about the buggy. I see myself with the hammer. I see—"

He lifted his shackled hands and thrust them out to her. His face was twisted in pain. "I don't want to see it anymore. I want to die. I want it to be over."

Josie caught her breath, her hand at her throat.

"I told Mr. Richards not to fight for me. Just let them get to it. I was arrested twenty-six days ago. I've been in jail for more than 624 hours. That's 37,440 minutes. I don't want to be here one minute longer. It doesn't matter if I go to hell after they hang me. I'm there already. I'm begging you. You said you were going to see Mr. Richards after you spoke to me. Tell him I want him to stop. Tell him I want him to leave me be."

"Why—" Josie broke off. It was cruel to ask someone in such pain, but she couldn't stop herself. She had to know. "Why did you do it? Why did you kill her?"

"I don't know." He swept his manacled hands across his face. "I ask myself that every day. Don't you see? I just don't know."

The mask was off, leaving the man's true face: a picture of unrelenting anguish. Josie couldn't bear to see it. She was shaking. She rapped on the door, and the jailer came in. "Take him," she said hoarsely. "Take him away." She stood as if stuck to the floor as the jailer escorted Ruben Ashford from the room. At the last moment he turned back to her. "Tell everyone I'm sorry. Tell them I said that." Then he was gone.

Josie followed the jailer to the exit of the jail. When they came to the courtyard, she saw a group of prisoners at work, converting the loose pile of lumber into a gallows. Who would hang this time? One day, sooner rather than later, unless she could find a way to help Ruben Ashford, he would hang there too.

But she couldn't find a way to help him. And he'd been explicit. He didn't want her to.

She left the jail, relieved to see the mob was gone. She was still shaking, and she stood for a moment in the shadow of the walls, steadying herself. She would have to tell Norbert Richards what

Ashford said: that he wanted him to drop his case. She had a duty to do so. But first she would go to the hospital and tell Dr. Meyer that she had failed. She hated to disappoint him, especially after he'd shown such confidence in her, but she didn't have a choice. She certainly hadn't arrived at any answers. The hospital was about a mile to the east, and as she walked there, Everett Crane's words returned to her. Are you blinded by hope? he'd asked her. Yes, she wanted to say, I was, but not anymore.

Soon the Johns Hopkins Hospital came into view, sitting high on the hill, the iconic dome reaching for the sky. There was some kind of commotion out front. Ambulances, trucks, and horse-drawn carts lined the circular drive. A woman stood in the middle of the street, waving her arms. Had there been an accident? Josie hurried forward. She dashed up the steps, passing a pair of men carrying a patient on a stretcher. A nurse was helping another patient through the front door. Inside a man had fallen to the floor. Josie saw no obvious trauma linking the three, no wounds, blood, or broken bones. Then with a stab of fear she realized the link between them—and to the woman who had collapsed that morning on the streetcar. Each of them was gasping for breath, and each one was tinged with blue.

Fourteen

Margaret was gone. In the end Nell could do nothing but sit by her side as she gasped for breath, her lungs full of fluid, her skin dusky with cyanosis. By the time she succumbed, drawing her last breath at the break of dawn, Nell was relieved. At least Margaret's suffering was over. But then Margaret's mother began to wail, and her father turned his face to the wall. For this family, the suffering had only just begun.

"I'll send someone to come for her," Nell said. For Margaret's body, she meant. She couldn't bring herself to say it. She knew Margaret's parents wouldn't want to hear it. They weren't ready to let their daughter go. Nell had seen it over and over again in the three weeks since the influenza epidemic took hold in Baltimore. The flu came on too quickly, and the dying happened too fast, leaving people no time to cope. One day their beloved was with them, warm and alive. The next day they were gone, cold and dead. How was anyone supposed to react under those circumstances? Numbness set in, a kind of vacancy, the mind simply shutting down. If Nell could, she would go numb herself, crawl into bed, pull the blankets over her head and never come out. She'd never experienced anything like this before in her years as a doctor—never expected to experience anything like it in her lifetime. Nothing she'd learned in medical school had prepared her for a tragedy as all-encompassing as this. But she had no choice but to move forward. Too many people depended on her. All day long they came to her door, filling her waiting room, lining her steps, spilling out onto the sidewalk. At night knocks came to the door—both front and back. Already three people on McCulloh Street were dead, and at least a dozen other families were caring for sick relatives at home. She needed to get back home.

She slipped out of Margaret's house, leaving her parents with the promise to send someone to come for their daughter. It was a promise she knew very well she might not be able to keep. According to the *Baltimore Sun*, well over ten thousand people in the city were ill, with nearly a thousand already dead. Every day the numbers rose. At the beginning of the epidemic the black horse-drawn hearses had been a familiar sight, wending their way to the Greenmount and Baltimore Cemeteries where the bells on the gates tolled their mournful arrival. But lately even the hearses had disappeared, the funeral parlors closing one after another, their directors felled by flu. The entire city was beset by shortages of caskets and gravediggers. The mayor had proclaimed burials must be done as quickly as possible, to allow for more of the dead to be cared for. But proclamations were one thing. Carrying them out was another. In the alleyways it was worst of all. Nell had seen black bodies abandoned on porches, heaped in piles on the curb.

Only please, she thought, please not Margaret. Let there be a burial for her.

With dawn had come a soft blue sky, a fresh tang to the air. It was a lovely day in mid-October, or rather would be if any day could be called lovely at a time like this. West Baltimore had a ghostlike feel, the streets and alleyways all but deserted. People were too ill—or too afraid—to come out. A masked woman walked by, her shoulders hunched, her eyes downcast, keeping her distance. A lone man drove an empty cart. A pig rooted forlornly in the gutter, looking for garbage to eat.

Just that morning Nell had read in the *Sun* that flu had infected the city jail, rendering dozens of prisoners ill along with their guards. The courts had shut down, bringing criminal proceedings to a halt. As far as Nell knew, nothing more had happened in the Ruben Ashford case. She didn't even know if he was still alive. Influenza might have claimed him too. She was ashamed to admit it, but she hoped so. To die of the flu might be a kindness. One day, no matter what, he would hang. Of that she was sure. At least Josie had decided to drop his case. So she'd said after she interviewed him in the city jail. She hadn't told Nell the reason why. The epidemic struck, and there simply wasn't the time to talk anymore about it.

A few days after the day Josie interviewed Ashford at the City Jail, she'd moved into the hospital, where she worked night and day, pitching in wherever she could. She mopped floors, washed bed linens, cooked pots of broth. Meanwhile Nell worked night and day too, tending to as many patients as she could, making house calls on the ones who were too sick to go out, and seeing the others who made it to her door—both front and back—in her examination room. She hardly slept. Even Esme, who famously survived on little sleep, had been working to the breaking point, cooking and carrying food to the housebound.

The list of the dead grew until it was heartbreaking. Maxwell Donauer, the haberdasher who once called for Ruben Ashford's early execution, lost his wife. Edith Moskowitz fell ill and became bedridden. With no one to look in on her, she starved to death. Overcome with despair, a man shot his ailing wife to death and then turned the gun on himself. The flu delivered one unimaginable horror after another. Then the most unimaginable thing of all happened, and the Johns Hopkins Hospital closed down. They simply couldn't take any more patients. Too many nurses and doctors had fallen ill, and the wards were overflowing. But the closure filled Nell with despair. It felt like a betrayal—especially for the people of the alleyways. With Hopkins shut, Provident became the only hospital left still taking people of color. Then Provident closed its doors, too. Meanwhile the flu raged through the alleyways, feeding on the crowded conditions like unchecked fire.

Nell hurried down one alleyway after another. She had to see to

Margaret's burial. But first she had to get back to her patients. She had to get home. All at once she heard a voice.

"Miss. Please."

Don't stop, she thought. Keep your head down and keep walking. You can't help everyone. You can't possibly—

"Please. Miss."

She stopped and turned. "Yes?"

A black man was standing in the doorway of a shack, clinging to the frame, barely able to stay upright. He was tall and thin, would be thin even under the best of circumstances, Nell thought, but from illness had become skeletal. His eyes were bloodshot, his lips dry and cracked. If nothing else, he needed water. Nell knew how hard it would be to get it into him. It was one of the worst symptoms of the influenza, people refusing to eat or drink. Then she realized—it was in his face—he wasn't asking for himself.

"Please. Miss." He held out his hand.

"Yes." She took a deep breath. "Of course."

She followed him inside. The shack was a storage room. It smelled faintly of earth; bales of straw and bags of corn were stacked against the walls. Someone must have kicked him out of the place where he was living when he got sick, and he had ended up here. The floor was dirt, the ceiling exposed rafters, the walls nothing more than wooden slats nailed up haphazardly with light leaking through the seams.

In the center of the room was a woman stretched out on a blanket. Dead. Newly dead, Nell guessed. Only a few hours most likely, sometime in the night. The flies were only now finding their way to her; she hadn't yet started to smell. Nell felt a surge of hopelessness and frustration and finally anger at the man who had called her in here. Surely he must know there was nothing she could do. He must be mad from shock. "I can't help you. She's gone."

"No." He pointed to a pile of rags in the corner. "Miss," he said again. "Please."

Nell drew closer. Nestled in the rags was an infant. Three months or so old, as far as she could tell. The baby looked up at her, bright-eyed, the mouth working, the fingers clasping and unclasping. Nell had been taking care of sick people so long, she'd forgotten how good it felt to see someone well. The baby cooed, wriggled happily, offering her a crooked smile.

"Please," the man said again.

She knew what he wanted, just as she knew what her answer must be. She couldn't possibly take care of this child. "Isn't there anyone else?" she said, even as she knew there wasn't. If there had been, they would have come already and taken the baby away.

The man's lips moved. "Please," he was saying. He mouthed the word silently.

Milk. Nell would need milk, and where was she to find it? Most of the stores were closed, and the ones that were still open had shortened hours. Supplies were low, the shelves bare, milk gone along with everything else, and there was no one left to bring more. How quickly the world had come to a halt! The carters and drivers were ill just like the gravediggers and the funeral directors and the firemen and the streetcar conductors and the teachers and the merchants. The city had simply shut down.

She rummaged in her bag for a pen and her prescription pad. Not for a prescription—there was no point in writing one. Medicines were gone: aspirin, Epsom salts, quinine, bicarbonate, epinephrine. All scarcer than dragon's teeth. Pharmacies were experiencing shortages just like everyone else. She wrote her name and address on the page, ripped it off, and handed it to him. "When you are better, come and get your baby."

He didn't have the strength to thank her. She saw it in his eyes.

She pulled a packet of aspirin from her bag. "Take this. With water. As much water as you can. Do you understand?"

He shook his head. He didn't want to take it. He wanted her to keep it for others who still might be saved.

She pressed the packet into his hand. "Take this. Do you hear me?

And when you are better, come and get your baby."

She bent over and picked up the baby. She was surprised at how comforting it felt to hold someone so warm and alive.

"Thula," he said.

"What?"

"Her name is Thula." He glanced towards the corpse on the floor. "Like her mother. Tell her that."

"You will tell her yourself," Nell said firmly. But she knew he wouldn't. As she left the house, she looked back and saw Thula's father, his great responsibility discharged, lie down beside his wife and close his eyes.

Nell hurried home, Thula tucked securely in her arms. They emerged from the alleyways onto Eutaw Place, the grandest of the west side avenues. In the center ran a park-like median, studded with fountains. Normally Eutaw would be bustling at this time of the morning with carriages and motorcars and nannies pushing prams. Today it was all but deserted. Only the children were out. They'd been gathering on the avenue for days now, ever since the schools closed, the girls playing hopscotch or skipping rope, the boys hunched over games of marbles or stick ball. It was one of the things that surprised Nell most about the flu: the age of its victims. Normally epidemics took the oldest and the young, but this influenza killed people in the prime of life—people like Margaret and Theo. And Thula's parents. How many more children would be left orphaned when it was over?

A my name is Alice, my husband's name is Albert, we live in Annapolis where we sell apples…

The girls sang as they skipped rope. Suddenly Nell felt dizzy, the world turning. She sank onto a bench by a fountain. She must be more tired than she thought. She would rest for a minute with Thula in her arms. She closed her eyes, listening to the girls chant.

B my name is Betty, my husband's name is Byron, we live in Birmingham where we sell bottles…

Nell peered down at Thula, and Thula looked back, her gaze open and trusting.

C my name is Clara, my husband's name is Carl, we live in Cumberland where we sell cotton…

Thula whimpered, and Nell pressed the baby closer. "Milk," she said. "Yes, I know. You need milk." She would find milk, and then she would talk to Esme about finding a place for the baby until—well, if her father came for her.

As Nell stood, the world turned again. The sun was so bright now, hurting her eyes. She leaned against the bench, steadying herself. Then she tucked her head, tightened her grip on the baby, and headed for home.

Some of the girls on the avenue had joined hands and were skipping in a circle while they sang. *Ring around the rosy, pockets full of posy, ashes, ashes, we all fall down.* The song, Nell had heard, dated to the years of the black plague. *Ring around the rosy*: the distinctive rash that announced the onset of the illness. *A pocket full of posy*: the flowers sufferers would conceal in their pockets to mask the smell of the disease. *Ashes, ashes, we all fall down.* That was self-explanatory. Then Nell heard another group singing. *I had a little bird. Its name was Enza. I opened the door and in-flu-enza.*

What would the world be like when the influenza epidemic ended—if it ever did? What would survive? What would be remembered, and what forgotten? Hundreds of years from now would little girls skip rope and chant, *I had a little bird. Its name was Enza?* If they did, would they know where the words came from? Would they know how much grief and loss and sickness and dying lay behind each one? Would they even know what the words meant?

By the time Nell got home, Thula was wailing. Nell slipped in the back door, avoiding the line of patients at the front. Esme was in the kitchen. She looked at Nell then at the baby, then at Nell again. "We need milk," Nell said. She didn't have the energy to explain. She would have to tell Esme about Margaret, but she couldn't even begin to think about that now. "Please tell me we have milk."

Esme didn't answer. She stepped to the side, gesturing behind her. There, standing at the back of the room, was a man. "Mason?" Nell said. What was Mason Fordham doing in her kitchen? Then she remembered: his wife. She was due around this time. "Lily," she said to Mason, "is she all right? Is she—?"

Mason smiled, a shy grin that lit his face. "Lily's fine. Lily and the baby. It's a boy. She wanted you to be there when it came. She wants you to know she's sorry about that. But my sister helped, she's birthed babies before. And Lily was strong. She was so strong." His eyes shone with pride. "She told me to come tell you that everything is all right, and when you can, if you could please come see the new baby. Our son."

"Oh, Mason." Nell couldn't begin to tell him how much this news meant to her. As Margaret was dying, Lily was giving birth. Death and life: they always came intertwined. Nell must never forget that.

Thula didn't care. She was no philosopher. She just needed to eat. Her wailing had taken on a higher pitch now, a frightened urgency. "Milk," Nell said to Esme. "Do we have it?" Then she looked at Mason. "Do you think?" She held the baby out to him. "Do you think that you and Lily—?"

Mason grew serious. He didn't ask; he just took on the responsibility offered to him. It was the one silver lining to the flu: how people stood up for one another.

"Like I said, Lily's strong. She's real strong." He took the baby from Nell's arms, bent over her, gentling and hushing her. "Shh, shh, you'll be all right."

"Her name is Thula," Nell said. "Tell Lily—" Tell Lily I will come soon, she wanted to say, but she couldn't. The world was turning again, and this time it didn't stop.

Fifteen

Mrs. Charles Forester
226 Commonwealth Avenue
Boston, Massachusetts

November 19, 1918

My dearest Adele,

I can't tell you how sorry I was to hear about the death of your dear husband Charles. It must have felt like an especially cruel trick of fate to lose him so soon after you had begun your life together. I'm glad to hear you will keep his sons, it was what Charles wanted, and his family agrees. They will be a comfort to you, as I know you will be to them.

I was sorry also to hear about Eleanor's sister. What a terrible loss that must be. They were always so close, and Eleanor depended on her greatly. Is there anyone who has come through this epidemic untouched? I used to think nothing would be the same after the war, but now I think it's influenza that has changed us. When news came that the Germans had surrendered, I confess it meant nothing to me. That same day I learned over twenty thousand people had been struck with flu in Baltimore, and at least three thousand dead. We'll never know the exact toll, since so many of the doctors have been overwhelmed or sick themselves and unable to keep records. The good news is that Calvin's well and will be coming home after the first of the year. That's a comfort. We're all survivors now and must shore each other up as best as we can.

Life is finally returning to normal here—or what passes for normal these days. The schools have reopened, as have the churches and stores. They sent Negro soldiers from Camp Meade to bury the dead in Mount Auburn Cemetery, over two hundred colored people whose bodies had been left in sheds or stacked outside in coffins. No one knows what will become of all the abandoned children since the orphanages are full and have no more beds. Some I hear have been sent out to work.

Dr. John Blake, our health commissioner, reports that the city's death rate is no longer elevated. At the peak of the epidemic, it was the highest in the country. I freely admit I blame him for much of it. For a long time he denied the flu was here, and insisted it was no cause for alarm, even after people had begun to die. Then he dragged his feet, refusing to set up quarantines or curtail public gatherings. Apparently he ascribed to the ridiculous theory that closures would cause panic, which would lower people's immunity, leading to more illness. No scientist worth his salt, certainly none at Johns Hopkins, subscribes to such bunk. Honestly I think Blake's real fear was that the flu would interfere with the war effort. No matter what, the Liberty Bond rallies and parades had to go on, never mind the lives that could have been spared if he'd only taken common sense measures. I will never forgive him.

The hospital is finally returning to normal, too. The medical students have returned from Western Maryland, where they were sent to man emergency clinics for the B&O Railroad in hopes of keeping the lines of transportation open. At the height of the epidemic, we closed our doors. It was a terrible thing to do, but we were shorthanded to begin with, so many medical personnel working overseas, and simply couldn't take in more patients. The shortage of nurses was particularly bad. We filled six wards with our own staff, all who were desperately ill. They looked absolutely shot-to-pieces. In the end we lost three students, three doctors, and four nurses, one who looked as if she'd been gassed when she died. Even Dr. Meyer fell ill, went home, and took to his bed. Thankfully I hear he's expected to enjoy a full recovery. At Phipps we closed the dispensary so that all hands could treat the flu. The clinic itself escaped the worst of the outbreak, although one woman suffering from delusions came down with a dangerously high fever. When she recovered, to our surprise, her delusions were gone, and the doctors sent her home.

What scared me most was how little we could do. Despite their best efforts, the doctors could find no treatment to make a difference, neither anti-toxins nor vaccines. They couldn't even agree on what caused the flu, some saying the Pfeiffer's bacillus of epidemics in the past, others saying a new kind of virus. All we could do was minister courage, cheerfulness, and a sense of peace to those who were stricken. It broke my heart, Adele, to see so many suffering, especially the ones who gave up, saying it was no use, they would never live. Without hope, there is nothing.

I'm sorry to tell you we lost Nell's housekeeper, Margaret. We almost lost Nell. In the end it was no surprise she got sick. For weeks she ran herself ragged, hardly sleeping, giving everything for her patients. I was working night and day in the hospital and didn't even know she'd fallen ill. Esme was so frantic caring for her, she could think of nothing else. More than once she thought Nell would die. But then Nell rallied and asked for me. Esme sent James to the hospital, and when I heard the news, I came straight home. When I saw Nell's face—I've never been so frightened in my life. Esme didn't want to leave her side but I insisted and finally she turned the nursing over to me. She had been running herself ragged too, caring not only for Nell but also for the families she helps through her church, gathering donations of clothes and cooking food for the bereft.

Nell was bedridden for weeks even after the worst of the

symptoms had passed. She was so weak, lost so much weight, and altogether became a paler version of herself. Lately she has begun to recover and is seeing patients again for a few hours in the morning. She wants to do more, but Esme and I forbid it. On this we see eye to eye. Nell is still too easily exhausted. In the meantime James has been handling her practice, doing a workmanlike job, showing how much he has learned and what an excellent pharmacist he will become.

How can you find meaning in something that is so meaningless? Over and over I ask myself that. So many people, it seems to me, have used the flu for their own purposes, twisting and turning it. Some call it a plague and say God has visited it on us for our evil ways. But what evil exactly? When colored people die, white people say it proves their perfidy. When white people die, colored preachers say God is punishing them for Jim Crow. Some say the flu is here to show us God's great mercy—at least for the survivors. Others see it as nothing more than a random act of nature, a storm or conflagration, or another war like the one we fought overseas. For me it was a nightmare. Words simply can't convey what it was like. I don't need to tell you that. If in the end it is forgotten that, I think, will be a blessing.

I will confess, dear Adele, that the epidemic affected me another way. I won't go into details—this letter has gone on long enough. But before it struck, I took on a new case, one that led me to see Baltimore in a new way. Suddenly everything about it depressed me, especially the insidious Jim Crow. How I missed you then, how I missed all of you, even Freddie. I thought I wouldn't be able to bear living here and was overcome with a desire to come back to Boston—to come *home*.

Then, when I saw Nell suffering, when I came so close to losing her, everything else fell away. Do not blush, dear Adele, if I confess to you openly that when I fell in love with Nell, I felt only the excitement of our union, the blurring of boundaries, the joining of one soul to another. I tell you these things because you are one of the few people I can speak to so fully and honestly about my feelings. The intoxication I felt with Nell was only that much deeper as we didn't have to overcome the natural divide that separates women from men. I believed we had found ourselves in each other.

Now we have changed and matured, coming to a place that is sadder but wiser. We will never agree on everything, Nell and I. I know that now. We are two very different people, just as Baltimore and Boston are two very different cities. Still I remain convinced of the rightness of our union. Whatever I may face in life—including the difficulties of living in this southern city—I will face with her at my side.

I once told Nell I never wanted an ordinary life. How wrong I was. An ordinary life is the most any of us can hope for, especially if we are fortunate enough to spend it with the ones we love. Each and every one of us is precious—and fragile. The flu has taught me that. There is a kind of terrible beauty to our existence on this earth. It's all we have left to cling to. I hope it is enough.

I remain, with great affection,

Your Josie

Sixteen

On the first of December, the courts finally reopened and addressed the backlog of cases. The next day the *Baltimore Sun* reported that Ruben Ashford had been sentenced and would hang by the neck until dead for the murder of Constance Prentiss.

That night Josie finally told Nell about her interview with Ruben Ashford in the City Jail over two months earlier—before the epidemic struck—a lifetime ago.

"I would have told you before," Josie said, "but you were so busy with your patients, and then you were so ill." Scaring me to death, she might have added, but she didn't. She didn't have to. Nell knew. She reached over and ran her hand down Nell's cheek. "It wasn't the right time. But now that the sentencing has come out…" She gave Nell a small smile. "We need to talk about it."

They had just finished dinner and were having tea in the parlor, a cold wind blowing outside, rattling the windowpanes. But in the hearth a fire burned brightly and the room was warm.

"He asked me to drop his case," Josie said. "He said he didn't want my help—he didn't want anyone's help. He asked me to tell Norbert Richards to stop making efforts on his behalf, too. It was terrible. He begged me. He was in so much pain." She lifted her tea cup then put it down. "But he remembered you. That was something. I don't think he would have talked to me at all if he hadn't."

"I still remember him, too," Nell said softly.

For a time they were silent. There didn't seem to be anything else to say.

Finally Nell spoke. "What will happen now?"

"I don't know. I assume the sentence will be carried out, but I don't know when. But I'll go see Mr. Richards and tell him what Mr. Ashford said. And I'll tell Dr. Meyer too, although I'll be sorry to do it. He put such faith in me."

Josie stood up and walked to the hearth, speaking to Nell with her back turned. "If only there was something I could have said, something I could have done to make him change his mind…" She poked at the fire unnecessarily, ineffectually. Then she turned around and raised her hands in a helpless gesture. "I know, there was nothing I could have done. Still, I'm the one who talks so much about choice, about why people do the things they do, and the values that underlie their decisions. Only in this case, the choice wasn't even mine to make. It was his. I have to respect that. Still I can't help feeling as if I've failed all of them, Ruben Ashford most of all."

Nell stood up and put her arms around her. "Don't blame yourself."

Josie nodded. "Anyway, now he's been sentenced, and I suppose that puts an end to it."

The two women walked upstairs. Nell, Josie knew, would be glad to see Ruben Ashford's case come to a close. She'd been against Josie's involvement from the start. And Ashford would finally get what he wanted. He would die. No doubt he was already counting the minutes, the hours, and the days to the hanging. There was nothing left for her to do but put it all behind her.

But putting it behind her was something she found she couldn't do.

Three days later she was in Norbert Richards's office, a dimly lit room in the basement of a Redwood Street row house, dominated by a desk piled high with papers, files, and folders, with more of the same heaped on chairs and on the floor. There was hardly room for the lawyer to sit, let alone her. Outside it was cold, a dreary rain falling. It wasn't much warmer inside. Josie kept her coat on as she perched on the narrow chair Richards provided her, wondering how many prisoners like Ruben Ashford the lawyer was defending in his attempt to usher justice into the world. And how many—if any—were in a position to pay his bills.

"Miss Berenson." The lawyer gave her what she knew was his best attempt at a smile. "I'm happy to see you."

She smiled back. "As I am to see you. After influenza, I take nothing for granted."

"Nor do I."

She folded her hands in her lap. "I wanted you to know that I met with Ruben Ashford a few months ago. He asked me to drop his case. He asked me to tell you to do the same."

He eyed her gravely. "Go on."

"I meant to do so at once. Under the circumstances, it seemed the only thing—the right thing—to do. Then influenza hit and…" She raised her hands helplessly.

"I understand."

"It's probably too late to even be talking about it now, since he's been sentenced. And I know I'm duty bound to respect his wishes. But I can't. I came here this morning to tell you that, despite everything, I'd like your permission to go on."

He seemed surprised to hear it. "Please, explain."

She gave him a small smile. "I don't know if I can. Sometimes I think it's because of the flu. I've seen—we've all seen—so much death over the past few weeks, and it's hard to think of even one more person dying. I've never believed in capital punishment, and while it's true Mr. Ashford has asked me to abandon him to his fate, I ask myself: if a man holds a gun to his head and begs you to leave him to it, do you simply walk away?"

He sat quietly, waiting for her to continue.

"I believe in the quest for justice you spoke of, and the perfection of the law. I share your goals. Lately I've taken them to heart in a way I never have before." She grew silent in acknowledgement of her own shortcomings. "But all that is everything and nothing. All I can tell you is that ever since I met Ruben Ashford, I can't forget him. His case has taken hold of me ways I can't explain. *Ruben Ashford* has taken hold of me. I simply can't let him go."

"I see." Richards fell silent, considering. He seemed to have aged in the months since Josie had seen him last. She was struck again with weight of his presence, how tired and heavy he appeared, as if gravity exerted a particularly strong force in the place where he sat.

"Three black men were hung in the courtyard of the city jail this week," he said at last. "Two more are scheduled for tomorrow." He gave her a grim look. "Apparently they're making up for time lost during the flu epidemic. Like you, Miss Berenson, I have no love of capital punishment. In my view, we've seen enough of these executions." He passed a hand over his eyes. "Would it surprise you to know that Ruben Ashford also asked me to quit working on his behalf? And yet immediately after his sentencing, I filed a request for an appeal in his case."

"An appeal?" She hadn't expected to hear that. "Have you found new evidence then?"

"I'm afraid not. But I am hoping to gain time. The judge has granted us thirty days. Barring any change, Mr. Ashford will hang in the new year. Under these circumstances, if you are indeed willing to keep working on Mr. Ashford's behalf, I'd be grateful."

Josie nodded. "Thirty days. That, at least, is something." She thought about it. "And if we succeed?"

"The most we can hope for is that the governor will commute his sentence. Ruben Ashford has confessed to murder, and no matter what, will spend the rest of his life in jail."

Counting each and every minute, each and every day, as she very well knew. "In that case, I fear we may only increase his suffering."

Mr. Richards inclined his head. Each of them had made their decision, and would have to make their peace with it, too.

"So you went to the jail and spoke to Mr. Ashford," the lawyer said. "I expect you met Everett Crane?"

Josie nodded.

"I'm sorry to tell you he died from influenza."

"Oh." She'd found the warden infuriating at times, but admired the way he'd injected a note of humanism into the most inhumane of places. "I'm sorry to hear it."

"As are we all. I doubt we will see his like again." Mr. Richards placed his hands on his desk. "Tell me about your interview with Mr. Ashford. What was it like?"

"Frustrating, I'm afraid. I didn't come away with any answers. I still don't know why he killed Constance Prentiss. But I wouldn't say the interview was fruitless."

The lawyer waved his hand. "Continue."

"Several things struck me. First of all, Mr. Ashford is remarkably consistent in the story he tells. He repeated almost word for word his confession. I believe he's telling the truth when he says Constance Prentiss sought him out because she wanted him to drive her to the train station. He didn't lure her to the stable with some kind of subterfuge, as the eyewitness Abram Sledge suggested. Apparently she wasn't the only white person at the asylum to use him for favors of this kind."

Mr. Richards rested his chin in his hand, listening.

"Ruben Ashford was lonely at Rosewood. He made no friends there; his position didn't allow for it. Isolation may have played a role in his crime, although I don't know how. I believe he also suffered from shame and resentment, although he didn't say so, but it's a natural outcome of living under Jim Crow."

"Indeed." Once again, the hint of a smile crossed his face. "I see you have come a long way from Boston after all, Miss Berenson."

Josie colored. "I suppose so." She hid a smile. Then she grew serious again. "But what concerns me most is that Mr. Ashford appears to have had no prior relationship with Miss Prentiss. Everyone agrees on this. I find it hard to believe. I can't believe the murder was a random act. He must have had some reason for choosing his victim. But why murder someone he hardly knew, someone he even says was 'kind'?"

"And now?"

"I'm thinking of writing to the superintendent of Rosewood. I'd like to visit the asylum and see what I might learn there."

Richards nodded. He seemed to be considering something. He lifted a paper from his desk, eyed it, then put it back down. Finally he spoke. "I think you should know that after I took on Mr. Ashford's case, I went to Owings Mills to speak to Frank Hopper, the sheriff who arrested him. Sheriff Hopper told me that when he first saw Mr. Ashford, he claimed he was innocent. He said the death was an accident—that Miss Prentiss had been killed by a horse."

Josie frowned. "That's strange. He said nothing about an accident to me." She grew thoughtful. "Although he does mention a horse in his confession. He said he was shoeing one when Miss Prentiss came into the stable. He told me the same thing when I saw him. He described it in such detail, it felt real. But neither of the eyewitnesses mentioned a horse, and when I pointed that out to him, he had nothing to say."

"Hopper concluded he was lying and had made up the story to deflect from his guilt."

"It's possible," Josie said slowly. "Mr. Ashford impressed me as the kind of person who is very timid around figures of authority, especially when they're white. It's possible that, in the shock of the moment, he was trying to appease the sheriff."

Richards raised a finger to his cheek. "Every time I've spoken to Ruben Ashford, he's insisted on the truth of his confession—and that includes deliberately killing Constance Prentiss. He's been unwavering on that fact."

"As he was with me."

Josie's thoughts turned again to the otherworldly recitation

Ruben Ashford had given her of his commission of the crime. It had been compelling—and chilling. The horse was certainly a puzzle, and she would keep her mind open on that account, but it was hard to see how it figured in. She stood. "Thank you, Mr. Richards. I appreciate your support—and your confidence in me."

Richards stood as well. "I wish you the best of luck in your inquiries, Miss Berenson. Dr. Meyer once said you possessed great skill as an interviewer and had insight into human psychology. I hope those talents will hold you in good stead now. But you do know the likely outcome of Ruben Ashford's situation. I must caution you not to hold unwarranted expectations."

You mean, Josie thought, don't become blinded by hope. She smiled. "I will do my best."

He inclined his head in a slight bow. "Until we speak again."

Seventeen

Miracle of miracles: Thula's father survived the flu. Early in December, a dismal day with rain coming down, he showed up at Nell's kitchen door, clutching the paper she'd given him with her name and address. He was gaunt and shaky, but very much alive. Nell was so overcome with delight, to his great embarrassment—and Esme's surprise—she embraced him. "I will direct you to the Fordhams. They're caring for your baby. I can promise you, she's thriving."

"But first," Esme said sternly, as she set a plate of hot food on the table, "you will eat."

Nell left him to it. Wilma Gantry, her first patient of the day, was already in the examination room, waiting for her. This was Wilma's second visit in as many weeks. Ever since she'd gotten married, she'd been suffering from hives. They appeared each day in the evening as soon as Herbert, her husband, a junior executive at the Mercantile Bank, came home from work. They cropped up all over her face and body, turning the normally collected petite redhead into a suffering, itching mess. All she could do was take to her bed—alone. In the morning, after Herbert left for work, she arose, skin clear. And so it remained until the evening when Herbert returned and the hives reappeared.

If Nell didn't know better, she would say the newlywed was allergic to her husband. She took a quick look at Wilma's skin. It was perfectly

135

fine—as it would be, since Herbert was nowhere in sight. "You've tried the Calamine lotion I suggested?" she said. "Oatmeal baths?"

Wilma nodded miserably.

"Have you tried changing your laundry soap?" Nell asked. "Your perfume?"

Wilma shifted on the exam table with a troubled air. "Yes."

"And nothing helps?"

Wilma shook her head.

Nell studied her thoughtfully. "Nursing school," she said. "It's going well?"

"Oh, yes." Wilma brightened. "It's wonderful. It means so much to me, especially after the influenza. Herbert's sister took ill, and if it weren't for the nursing I was able to give her, she might have died. I graduate this coming year. I'm hoping to work with children. I'm so taken by them." Then she grew serious. "I'd like to have a family of my own one day. But first I'd like to spend a few years working. Getting my sea legs, so to speak. Herbert agrees. He says I've done so much with my schooling, it would be a shame not to use it. Only Herbert's not willing to forgo those activities that might lead to children..." She reddened and lowered her eyes. "Truthfully neither am I. We both want to enjoy our marriage."

"I see." Nell thought for a moment. Then she said, "Wait here, please."

She left the examination room, went into her dispensary, opened a drawer in a cabinet, and removed a small package wrapped in brown paper. When she returned, she unwrapped the package and placed it in Wilma's hands.

Wilma looked at Nell. "Condoms? But isn't birth control—"

"Illegal? Yes." Nell smiled. "But no one need know about it, do they?"

"Oh," Wilma said. She smiled shyly. "I suppose not." Then she frowned. "But what does that possibly have to do with my hives?"

Nell patted her hand. "Why don't you give it a try and we'll see."

Wilma snuck out of Nell's office as furtively as a spy, the condoms safely hidden in her purse. She knew not to mention them to anyone. It could cost Nell her medical license. Just last year a Brooklyn practitioner had served thirty days in jail for defying the Comstock laws and providing women in her clinic with contraception. As a doctor, Nell was allowed to prescribe condoms for the prevention of disease—but not for the prevention of pregnancy. Fortunately, she knew a friendly pharmacist who shared her aversion to the birth control ban and supplied her with condoms without questions.

This interference in a woman's—in a married couple's—private life was simply beyond outrageous. Dangerous, too. Most troubling of all were the women Nell had treated over the years after self-induced abortions. Some were unable ever afterwards to have children. One had almost died. It had never occurred to her, when she became a doctor, that politics would affect her practice as much as medicine. Maybe once women gained the vote they would be able to effect real changes and take control of their lives.

Maybe. She'd yet to see any tangible fruits from the rally she'd attended with Josie before the epidemic hit. But in other corners, there were murmurs of change. She could only hope.

As for Wilma's hives? Nell had a feeling that once Wilma's fears over becoming pregnant dissipated, they would too. Wilma had promised to come back in a few weeks to let Nell know.

All morning long, the waiting room was full, patients coming and going. James brought each one to Nell in proper order. The Goldberg twins suffered from stomachache. Mr. Blount's lumbago was acting up again. Flora Grant had been feeling poorly and feared she had the flu. She was much relieved when Nell diagnosed an ordinary head cold. Two of Nell's patients did have flu symptoms, but neither was dangerously ill. Nell prescribed bed rest, plenty of hot tea, and a light diet.

More than once during the course of the morning, Ruben Ashford came up. Several of Nell's patients had seen the news of his sentencing in the *Sun* that week and wanted to talk about it. Some, mostly the ones who knew the Ashfords, were sorry to hear it. They remembered Ruben as a kind, exceedingly polite young man, and had trouble reckoning with his criminal turn. Others weren't afraid to admit they were glad to hear he'd finally been sentenced. One man, a Bolton Hill merchant, was quite outspoken about it. "Death is too good for that boy," he growled, "after what he did to that woman."

Nell didn't answer. She had no appetite for another hanging in the Baltimore City Jail, especially not of someone she knew. But she had to admit she was relieved that the case was finally coming to a close. She'd never expected it to end any differently. And it had been so hard on everyone—especially Josie. At least they could put it all behind them now.

Nell's workday ended at lunchtime. She'd been itching for weeks to resume a full schedule, but both Esme and Josie forbade it. They feared she needed more time to recover from the flu. For once Nell was glad. The morning had tired her out. She bid James good-bye, went into the kitchen to have lunch with Esme, then went upstairs to lie down.

That night, as she and Josie sat at dinner, Nell bubbled with good spirits. Rain had been falling all day, and now it drummed against the window with a soothing, rhythmic sound. "I had the most interesting patient today," she said as she tore into the baked Rockfish Esme had prepared. It was such a pleasure to have her appetite back after the weeks of flu. "She's been suffering from hives. But I couldn't find anything wrong with her. I think it's what you've always said, a case of the mind affecting the body. I—"

Josie didn't seem to be listening. She fiddled with her food, her thoughts elsewhere.

"What is it?" Nell said quietly.

"I'm sorry. It's just that I have something to tell you."

Whatever it was, she wasn't happy about it. Nell put down her fork. She felt a stab of anxiety. "Yes?"

"I saw Norbert Richards today. I'm going to keep working on Ruben Ashford's case after all."

"But I thought—"

"I was going to drop it? Yes, I know. But I changed my mind." Josie looked away. "I'm sorry. I know it's not what you want to hear."

Nell didn't answer. She lowered her eyes, her fingers running across the tablecloth. She felt herself growing irritated. Would Josie never let it go? When they met, she had told her how she always insisted on being right, how she inevitably drove everyone she knew crazy. Nell was beginning to agree.

Then an image came to her mind of the day she finally emerged from her flu delirium. Sitting by her side was Josie, her face pale with worry, her hands twisting the cool cloth she'd been using to bathe Nell's forehead. "Dear heart," Josie had said as Nell's eyes opened. Then she dropped her head down to the bed and wept.

"I don't know what to say," Josie was saying, "It's complicated, and I don't know how to explain—"

Nell pushed back her chair. "You don't have to." She walked to Josie and put her arms around her. "I never wanted you involved in this case. Not just because it's murder. I was worried about what it might do to you—what it might do to *us*. But the flu has changed me. It's changed all of us. We have to rely on each other. I know that now. We have to trust one another. That means I have to learn how to trust you. If I can't…" Her voice trailed off.

"Lately I've seen things I'd never seen before," she said finally. "I hope I never go through that again. But my eyes are open now. And one of the things I can see, for the first time, really see, is *you*." She took Josie's face in her hands and kissed her. "Josefa Berenson, you are passionate, and that passion is the last thing I would ever want to take from you. Follow it wherever it leads you. I promise to be with you no matter what."

"Dear heart." Josie smiled.

Nell wiped away a tear. Then she sat down, and for a time they ate in silence, listening to the rain.

"What will happen now?" Nell said at last.

"I don't know," Josie said. "It all seems so unsure. I want to go to Rosewood, to see what I can find there. And I'd like to speak to Ashford's parents, if I can. There's not a lot that Dr. Freud and Dr. Meyer agree on." She smiled. "The two men are very much rivals. But they both say people are formed in childhood. I'd like to know more about what Ruben Ashford was like when he was growing up." She tapped a finger thoughtfully on the table. "But I'm afraid the Ashfords might not speak to me. They've been through so much. I can well imagine they may not trust people they don't know, especially when they're white."

"Yes, that's true," Nell said, "they don't know you." Then she smiled and took Josie's hand. "But they do know me."

Eighteen

Early the next afternoon, Nell closed her practice, bid James good-bye, and told Esme she would be out for a few hours. Then she stepped outside to McCulloh Street and headed south. Overnight the rain had stopped, delivering a bright, sunny day. A breeze came from the north, clearing the harbor vapors. Nell fixed her hat firmly on her head and tightened her shawl. Ruben Ashford's parents lived on Lemmon Street, two miles away. Normally she would walk, taking advantage of the crisp winter weather, but she wanted to save her strength. She walked to Lafayette Avenue, boarded the streetcar for whites, then transferred at N. Calhoun Street.

The streetcar rattled cheerfully down the avenues, with patrons boarding and disembarking at each stop, jostling and chattering. How delightful it was to be out and about in the crisp winter air. She had missed that during the weeks she was bedridden. Mr. Tillerson, she was happy to see through the windows of his drugstore, was restocking his shelves. On the corner of Edmondson Avenue, a black man stood by his pony and cart, selling bundles of greenery and firewood; people in the city called the peddlers Arabbers, although Nell never knew why. The markets had fresh produce again in their sidewalk displays, baskets of chestnuts and apples and potatoes and pears. Grasmere's butcher shop was back in business, but Foster's bakery was still closed, with black bunting hung on the door. Nell wondered if it ever would reopen. Everywhere she looked, people greeted each other with smiles of pleasure and surprise. They were like the survivors of a shipwreck. Nothing was taken for granted, least of all the fact that they were still alive.

Her mood changed as she disembarked at Lemmon, and she felt herself fretting, growing anxious. She still didn't know how she would present herself to the Ashfords, what she would say. She was used to visiting the homes of the sick, homes harboring death. She prided herself on bringing hope to her patients—or if not hope, at least a kind of comfort. But Violet and George Ashford faced a tragedy of an entirely different sort. Death, in the normal course of things, left grief in its wake, but also, in time, the consolation of memory. But Ruben's fate was hardly normal. There would be no consolation if he were hanged, and his memory would be nothing more than an open wound.

Lemmon was a narrow alleyway bordered by a hodgepodge of small, cramped houses leaning into one another. Some had chicken coops or pigpens or stables out back; all had outhouses. The air was redolent with the smell of animal feed and manure. Nell walked past a man with a cart and pony collecting nightsoil and another chopping wood. A knot of children dashed by on their way home from school. The children made her smile. It was good to see the return to normalcy after the epidemic, the reassertion of life.

The last time Nell had seen the Ashfords, Ruben had been just a boy. That was over ten years ago now. She remembered their house as being one of the nicest on the alleyway, a two-story clapboard cottage painted saffron yellow, testimony to Violet's love of color. The Ashfords had done well for themselves. Violet grew vegetables and herbs and kept chickens. George fashioned metalwork and tools. He took pride in his work and was as talented with wood as he was with iron. He had built their house himself and some of their furniture too. Nell remembered a deep sense of peace and contentment reigning inside, even in the midst of Violet's illness, the sign of a home where love was freely given and received.

Any peace the Ashfords had experienced seemed to be gone now. Violet's garden was overgrown with weeds, her chicken coops abandoned. One of the windows on the house had a broken pane and had been crudely covered in tarpaper. The George that Nell remembered never would have stood for that. At the back of the yard, a trashcan had been crudely overturned, spilling ashes, scrap paper, and cans. The sun still shone down cheerfully and brightly on everything, but it felt like a mockery.

Nell put her hand on the gate. Had she made a mistake coming here? In her mind she had imagined the Ashfords glad to see her, overjoyed—or at least relieved—to know people were still working to save their son's life. But that was nothing more than a fantasy she'd concocted for herself. She had no idea what Ruben Ashford's parents would think when they saw her. She might not be welcome at all. Still, she'd told Josie she would speak to them, and she was determined to follow through. She went up the walkway to the front door, pausing to right the trashcan. Then she knocked.

Her knock was met with silence, long enough she thought it might go on forever. The Ashfords must not be home. She was about to turn away—filled with a coward's relief—when a woman's voice, low and hesistant, called out from inside. "Who's there?"

"Mrs. Ashford?" Nell tried to make her voice sound light and upbeat, but feared it did nothing but betray her anxiety. "It's Dr. Winters. Nell."

Silence fell again, as thick and dark as the tarpaper on the windows. Then Nell heard a chain fall, the door opened, and Violet Ashford stood before her. Like her house, she too had changed. Nell remembered her as an attractive woman, a bit plump, with a crown of thick, dark hair that she'd gloried in, and coiffed with perfumed pomades, a pearl-handled comb, and silver mirror. She'd been as talkative as a magpie and as resolutely cheerful, even in the midst of her illness. She'd had a touch of vanity, and even while bedridden had sported a dressing gown in rich tones of lavender she'd sewn herself. Now her face was drawn and gaunt, her hair uncombed. She wore a stained housedress and a sweater that hung loosely on her frame. "Dr. Winters? What is it? Is someone sick?" She pulled nervously at the hem of her sweater.

"No, Mrs. Ashford, it's nothing like that." Nell forced herself to hide the shock she felt, employing the doctor's trick of turning her face into an impassive mask, showing no emotion, no matter how grim the prognosis. "I've come about Ruben. I was hoping I might talk to you about him."

"Ruben?" Violet stepped back, her hand at her throat, her body stiffening. "Did something happen to him? Did they already—?" Her voice dropped to a whisper. "They're going to hang him, you know. It said so in the papers."

"I know," Nell said. "But I have some news about that." She held herself back from saying more. She would have to frame her words carefully. She didn't want to raise hope where it might be unwarranted or promise something she couldn't deliver. "Would it be all right if I came in?"

Violet twisted her sweater. Then she dropped her hands, nodded, and stepped aside.

As Nell recalled, the Ashfords had a parlor and kitchen on the ground floor, two bedrooms upstairs, and a cellar in the basement. Once the parlor had been crammed with bookshelves—Violet loved to read—and decorated with watercolor landscapes she had painted herself. The walls were a vibrant rose color, and hand-knitted throws softened the chairs. Something good to eat, a stew or pudding or cake, was always waiting on the table, cooked by Violet when she was well and brought by neighbors when she was sick. George was always pressing Nell to eat. All that was gone now. The room had been emptied out, with nothing but dust collecting in the corners. The curtains were drawn, the light dim. The fire in the grate had gone out, leaving a chill in the air.

"We had to sell everything," Violet said. She lowered her eyes. "We're leaving. We can't stay here anymore."

Nell heard footsteps on the stairs, and George came up from the cellar, dressed in heavy work clothes and boots, carrying a crate of tools. He looked at Nell in surprise then turned to Violet.

"It's Dr. Winters," Violet said. "She has news about Ruben."

George put the crate down. He looked thinner than Nell remembered, and spent, as if even moving forward had become a chore. His face was flat, his voice too. "I can't much see the point of hearing that." He rubbed a hand over his eyes.

"I don't want—" Nell said. I don't want to make this any harder for you, she meant, although it was clear she was doing just that. "I came to tell you Ruben's lawyer is working on an appeal on his behalf. I don't know if you'd heard. A friend—a dear friend of mine—is helping him with it. I promised to help, too.'"

"Norbert Richards," George said. "I remember him." He rested his hands on the small of his back. "He came to see us after Ruben was arrested. Said he wanted to represent him. I said we didn't have money for lawyers. He said that didn't matter, he would take Ruben on anyway." He shook his head slowly. "Craziest colored man I ever did see. Went on and on about equality and justice and the law. As if white people cared anything about that." He looked at Nell. "No offense, Dr. Winters. I appreciate what you did for Violet when she was sick."

"An appeal?" Violet said. Her hand flew to her throat. "So they're not going to hang him?"

"Oh, they're going to hang him," George said. "You can count on it." He bent down and lifted the crate. "Sorry, Dr. Winters. I know you mean well. But I don't have time for this. I have work to do." He turned his back and stiffly left the house.

Nell stood awkwardly in the middle of the empty room, not knowing what to say. Her hands fell limply to her sides.

"Please don't mind George," Violet said. "This has been hard on both of us. But George—" Her voice broke. "We've lost our way." She covered her eyes. Then she raised a hand to her hair, smoothing it down. In that gesture Nell saw a remnant of the woman Violet had once been, the one who'd pressed bunches of dried rosemary and thyme into her hands "for your kitchen" even when she was racked with fever. "Won't you stay? I'll make tea."

Water boiling on the stove brought a sense of normalcy into the house. Violet fetched a teapot from a cupboard and added tea from a tin. The kitchen table was gone—they'd had to sell it too, she said—but they still had a pair of chairs. Nell sat in one, Violet in the other. The stove at least brought some warmth, and dried flowers hanging by the window spread a bit of cheer. "We're going to my sister in Virginia," Violet said. "She said we can find work there. There hasn't been any since Ruben…" Her voice trailed off. "I lost my job right after the news of his arrest came out. And George—no one wants to hire the father of a…" She skewed her eyes away. "Not colored or white. I can't blame them. George isn't the only one who lost work over Ruben. Lots of colored folk did. White people don't want them in their homes anymore. They're afraid. We got blamed for that."

A few people, Violet said, had come around from their church. "They took up a collection for us. We wouldn't have made it without them. But we can't rely on charity forever." Most people kept their distance. Some muttered threats, and some did more than that. Violet glanced at the broken pane of glass in the window. "Someone put a rock through that. They want us gone. George wants us gone, too. He says it's too dangerous here." Violet lowered her eyes. "But I don't want to leave my boy. I can't help thinking something has to change. They'll realize they made a mistake. They'll let him go." When the news of the sentence came out, she agreed to leave. "I don't want to be here when—" She raised her eyes. "But now, with the appeal you're talking about—" A glimmer of hope came into her face. "Maybe we should stay?"

Nell wanted to believe Ruben had a chance. She knew Josie did. Or rather, Josie refused to accept that Ruben didn't. It was her Boston sensibility coming through, her northern idealism. But this was Baltimore, and in her heart, Nell knew George was right. No matter what she and Josie did, the appeal would most likely fail, and Ruben would hang. "I'm sorry. I don't know what to say."

"That's all right." Violet took Nell's hand, a cool and papery touch. "I just won't believe Ruben is what they say he is. That's not my boy." She let Nell's hand go.

Nell felt a growing sense of anger—an inkling of the passion Josie felt about Ashford's case. No matter what their son had done, Violet and George didn't deserve this. No one did.

Josie, Nell knew, was working on the motive for the crime. If they could find that, Norbert Richards might be able to convert his hanging to a life sentence. Nell turned her attention to that, probing carefully, arranging her questions so as not to alarm Violet or cause her any further pain. "I remember Ruben as a boy," she said. "He always seemed so kind."

"He was," Violet said firmly. "He was kind to everyone. Even animals. Ruben would never hurt anyone."

"Did he ever give you any trouble?" Nell smiled. "Most boys do."

"Never. Not Ruben." Violet shook her head. "He was always respectful. Just ask George. Ask his teachers, ask anyone who knew him. No matter what people asked of him, he did it. He never said no."

"Did he have friends?"

"A few, but Ruben was a quiet boy. He was shy. He reminded me of my father in that way. Mostly he kept to himself."

"And girls? Did he have anyone special? Anyone he walked out with?"

Violet gave Nell a sad smile. "I always hoped he would, but like I said, Ruben was shy. I figured that would come with time."

Nell ran her finger around the rim of her cup. She needed to ask Violet about the murder, but it would be tricky raising the topic without distressing her. "The teacher at Rosewood," she said finally, "the one they said Ruben—" She broke off. "Do you have any idea if

Ruben knew her?"

"He didn't." Violet looked at her fiercely. "That's just it. He couldn't have. Not a white woman. George and I—we raised Ruben right. We taught him to stay out of trouble. We said, if there's a white woman coming down the sidewalk, you step into the street. If there's one on the street, you go to the other side. You keep your eyes down. You keep your distance. You say, Yes, ma'am, No ma'am. You keep your thoughts to yourself."

Ruben must have absorbed the lesson early. Nell remembered him as a young boy, standing at the back of the room while she tended to his mother. He'd refused to look at her or meet her eye. She'd attributed his behavior to shyness, but could it have been more than that? Could he have been afraid of her?

"I blame myself." Violet's voice caught in her throat. "George never wanted Ruben to go to Rosewood. He said no good would come of it. Ruben didn't want to go either, but he was smart, and I wanted more for him. I was going to be a teacher once. It didn't work out for me, but I thought it could work out for Ruben. I told him to go." She covered her eyes again. "I should have listened to George."

Nell sat quietly, waiting for Violet to compose herself. At last she stood, wiped her eyes with the back of her hand, and put her cup in the sink. "I never even went to see him there." She spoke with her back turned. "I wanted to. I should have, but I never got the time. If I had—if there had been something with that woman—he would have told me. I would have made him come home."

Had there been something between Ruben and Constance Prentiss after all? Violet, perhaps inadvertently, had opened the door to the idea. Nell thought about that. Then she carried her cup to the sink. Violet was shaking. Nell rested a hand on her shoulder. "I'm sorry about Ruben," she said softly.

"I know you are." Violet reached up and covered Nell's hand with her own. "Thank you for coming. It felt good to have you here, to talk to someone who remembers Ruben the way he was."

Nell stepped back. "I promise to do my best for him."

"Yes, Dr. Winters." Violet turned so that Nell could see her face, a view of the lost, or the damned. "I believe you will."

Nineteen

Head held high, Josie marched through the B&O railroad station to the platform where the train for Owings Mills, which would take her to the Rosewood Asylum, departed. She walked deliberately past the cars for whites and boarded the colored car at the back. No matter that it contained nothing but hard benches while the other cars had cushioned seats. She'd taken only colored transportation ever since the day she met Ruben Ashford. She sat down and looked defiantly around her, daring anyone to notice, to raise a ruckus, or even arrest her like Dorothy Day, Lucy Burns, and the other suffragists who had been thrown into jail just last year after picketing for women's rights outside the White House. But no one arrested her. No one even paid her any attention. The conductor came through, gave her a look that was half curiosity and half exasperation, then took her ticket without comment. Apparently white people were free to sit wherever they wanted to in the Baltimore transit system. Only black people were restricted.

She settled back in her seat with a sigh of fury as the train left the station. It was all so frustrating. She was determined to make Jim Crow disappear, while it was just as determined to remain. This, she feared, was a war she would never win. Perhaps some future generation would vanquish the enemy, long after she was gone. She would be sorry not to be there when it happened.

The colored car was only lightly populated, and Josie looked with curiosity at her fellow passengers. She smiled at a young girl in a blue coat who was sitting quietly nearby, beside an elderly woman in a grey hat. The woman ignored her, but the girl smiled shyly back. At the back of the car, a man in a suit clutched a leather case on his lap. A boy in a straw hat sat on his knees, looking avidly out the window. Meanwhile the train chugged steadily northward out of the city into the countryside. After twenty minutes or so, it stopped at Windsor Mill, where a woman in a muslin skirt boarded with a basket of cabbages, trailing the smell of wet earth behind her. At Hebbville the boy in the straw hat got off and a man in overalls with thick, calloused hands, sat heavily in his place. Outside the window, creeks and farms and stands of trees flew by. A herd of cows, gathered by a fence, looked up curiously as the train whistle sounded. A lone horse, grazing, paid it no mind. They passed a willow tree which cast long limbs like fishing lines into a pond. In the distance a fire smoldered, releasing a finger of smoke into the sky.

It was early in the morning, a bright, sunny, wintry day, the kind of day that normally Josie delighted in. But she was too busy thinking about Ruben Ashford to think about that. Just that week Nell had spoken to the Ashfords. Much of what Nell said about her visit confirmed what Josie already knew. Ruben Ashford was shy, excessively so, and overly respectful of authority, incapable of asserting himself or saying no to requests, even the most unreasonable ones. Josie had not been surprised to learn he had few friends growing up; she suspected loneliness was a trait embedded deeply in his personality early on. She had not been surprised either to have her hunch confirmed, that Ashford might very well have known Constance Prentiss; Violet all but admitted it. Josie also found it significant that Ashford had little experience with women, especially white women, and might even have been afraid of them. She wondered if he'd found something about Prentiss threatening. Perhaps the murder was an act of self-defense. If so, Norbert Richards might finally have the angle he needed for his appeal.

The very idea lifted Josie's spirits. She knew she should be cautious and not get her hopes up—Richards had been adamant about that—but she couldn't help feeling good about her chances. She felt as if she were growing closer to an answer to Ruben Ashford's predicament, closer to the truth, as if it were an egg ready to hatch, releasing a new chick into the world. As the train rocked on the rails, sunlight glinted on the window, a shifting rainbow pattern. Josie's thoughts drifted back to the laboratory where her father had conducted his experiments. Bottles of dye sat on the shelves, glowing in the lamp light in a full range of colors, from magenta to sapphire. She remembered the smell of camphor from his chemicals, the steadiness of his hands as he worked, the warmth of his skin. Like a magician, he transformed one thing into another, powder into flames, clear liquids into colorful gels, ice into smoke. You never knew what anything was, he said; in the blink of an eye, it could become something else entirely different. But at the same time he told her cautionary tales of alchemists and charlatans who promised to turn lead into gold. Everything she believed, he said, must be conditioned on scientific proof. At the moment when he made the magic happen, however, she didn't want to think about that. She wanted to believe that anything was possible—

Even that Ruben Ashford might be saved.

The conductor strolled idly by, checking tickets on his rounds. Josie reached into her pocket and pulled out the letter she'd received the day before from Aubrey Foyle, superintendent of the Rosewood asylum. Foyle had been most cooperative when she wrote to him explaining that she worked at the Phipps Psychiatric Clinic, was assisting Ruben Ashford's lawyer with his inquiries into the murder of Constance Prentiss, and would like to visit the asylum. He'd promised to meet with her personally and also said he would arrange for her to speak to Ida Crofter and Abram Sledge, the two eyewitnesses to the murder. The visit had been set for today, beginning with a meeting with Foyle at ten o'clock.

She'd taken extra care that morning as she dressed, deciding finally on a formal tweed woolen jacket and skirt; as ever, she worried about what people would think of her, just as she chided herself for her silly vanity. Mostly she was glad for the skirt's pockets. One held her train ticket and fare for the return, the other a handkerchief and business cards. If ever she could influence the people who designed women's clothing, she would beg for more pockets. It was such a pleasure to move about without the encumbrance of a handbag. She was wearing the scarf Nell had tucked around her neck that morning, "Just in case it's colder in the country than it is here," and comfortable boots for walking. The Owings Mills train station, Ruben Ashford had said, was two miles from the asylum on country roads. As always, stray locks of her unruly hair escaped from the modest cloth hat she had pinned on so carefully before she left the house.

The hat made her think of her mother, who never left the house without one. Just recently Josie had heard from her father, who wrote that they'd both survived the flu. Josie had been relieved to hear it, and wrote immediately back. What she didn't say—although she didn't have to; he knew—was that she had yet to hear from her mother. At the thought, her heart ached.

Forty minutes later the train rattled across a bridge, sending ducks on the river below into panicked flight. Then with a burst of steam and cinders, it rounded a bend, and the Owings Mills train station, a low wooden building with a peaked roof, came into view. Josie disembarked and walked inside the station, where she found a lone man behind a counter, sorting mail. When she asked for directions to Rosewood, he pointed silently down the road to the east, and she set out walking.

The road took her through the village of Owings Mills, a dozen cottages ringed by a stable, a tinsmith, a produce market, and Creedwell's General Store. The sheriff, Josie remembered, had left word for his deputy with Micah Creedwell when he got the call about the Rosewood murder. The sheriff's headquarters was in a cottage across the way. Josie considered stopping by to see if he was in, but decided against it. She didn't want to be late for her appointment with

Dr. Foyle. Besides, Richards had already spoken to Frank Hopper, and she suspected she would learn nothing new. Still it reminded her of the puzzle about the horse; had there been one in the stable at the time of the murder or not? And if so, had it played a role in Constance Prentiss's death? She hoped to find out more at Rosewood.

Soon the village gave way to fields and farms. At the end of a rutted road, a sign pointed to a dairy. The growing season was over, and the earth was brown and barren. But the sun was strong enough to warm her, and as she walked, she loosened her scarf. Down the road came a wagon, pulled by a draft horse, with a farmer walking at its head. He eyed her curiously as he passed by. The mark of village life: people taking note of strangers. She encountered no one else. Crows squabbled in a patch of pumpkin vines. Chickens pecked and scratched outside a coop. In the orchards the limbs of the apple trees were bare.

In time she came to a small stone church, sitting at a crossroads. Was this the one Ruben Ashford had attended? Beside it was a small cemetery. On impulse she left the road and walked to it. At the back was a line of graves for children. They had come from Rosewood; the asylum's name was marked on the stones. Most of them bore a name and dates, but a few said simply *Child*. How sad to live and die in such anonymity, to be buried alone, so far from your family. Any number of things could have claimed these young lives: measles, tuberculosis, pneumonia—or influenza. At the end of the line were three new graves, freshly dug. Flu must have come to the asylum, too, despite its remoteness. It would have made its way in the arms of deliverymen, on the backs of visitors. The graves brought back a memory of Nell at the height of her illness, racked by fever, struggling for breath. How close she had come to ending up in a cemetery, too. Josie ran her fingers along the scarf Nell had tied on her that morning. How lucky they were to have each other. She would never take their life together for granted again.

She left the graveyard and returned to the road. Past the church the road ended in a T. A small sign reading Rosewood pointed to the north. Here the road narrowed to a lane with woods on one side and fields on the other, stretching across low hills to the distance. In the fields, boys were working, cutting dried cornstalks, binding them into sheaves, loading them into wagons. A few colored men worked alongside the boys, while a white man on horseback looked on. This must be the Rosewood farm.

The boys, Josie recalled, provided free labor to the asylum. It was essential, Ruben Ashford said. The asylum was always short of funds, and there were always more children waiting for its services. The work was meant to benefit the boys, to improve them, and train them for future employment. Still there was something disconcerting about it. There was a repetitive sameness to the work as the boys went down the rows of corn, bending, cutting, binding, lifting. It seemed both dull and dulling, as if the boys had been robbed of their individual vitality and were employed simply as parts of a larger machine.

The entrance to the asylum was farther down the lane, marked by a cast iron gate with an iron vine of roses twisting through the bars. Past it a long drive led in the distance to the top of a hill. As Josie walked up it, she thought of Ruben Ashford doing the same the first day he came here. She tried to see the place through his eyes. She remembered him saying he liked it here, that it was quiet and pretty. She could see why. The property was quite lovely, with grassy meadows stretching on either side. Through one a creek ran prettily. She passed a group of girls who were sitting on the ground in a circle in the sunshine, sewing, while a woman in a chair read out loud to them from a book. The girls were dressed in identical uniforms of grey dresses and white pinafores, their hair neatly braided. The teacher looked up curiously as Josie walked by, and some of the girls looked up too. One gave her a somber wave, and Josie smiled and waved back. Smiles from the children, she recalled, were one of the few touches of humanity Ashford had experienced when he lived here, and he had remembered them with pleasure.

The drive ended at the top of the hill, where a dozen two- or three-story buildings, built of brick or stone, stood together around a half circle like a crescent moon. They must come from different eras; some looked quite old, while others still had a freshness to them. But all were equally drab, without decoration or ornament, built with a depressing, institutional sameness, as if to distinguish oneself would be severely frowned upon. From one, where the windows had been thrown open to the fresh air, came the sound of girls chanting. Another rang with the voices of boys laughing and shouting. A door at the front of one of the buildings opened, and a woman emerged, holding a small child by the hand. Without even a nod at Josie, she towed her charge busily to another building and disappeared inside. A colored woman trudged past pushing a cart piled high with linens. Somewhere a dog was barking.

At the far end of the circle was a clapboard cottage marked *Inquiries*. This, Josie thought, must be the Great House, although if so, it was quite poorly named. It was hardly great at all, most likely the farmhouse that had originally sat on the property before it was converted to an asylum. She paused at the door to straighten her hat. The windows were open here too, and from inside came the sound of typing. When she rang the bell, the typing stopped, and the door opened, revealing a woman with grey hair pulled into a severe bun. "Yes?"

"Josefa Berenson, from the Phipps Psychiatric Clinic." Josie dug into her pocket, pulled out a card, and presented it. "Dr. Foyle is expecting me."

The woman studied the card, frowning. "I'll tell him you're here."

She turned her back on Josie and disappeared down a long hallway, leaving Josie to see herself in. Inside was a room that might have once been a parlor but now served as a reception area. To one side a sofa and chairs flanked a grate, where a fire had been set. The typewriter Josie had heard sat on a desk at the back of the room. Past it was a staircase leading to the second floor. Distantly she heard a phone ringing. There was the sound of muffled voices, a door opening and closing, then a man came down the stairs, glanced coolly at Josie, and without a word exited the house. It was cold inside—much colder than outside where the sun shone. Josie drew closer to the hearth. Above it hung a portrait of a man with a somber expression. A governor, perhaps, or board chairman. On men like these, Ruben Ashford had said, the fate of the asylum's budget depended, and on that depended everything else.

Where had Ruben Ashford worked? He had an office in the Great House near Dr. Foyle, he'd said. Upstairs? Down the hall? Josie tried to imagine Ashford coming in the door, crossing the parlor, going to his office, greeting others, exchanging pleasantries as people who work together do. It was impossible. Whom would he speak to? The woman at the typewriter? The man who hurried past so rudely? Neither seemed like the kind of person to engage in idle conversation, especially with a black man. Ashford would have found another way into the house, through the back door perhaps, where he could come and go unseen.

The typist returned. "The superintendent will be with you shortly." She sat down and resumed her work, leaving Josie to wait to the accompaniment of the clacking keys. Soon a man came down the hall towards her with a quick, efficient step. He appeared to be in his mid-fifties, tall and angular, with sharp features, a bony forehead and eyes. He exuded an air of importance: a man with little time to spare. "Miss Berenson." He pressed her hand. "Aubrey Foyle. So sorry to keep you waiting. I was called to the telephone. If you'll just –?"

Josie hurried after him down the corridor, struggling to keep up with his long strides. He led her to his office, which might have once been a dining room, but was filled now with the detritus of a busy man: filing cabinets piled high with folders, tables stacked with papers, overflowing bookcases. At the back of the room sat a desk with more papers, a lamp, and a telephone. In keeping with the institutional drabness that permeated the asylum, the walls were devoid of decoration, except for a framed diploma, quite prominently displayed, which identified Aubrey Foyle as a doctor of education. The windows were shielded by drapes, as if the pleasure of a view were too distracting to be allowed. The light was dim, the air cold. In the hearth, the remnants of a fire smoldered. The superintendent guided Josie to a chair in front of the desk then seated himself behind it.

"Coffee?"

"Yes," Josie said, giving a final tug on her hat and smoothing down her skirt. Something warm would be well appreciated. "Thank you."

Foyle rang a bell, and a moment later a colored girl in a uniform and cap opened the door. "Yes, doctor?" She waited in the doorway to receive his instructions, then curtsied and exited, closing the door behind her.

"Now, then. Welcome." Foyle gave Josie a smile that was clearly meant to be warm, although she found it distinctly lacking. There was something false about it. She much preferred Norbert Richards's grimaces, which were strained but also genuine. "We're always pleased to have visitors from the Phipps Clinic. Your Dr. Meyer has been a great help to us over the years, making recommendations for the children, helping with evaluations. How is he?"

"Quite well," Josie said. "Thank you." This was the first Josie had heard of Meyer's work at Rosewood. The great doctor was like a magician himself, appearing everywhere.

"I'm glad to hear it. Nowadays, with the flu, one is almost afraid to ask." He lowered his voice. "We were so grateful when Dr. Meyer agreed to examine Ruben Ashford after the…" His voice trailed off. "To be honest, I thought he would surely find Ruben insane. It's hard to imagine otherwise how—" He lifted his hands in a helpless way and let them fall. "I understand from your letter that you are working on his case. I'm wondering—"

Just then the door opened, and the girl appeared with a tray. Dr. Foyle pushed aside a raft of papers, making room on the desk. "Thank you, Molly." She put the tray down. "That will be all."

Molly left with a curtsy, closing the door again behind her.

"Cream? Sugar?" Foyle said.

"Yes, please. Both."

He busied himself, preparing the coffee. "As I was saying, I understand you are here on Ruben's behalf." He handed Josie a cup. "I'm glad to help, but I don't see how I can. I heard just last week that he'd been sentenced. Doesn't that mean his case is over?"

"Perhaps." Josie balanced her cup on her knees. There was nowhere else to put it. The cup brought a welcome warmth, and she was glad to hold it. "Ashford's attorney is working on an appeal. The reason is as you say. Ruben Ashford is quite sane, and yet he killed Constance Prentiss. No one seems to understand why, least of all himself. What was his motive? That's what we're trying to determine. I don't suppose you have any idea?"

Foyle shook his head sadly. "I've been asking myself the same thing. How could this have happened? It's like a nightmare one keeps hoping to wake from." He took a sip of his coffee then put the cup down, walked to the hearth, and poked at the fire. With an air of annoyance, he returned to his desk and rang the bell. Again, Molly appeared. "The fire has gone out," he said.

"Yes, sir. So sorry, sir. I'll see to it right away." She curtsied and exited.

"I don't know if the school will ever recover." He seated himself and recovered his line of thought. "You can't imagine what it has been like here. Two teachers left us immediately after Miss Prentiss…" He raised his cup then lowered it without drinking. "They said they no longer felt safe here. Who was I to disagree? I have tried to replace them but to no avail. I sent out notices from Virginia to Connecticut. Not a single candidate applied. Meanwhile twelve families withdrew their children when they heard the news, and we lost three more from the flu. As long as we're shorthanded, I can't possibly replace them. The governor has docked our appropriations, even though I explained to him that our needs are every bit as great. He insists no additional funds are to be forthcoming until—"

The door opened and Molly returned with an armful of kindling.

Foyle fell silent as she bent down and relit the fire. Once again she curtsied as she left, closing the door behind her.

He gave Josie an apologetic smile. "I'm afraid I've burdened you with my concerns. Please forgive me."

"Not at all," Josie said. "I can see you are doing important work here."

The superintendent inclined his head. He seemed pleased, and smiled with a feigned modesty. "May I ask what you know about Rosewood, Miss Berenson?"

"Very little, I'm afraid. I know you care for feeble-minded children here."

Foyle nodded. "We are in our thirtieth year. I've been superintendent for the last six. We opened with twenty children. Now we have over three hundred, and the needs are only increasing."

He walked to the hearth and poked at the fire, heightening its blaze with an air of satisfaction. "Every child here requires—deserves—our particular attention. Their families can't possibly provide for them. They exhaust themselves, expend their funds, doing their best to care for a child who simply can't be cared for in the usual way. No school will have them; even the most loving mother falls into despair when she sees how her ministrations fail. These children require the hand of the expert, the attention of the professional."

His gaze migrated to his diploma, and he seemed gratified when Josie's did as well. With great dignity he returned to his chair. "Some of our colleagues in Virginia have taken to sterilizing their feeble-minded. They see in this manner an end to the burden on the public trust. In Maryland we have chosen a different path." He gave a light shrug as if he were very much unsure of the wisdom of that decision. "So be it. Under the circumstances, we do our best. We give every child, even the most impaired, the opportunity to improve. Rosewood provides hope. Children who fail to find sanctuary at a place like ours often come to a very different end. There are stories I could tell you…" He looked at her with an air of embarrassment. "Although, as a woman, perhaps you would rather I not?"

"Please," she said. "Go on."

"Very well." He nodded. "One farmer in our county had three girls, all idiots of such a severe nature as to be hardly above animals. Left on their own, the girls multiplied until there were seventeen of them, children and grandchildren. In the town of Frederick, a father induced an imbecilic man to marry his similarly impaired daughter, in the hope he would provide for her. The result was three more simpletons on the poor list." He placed his hands firmly on his desk. "Every dollar spent at Rosewood saves the state hundreds of dollars in incarceration, social welfare, and the like. So I have told the governor. Many times."

He refilled his coffee cup and offered the pot to Josie. She shook her head.

"No child deserves to be discarded. This I believe. Given proper instruction, every single person on this earth can improve, better themselves, become their best version."

"Even Ruben Ashford?" Josie said softly.

"Yes." He put down his coffee with an air of regret. "Once I believed Ruben was capable of improvement too."

Although, Josie wondered, what was improvement supposed to mean in Ashford's case? All he had ever wanted was to be a blacksmith. He would have been quite content in that life—and, no doubt, much better off.

"Tell me about him," Josie said. "What was he like when he worked here?"

"Ah, Ruben." Foyle gave her a sad smile. "If only you could have seen him then. Bright! I'd never seen anyone like him. What he could do with numbers. A prodigy. Truly remarkable. He was shy, overly so. But I was sure given time he would come out of his shell. And he was hardworking. Agreeable to any task. An exemplary employee. No matter what I asked him, he never said no."

"Including shoeing your horse?"

Foyle seemed taken aback by the question.

"Ashford claims he was shoeing your horse on the day of—of Miss Prentiss's death. Frankly, it's a bit of a puzzle. I thought you might be able to enlighten me."

"Shoeing my horse?" A guarded note crept into the superintendent's voice. "It's possible. Ruben did perform small tasks like that for me from time to time. But on the day of Miss Prentiss's death?" He shook his head. "No. I don't think so. The next time I came to ride the mare, she was missing a shoe, which would hardly have been the case if she'd just been shod."

"Or perhaps Ashford started the job but was unable to finish it."

"Perhaps," Foyle agreed, although he seemed reluctant to do so.

"Ruben Ashford told the sheriff that Constance Prentiss's death was an accident. He said a horse had killed her. Later, of course, he changed his story and confessed. I wonder if you knew about that."

The superintendent shook his head.

"I thought perhaps if he'd been shoeing your mare, something untoward might have happened—something that resulted in Miss Prentiss's death. But I admit it doesn't seem likely. Neither Abram Sledge or Ida Crofter mentioned seeing a horse in the stable. And we also have the murder weapon and the blood on his shirt to account for."

"Indeed." Foyle considered this soberly. "I've never known Mrs. Crofter to be anything but truthful. She's quite devout. If she says there was no horse, she's no doubt right. As for Abram Sledge—he's a colored man. I can well imagine he would lie if he thought it would aid a man of his race. And yet he too says there was no horse."

It was an odd thing to say, and Josie thought about pointing it out to Foyle, then decided against it. No reason to turn the man against her. The fire was beginning to warm the room, and she loosened her scarf. "You said Ashford was an exemplary employee. What about Constance Prentiss? Was she also satisfactory?"

The superintendent seemed surprised—and somewhat affronted—by her question. "No one ever lodged a single complaint

162

against her. Miss Prentiss was a lovely woman and a wonderful teacher. The children adored her." He dropped his eyes. "I had to call her parents after she... Later they came to retrieve her—her body. I met them at the train station. I've never seen anyone so undone." He pulled a handkerchief from his pocket and pressed it to his eyes.

Josie gave him a moment to compose himself. At last, as Foyle sighed and gave a last wipe to his eyes, she said, "You said in your letter that you knew of no relationship between Mr. Ashford and Miss Prentiss."

Foyle shook his head firmly. "None at all."

"And nothing has surfaced since then to make you change your mind?"

"No." He folded the handkerchief and put it away. "I blame myself, you know. I knew very well hiring Ruben was a risk. I heard all the arguments against it. They said he wouldn't fit in, that I was being unfair to the others who worked here, that I was raising expectations that couldn't be fulfilled. They said there was no point in trying to mix the races that way, that no good would come of it." A note of defiance crept into his voice. "But Ruben was competent. I saw no reason to deny him the chance to better himself just because he was black."

Josie sympathized with the superintendent's desire for social engineering, to effect racial parity on his staff. But it came at a price. *Better yourself.* Such was Foyle's expectation for everyone at Rosewood, Ashford and the children too. But what happened to those who failed? According to Ashford, some of the girls who were sent out to work as maids ended up on the streets—exactly the kind of outcome Foyle claimed his methods prevented. As far as Josie could tell, the boys were expected to become farm laborers. Any other sign of initiative, any other personal choice or preference, was methodically ground out of them.

And what did betterment mean in Ruben Ashford's case? Social isolation. He was not to associate with the other colored men at the asylum; they were beneath him. He was forbidden to form attachments with colored women—such things spoke of sexual immorality. And he was expressly forbidden to associate with white people. That was simply unheard of. Again, Josie found herself thinking of how lonely Ashford must have been at Rosewood, and wondered whether or not loneliness had played a role in Constance Prentiss's death.

"Did Mr. Ashford have any friends while he was here at Rosewood?" she asked.

Foyle seemed surprised to hear the question. "No," he said, "I don't—" He paused, considering. Then he lowered his eyes. "Not that I know of."

Josie nodded and returned her cup to the tray. "I'd like to see where he worked, if I may."

"Of course."

The superintendent rang the bell, and Molly appeared and cleared the tray away. Then he led Josie to a room farther down the hall and stepped back so that she could enter before him. This was a small, narrow space, perhaps originally meant as a storage room or pantry. There was no window, and little air or light. The room held a desk, a cabinet, a pencil and sharpener, a pile of ledger books. Nothing else. Certainly nothing at all personal. If Ruben Ashford had ever left his mark here, it had been erased.

Foyle followed her into the room. He lifted one of the ledgers with an air of exasperation. "I have yet to replace Ruben," he said. "It's been difficult to hire bookkeepers too. I've had to manage my own accounts, when I hardly have time…" He put the ledger down and gave her a small smile. "Forgive me. As I said before, these are hardly your concerns."

"Of course," Josie said, although she found herself wondering if Foyle were more upset by the murder or the inconvenience it had caused him.

They left the room. As they walked down the hall, Molly passed by, toting a bucket and a mop. "Will there be anything else, Dr. Foyle?" she asked.

The question seemed to annoy him. "If there is, I will ring."

She curtsied. "Yes, sir. Of course, sir."

When they returned to Foyle's office, he remained standing, and so did Josie. The interview was clearly over. "I've asked Ida Crofter and Abram Sledge to speak to you as you requested," he said. "One of our teachers will take you to Mrs. Crofter. You will find Abram at the farm. Martin Rutledge, our farm manager, can direct you."

"Thank you," Josie said.

With extended arm, the superintendent guided her back to the reception area. As he bid her good-bye, he attempted the warm smile again. "The Ruben Ashford I knew was a kind man." He had the look of a person who feared he had been misunderstood. "A gentle man. I can't help believing that man is still somewhere inside him. If there's anything you can do to help him, I would be most pleased." He nodded his farewell and turned to go.

"Was he happy here?" Josie said. The question came to her suddenly, and she felt beholden to ask it, although she had a feeling she already knew how the superintendent would answer.

"Excuse me?" He stopped and gave her a puzzled look.

"Ruben Ashford. Was he happy at Rosewood?"

"Happy?" His face fell as he seemed to realize what he was about to say. "I have no idea. It never even occurred to me to ask."

Twenty

While the receptionist furiously typed, Josie waited for the teacher who would take her to see Mrs. Crofter. Josie wasn't entirely devoid of sympathy for Aubrey Foyle. He did the best he could with the resources he was provided with—including his own very limited imagination. Despite fierce opposition, he had brought Ruben Ashford to Rosewood. He had meant well when he hired him. And yet what had that gained Ashford in the end? Josie could almost hear the superintendent's voice calling down the hallway, directing Ruben Ashford to do this or that, just as he ordered Molly about. Shoe my mare. Drive me to the station. Fetch this, fetch that. The bell summoning Ruben Ashford must have rung all day long.

The door to the cottage opened and a young woman in a brown dress covered by a white smock, her hair pulled into a tidy bun at the top of her head, entered. "Miss Berenson?"

Josie stepped forward. "Yes."

"Dr. Foyle asked me to meet you here. I'm Abigail Knowles. I'll take you to Mrs. Crofter now."

Josie nodded. "Thank you."

The teacher appeared to be in her early twenties, somewhat awkward and unsure of herself. She gave Josie a shy smile as she led her out of the Great House onto the crescent drive. It was midday now, the sun at its peak, shining on the brick and stone buildings. From her

166

vantage point Josie could see the farm in the distance, flowing from the bottom of the hill. The laboring boys must have finished their toil for the day. With the white man on the horse leading the way, they followed the wagons back from the fields in an orderly line. A pair of crows circled overhead, their caws delivered faintly on the wind.

The two women walked in silence, with Knowles giving Josie nervous glances. Finally, Josie smiled and said, "Is there something you wanted to ask me, Miss Knowles?"

The teacher colored deeply. "It's just that—well, Dr. Foyle said you had come because of Connie."

"Connie?" Josie said. Then she remembered. "Oh, yes. Miss Prentiss. I'm looking into the circumstances surrounding her death. I'm here on Ruben Ashford's behalf."

The answer seemed to surprise Knowles. She worried a loose thread on her smock. "But didn't he...?" Her voice trailed off. "I heard he was sentenced last week."

"Yes, that's right. But we still have some questions." Josie reached into her pocket, pulled out one of her cards, and handed it to the teacher.

Knowles studied the card. "Phipps?"

"It's a clinic for psychiatry, in Baltimore, at the Johns Hopkins Hospital."

"I see."

"We're trying to understand the reasons for Mr. Ashford's actions. That, I'm afraid, isn't clear at all. I don't suppose you have any idea why...?"

Knowles reddened and stuck the card in her pocket. "Oh, no, miss. I wouldn't know anything about that."

A buggy came up the drive, and a woman in an enormous hat disembarked and with an air of great importance hurried towards the Great House. Perhaps she was one of the dignitaries from the Ladies Auxiliary Ruben Ashford had mentioned. Foyle used to trot him out like a show pony when they came to visit. Josie wondered what he said about Ruben Ashford now.

"I heard Miss Prentiss was quite beloved here," Josie said. "Her death must have come as a shock."

"Yes, miss." Abigail Knowles seemed much relieved at this more favorable turn in the conversation. "Connie—Miss Prentiss—taught the 'bigs'."

"The 'bigs'?"

"The children older than twelve. That's what we call them."

"I see." Josie smiled. "And do you teach the 'bigs' too?"

"Oh, no. Mrs. Crofter says I'm not ready for that yet." Knowles looked at her earnestly. "I teach the 'littles'."

"And lucky they are to have you," Josie said. She found Abigail Knowles to be quite likable, despite her almost painful awkwardness. She wasn't particularly pretty, she had round eyes in a very round face, and was rather big-boned and ungainly. But she seemed naturally authentic and warm, and Josie could well imagine she would make an excellent teacher.

Knowles led Josie around the crescent drive. The Rosewood buildings, she saw now, were identified by function: Classroom Building A, Classroom Building B, Gymnasium Annex, Dining Hall, Girls' Dormitory 1, Girls' Dormitory 2, a pair of dormitories for boys. Outside one of these a dozen boys stood in a circle passing a ball while a teacher dressed exactly like Abigail Knowles, in a brown dress and white smock, her hair pulled into the same tight bun, kept watch. These must be 'littles'; the oldest looked to be no more than seven or eight years old. 'Littles' were young enough, apparently, still to get their exercise through play. They weren't required to work. But there was something mechanical and joyless to their game, with the boys diligently handing the ball to each another in perfect order.

As Knowles walked past, several of the boys turned to smile at her. One waved, and another broke free of the circle and ran to her, encircling her with his arms. "Miss Abigail," he cried.

"Now, Henry." She gently detached him and shooed him back to the circle. "You know you have to stay with your friends. I will come and see you later, I promise."

Henry returned with a frown of disappointment to the circle. "We're not allowed to show affection to the children," Knowles said to Josie as they walked on. "Mrs. Crofter has been most clear on that. She said it harms their development. The children must learn to regulate their emotions and control their impulses. I try not to grow attached to them, but sometimes…"

"I imagine it would be hard," Josie said.

Knowles nodded, apparently relieved that Josie understood.

"And Connie, too, did she struggle to contain her affections?"

Knowles colored deeply, her fingers worrying her smock, but didn't answer.

"Did you know her well? Was she a friend of yours?" Josie asked.

"A friend of mine? No, I can't say she was. We did talk from time to time. We both lived in the dormitory." She pointed to a stone building farther along the path. "All the teachers do."

"Was she happy at Rosewood?"

Knowles considered. "I think so. At least at first. But before she—before she died—I heard her say she was thinking of leaving."

One of the buildings was labeled Service. Where the washing must be done. Bouts of steam emerged from the chimney, lending a dampness to the air.

"It wasn't just Connie," Knowles said. "Most of the teachers leave eventually. The work is hard. The children are dear, but they don't always progress the way Dr. Foyle thinks they should. And Mrs. Crofter can be quite hard on us—as well she should be," she added quickly. "It's only for the children's sake. But some of the teachers find positions elsewhere, or leave because they get married. We're not allowed to teach at Rosewood if we're married." She looked at Josie earnestly again. "Mrs. Crofter is quite explicit about that. She says the children deserve our full attention, and a wife must be devoted to her husband."

Indeed, Josie thought with a huff. And were husbands expected to abandon their careers in order to demonstrate their devotion to their wives? There was more she could say on that subject, but now was hardly the time. "Isn't Mrs. Crofter married?"

"Oh, no. Mrs. Crofter is a widow."

The last of the buildings was labeled Kitchens. Past it, Knowles took Josie onto a path leading into a stand of woods. It was much colder there, the sun blocked by the trees, and Josie pulled her scarf closer.

"Why do you think Miss Prentiss wanted to leave Rosewood?" she said. "Was she planning on getting married too?"

Knowles considered. "I don't think so. Connie was from a town near Albany. It's far away. I think she wanted to go back to New York."

"Did Miss Prentiss and Mr. Ashford know each other? Was there any relationship between them?"

Knowles bit her lip. "Mrs. Crofter would never allow that."

They had come to a small stone cottage. Once it might have belonged to a game warden or grounds keeper. It looked well kept, surrounded by flowerbeds tended with care. The flowers had finished blooming, but the dry stalks had been left in place. A tiny yellow bird flitted from one to the next, feeding on the dried seed heads.

"Mrs. Crofter lives here," Knowles said. "She's expecting you."

Josie bid the teacher good-bye and watched as she hurried away, keeping her promise to Henry, Josie hoped. She was sorry to see her go. There was something appealing about Abigail Knowles. She felt like a rare warm spot in a very cold place.

Josie was having trouble controlling her feelings as she needed to do if she were going to maintain her objectivity. She couldn't help disliking the asylum, finding it off-putting. It wasn't just the regimentation and lack of human sympathy. It was the divisiveness of the place, the way people were separated into categories and then set against each other, white vs black, teachers vs servants, boys vs girls. Even the children were methodically categorized: imbecile, moron, idiot, simpleton. It made her faintly ill.

Josie knocked on the cottage door, and a woman in a black woolen dress, the kind that would have been fashionable in the previous century, answered. She was short and stout, with a plump face. A modest cap crowned her grey hair; at her neckline hung a small gold crucifix.

"Mrs. Crofter?" Josie said. "I'm Josefa Berenson." Once more a card was produced and proffered. "You have a lovely garden, if I may say so. It must be beautiful in the springtime when it's blooming."

Ida Crofter smoothed down her skirt, preening, a small smile of pleasure escaping her lips. "It's God's great earth. Any beauty I bring to it is just a poor reflection of the Lord's." She stepped aside. "Won't you please come in."

The cottage was cozy and tidy, amply furnished, although imbued with the quiet melancholy that often befell people who lived alone. Only one umbrella stood neatly by the door, one pair of rain boots occupied the corner, a lone cup and saucer sat on the table. By the hearth, where a cheerful fire blazed, stood a single armchair. Beside it was a table with a lamp and sewing workbasket. Nearby, within easy reach, was a Bible displayed prominently on a stand. It looked well thumbed. So did the Romance novels, the kind that sold for a few dimes in markets and train stations, that were piled more discreetly on a bookshelf.

"May I offer you a refreshment?" Crofter asked.

"Thank you," Josie said with a smile. "That would be lovely."

Josie sat at the small table as the matron directed, while she disappeared into the kitchen, then returned with a cake, which she ceremoniously sliced and served.

Josie lifted her fork then lowered it, her eye taken by a photograph of a young man in a naval uniform on the mantel. "Mr. Crofter?" she asked politely.

"Yes. My husband. He died in Cuba, in the war."

"I'm sorry to hear it." Josie had only vague memories of the Spanish-American war, which took place when she was a small child. Crofter appeared not to have recovered from it. It appeared the Crofters had no children. There were no photographs, toys, memorabilia, or other objects that accumulated in homes with families. Instead the matron's cottage seemed deeply embedded in solitude. Josie wondered if loneliness had become an integral part of her nature.

"Dr. Foyle said you wanted to talk to me about Constance Prentiss," Crofter said modestly, her eyes lowered.

Josie had worried the matron might find her visit disturbing. She'd been quite traumatized by the murder, as her testimony made clear. But she seemed content—even eager—to revisit it.

"Yes," Josie said. "I'm trying to understand what happened the day she died."

"I can certainly tell you that." Crofter raised her eyes and gave a delicate shudder—whether of terror or delight was hard to say. Then she launched into the story of how she had witnessed Constance Prentiss's death, telling each part in detail, leaving out nothing. She finished with an air of satisfaction. "That day is engraved on my soul. I can promise you that."

Apparently so. The account the matron had delivered was almost word for word the same as her written testimony, as if she'd spent a great deal of time polishing and rehearsing it. Listening to her, Josie was reminded of something that had struck her before. "Why did you go to the stable that day?"

"Excuse me?" She seemed taken aback at the question.

"You said you were on your way to the stable when you heard a commotion and saw Ruben Ashford with Constance Prentiss. But you never said why you went there."

The matron fell silent. "It was one of the children," she said finally. "A six-year old boy. He'd gone missing, and I was looking for him. He'd only been with us a few months and had yet to adjust to asylum life—to our training methods. He came from an orphanage in the city. Sometimes those children have a particularly hard time. Walter isn't a bad child," she hastened to add. "He's just difficult at times to manage. He likes animals, horses especially. I've seen other children like him.

They find animals soothing. Easier to get along with than people, I suppose." She gave a small laugh, as if difficulty getting along with people was something she understood very well. "He likes to go to the stable when he can—will creep off there if given the chance."

"And did you find him?"

"No. When I saw what happened to Miss Prentiss, looking for Walter Thursday went completely out of my head."

"I understand from your testimony," Josie said carefully, "that you saw no horse in the stable. Are you sure of that?"

The matron looked at her steadily. "Absolutely."

"So there's no chance Ruben Ashford was shoeing a horse at the time Miss Prentiss died?"

"None whatsoever."

"And did you know him?"

"Ruben Ashford?" Crofter seemed shocked at the question. "I should think not." Her hand flew to the crucifix at her throat.

"I understand he occasionally drove you to the train station."

She frowned. "There's hardly anything improper in that."

"No, of course not," Josie said. She was beginning to be put off by the matron, by her moral rectitude and self-righteousness. But she saw no point in arguing. Crofter was clearly set in her opinions.

"I know one thing," Crofter said, as if she could read Josie's mind. "Dr. Foyle never should have hired that boy. I told him so on many an occasion."

Yes, Josie thought tiredly, I know. No good would come of it. So said many people—including, according to Nell, Ashford's father. "I also heard he drove Miss Prentiss to the station occasionally. He might have been planning to do so the day she died."

"I wouldn't know anything about that," Crofter said stiffly.

It was hardly worth asking, but Josie did so anyway. "Were you aware of any relationship between them?"

"Absolutely not." A look of intense distaste crossed the matron's face. "If there had been, I would have let Miss Prentiss go. I can promise you that. I would have demanded that Ruben Ashford be let go too."

The source of Crofter's aversion was clear. It wasn't just her prohibition against married teachers; it was the implied mixing of the races. Josie hadn't touched her cake, but she'd lost her appetite. She pushed her plate away. She had only one more question to ask. "Do you have any idea why Ruben Ashford would want to kill Constance Prentiss?"

Crofter drew herself up with a look of horror, her fingers clutching at her crucifix. She had come to her favorite part of her story—the place where she proved her virtue. "Don't ask me. I have no insight into the evil mind."

Twenty-one

Ruben Ashford had disappeared from Rosewood without a trace. All he had left behind was his reputation as murderer. That, perhaps, was enough to erase the rest. Or perhaps he'd never made an impression on the asylum in the first place. No one remembered him in any detail— no one had anything useful to say about him. It was if he had vanished in plain sight.

Josie thought about that as she took the path through the woods back to the crescent drive. She was glad to be done with Ida Crofter. She never could abide false piety—the kind that elevated the believer at the expense of everyone else. Nor could she tolerate people who labeled others evil, as if that explained them, when all it did was obscure rather than illuminate their humanity. It rendered them worthless, beyond redemption—most certainly exactly what Crofter intended as far as Ruben Ashford was concerned.

Josie was beginning to tire of Rosewood, and she was hungry too. She'd had nothing to eat or drink since leaving Baltimore except the cup of coffee Dr. Foyle had offered. She was sorry now for turning down Ida Crofter's cake. But she couldn't go home yet. She still had to speak to Abram Sledge, and she wanted to see the stable and the cabin where Ruben Ashford had lived.

As she emerged from the trees, Molly come out of the Service building with a laundry basket in her arms. Josie hurried towards her.

"Miss—" she called. "Miss Molly."

The girl stopped, balancing the basket on her hip.

"I was wondering if I might speak with you a moment?" Josie said.

Molly was younger than Josie had originally realized, fourteen or fifteen at the most. She was a pretty girl, with a smooth brow and even features. Josie's question seemed to have disturbed her. A look of annoyance flitted across her face. Then it vanished, replaced by a blank passivity. She lowered her eyes. "Yes, miss."

"I'm from—" Josie said. Automatically she reached into her pocket for a card. Never mind that. Foyle's bell would be ringing. There was no time. "I'm here on Ruben Ashford's behalf. I'm trying to help him. I'm trying" —she was aware of how ridiculous she sounded— "to save his life. Did you know him?"

"No, miss, I can't say I did. But I always felt sorry for him."

Sorry for what? Josie didn't get a chance to ask. With the basket in her arms, Molly bustled away. Josie let her go. There was no point in calling her back. Whatever Molly thought or felt was hidden far beyond Josie's reach. It reminded her of how Ruben Ashford had been when she spoke to him, avoiding her gaze, answering her questions without answering them at all. It was maddening.

She continued farther along the circle at the top of the hill, looking for a way down to the farm. She found it behind the Gymnasium Annex, a rutted dirt track that wound in serpentine fashion down the long slope to the fields. She walked down, glad for her sturdy boots. Below her stretched a pasture with cows, hogs in a corral, chicken coops, horse paddocks, and the fields where the boys had been cutting the cornstalks. A creek ran through the middle of the farm, spanned by a stone springhouse. Other outbuildings lay scattered around the farmyard: a cow barn, storage sheds, a silo, a bunkhouse, the stable. The horses must be inside since the paddocks were empty. The boys were gone now, but the colored hired hands were still at work, unloading the sheaves from the wagons near one of the sheds. The white man Josie had seen earlier on horseback stood by on foot watching.

Josie walked directly up to him. "Good afternoon, Mr. Rutledge. You are Martin Rutledge, are you not?"

He took his time answering. "Gee up there now," he barked to one of the wagon drivers. As the wagon rolled away, he turned and grunted at Josie in a way she took as assent.

"I've come from the Johns Hopkins Hospital," she said. "I'm here to speak to Abram Sledge."

"Sledge." Rutledge's mouth worked over the name as if it left a bad taste. He was careless in his appearance, dressed in a soiled cloth jacket and pants. His skin was blotchy, from drinking no doubt. He smelled of it too. "I can't imagine what business a white lady like you could have with a nigger like him." He wiped his nose with the back of his hand.

Josie stiffened. The farm manager disgusted her, and she would have liked nothing more than to tell him so. But she contained herself. She drew herself up. "Dr. Foyle said you would direct me."

Rutledge grunted again. Then he shrugged. "Try the cow barn."

The barn was on the far side of the farmyard, a large and airy structure built of weather-beaten planks. Josie walked through the broad door at the end, finding no one inside. The milking stalls were empty, as were the wash and feed rooms. She walked past them, over patterned shadows cast by the sun on the floor, through air thick with the smell of hay and sour milk. When she came out the far side, she saw a black man working on a gravel yard, loading cans of milk into a paneled pickup truck. The truck had come from Seiler's Dairy—the one she'd seen near the village. The driver stood by idly, watching. He was a white man, in his early twenties, she guessed, rather good looking, with fair skin and startling pale blue eyes, dressed in white canvas trousers and jacket. He looked up as she walked towards him, his eyes resting on her in an insolent way, evaluating her, as if there were something transactional between them. It put her off to him entirely.

"Miss," he said with a simpering smile and a tip of his cap.

She ignored him and marched straight to the black man. "Mr. Sledge?"

The farm hand seemed surprised that she would speak to him. He looked up briefly with a can of milk in his hands. Then he put the can down and lowered his eyes. "Yes, ma'am."

"I'd like to have a word with you, if I may."

"He can talk as soon as he finishes his work," the driver said lazily. He hadn't forgotten her snubbing him.

Josie almost answered back, but then she bit her tongue. The only one to suffer if she got into a heated exchange with the driver would be Sledge, whose work would be interrupted. She nodded and stepped aside.

After Sledge loaded the last can, the driver took his time inspecting the load and securing it in the truck. Then he raked his eyes over Josie one last time in an ill-mannered way. "Miss." Once again she didn't answer. She was relieved when he drove away.

Abram Sledge waited for her on the gravel yard. He was thin and wiry, in his early thirties, Josie guessed, dressed in dungarees shoved into boots, a flannel shirt rolled up to the elbows, a broad-brimmed hat, and work gloves.

Josie proffered a card. Sledge glanced at it but didn't take it. It occurred to her that he might not be able to read. She put the card away. "I'm Josefa Berenson. I've come from Baltimore, from the Johns Hopkins Hospital. I'm here on Ruben Ashford's behalf. I understand you were the one who found him—who subdued him when he attacked Constance Prentiss. I read the testimony you gave."

The field hand nodded. He still hadn't met her eye.

"I was hoping you might answer some questions I have about Miss Prentiss's death."

With great care, Sledge removed his gloves. "I told that man at the courthouse all I had to say."

"Yes, but there are other things that you might have forgotten to mention. Like a horse. I'm wondering if you saw one in the stable."

"No, ma'am. I can't say I did."

"Ruben Ashford said he was shoeing a horse when Miss Prentiss came in."

"I wouldn't know anything about that."

"Did you know him at all?"

"Ruben Ashford?" The gloves seemed to be of infinite interest. Sledge studied them. "No, I didn't. He kept to himself."

"What about Miss Prentiss. Did you know her?"

Sledge raised his eyes to stare at her with an incredulous look on his face, as if it were impossible to believe anyone could be so obtuse.

"Did you ever see the two of them together?"

Sledge slipped the gloves into his pocket. "Ruben Ashford worked in the Great House. Up the hill." He spoke patiently, as if explaining a lesson to an exceedingly slow child. "Like I said, he kept to himself. He didn't have anything to do with the likes of me." There was a hint of resentment in his voice.

Up hill, down hill. Office work, field work. School, farm. White, black. The divisions at Rosewood ran even deeper than Josie had suspected. Everyone at Rosewood had a place—everyone, that is, except Ruben Ashford.

Sledge wiped a hand over his face. Then the expression on his face softened. "I'm sorry about what happened to that boy, but I never thought anything good would come of him. It's no good putting people like us with them. It doesn't work. Never did, never will. That white girl—"

"Miss Prentiss?" Josie said.

"She didn't understand that either."

"What do you mean?"

"There was something wrong with that girl—something wrong with that boy, too. He wasn't right." Sledge turned away, heading into the barn. "He never should have come here. He should have known better. He brought it on himself."

Josie watched him go. She would have liked to question him more, but it would do no good. He'd said all he had to say. Beneath that placid exterior, she sensed a conflict of emotions. Ruben Ashford had inspired pity in the field hand, but also humiliation. Sledge wouldn't have known that Foyle prohibited Ashford from socializing with the other colored workers at Rosewood. He would have assumed Ashford avoided him out of a sense of superiority. He certainly wouldn't have known that, given the choice, Ashford would have much rather worked side by side with him with the horses and cows, and lived in the bunkhouse.

She glanced up at the sky. The sun was still shining brightly, but it was advancing, and December days were short. She would need to leave soon if she wanted to get back to the train station before dark.

She crossed the farm yard to the stable, a low, rectangular building, made of rough-hewn timbers. Like the cow barn, it had a long central aisle with doors open at each end, but it seemed much older, as if it dated to the earliest days when the property was settled. She stopped at the entrance, reluctant to go inside. There was something chilling about a place where a woman had been so brutally murdered. But she could hardly call her investigation complete if she didn't see it. She squared her shoulders and walked in.

The stable was dark, deliberately so, she assumed, in order to be soothing for the horses. A series of small, grime-encrusted windows near the ceiling gave out little light, and beyond the door, the interior receded into gloom. She stood still for a moment, waiting for her eyes to adjust. Then she walked down the long aisle past a tack room and a washroom and a storage room for grain. The rest of the stable was given over to stalls, a dozen or so on each side. The horses were inside now, eating, and most of the stalls were taken. Their bodies warmed the air, which had the pleasant smell of molasses and corn. Now and then one blew out a breath or stamped a hoof. The sound of their chewing brought a feeling of contentment and peace to the place—a welcome relief, under the circumstances. Josie studied the ground as she walked. Somewhere here Constance Prentiss's blood had pooled.

180

There was no sign of it now. The floor was dirt, raked smooth. She stopped in the middle of the building to look around. She didn't know exactly what she was looking for. What had she expected to feel, to see? A ghost? Nothing struck her as out of the ordinary.

She reached the far end of the stable and stepped outside. After the darkness, the sun was blinding. She held a hand over her eyes. Then she turned around and went back inside, waiting again for her eyes to adjust. She stopped for a moment, thinking. Then she stepped outside and stood in the sun once more. After her eyes had adjusted to the brightness, she turned around and looked into the stable. The aisle running down the center disappeared into darkness.

She walked through the stable to the far side, where she repeated her experiment. She went outside and waited for her eyes to adjust to the sun. Then she turned and looked inside. From the outside, the interior of the stable was invisible. She recalled a line from the report of Frank Hopper, sheriff. "The sun was strong, and it was so dark inside, it took my eyes a few minutes to adjust." So he wrote on the day Constance Prentiss died. At first, when Hopper had gone into the stable, he hadn't even been able to see Constance Prentiss on the ground or Ida Crofter on her knees beside her.

Josie went back inside, waiting for her eyes to adjust to the dim light, imagining the sheriff doing the same. Just then one of the stall doors slid open, and a small boy came out, closing the door behind him. He looked at her, and she looked at him.

What had Ida Crofter said to Josie when she asked why she went to the stable that day? "I went looking for Walter." And did you find him? Josie asked. "When I saw Constance Prentiss," Crofter said, "looking for Walter Thursday went completely out of my head."

"Walter?" Josie said. "Walter Thursday?"

"Yes, miss." The boy dropped his eyes with the air of someone who expected to be scolded. He twisted his foot into the dirt.

Josie walked up to him, then bent down so that she could speak to him eye to eye. "Hello, Walter. My name's Josie."

Walter nodded. "Hello."

Josie smiled. "Shall we go now? They must be missing you at school."

Crofter had said Walter was six years old, one of the 'littles'. The boy was small, even for that age. He was tow-headed, a little bit bandy in the legs. Rather pale, with blue circles under the eyes. The runt of the litter, as Josie's mother would say, the one that always got pushed aside when the others came to eat.

Josie held out her hand, and he put his hand in hers. He seemed sweet-tempered and obedient. He came along without a fuss. Hand in hand, they walked up the long hill to the crescent drive.

"I'm wondering," Josie said carefully, "if you knew Miss Prentiss?"

"Yes, miss."

"And did you ever see her in the stable?"

Walter met her gaze, open and trusting. "I saw Miss Prentiss dancing with a horse." He raised his arms high over his head. "Ashes, ashes, we all fall down." He dropped his arms to his sides.

Just then Abigail Knowles appeared, leading a group of girls out of a classroom building.

"Miss Knowles," Josie called out. "I have someone for you."

"Oh, Walter." Knowles gave him an affectionate frown. "Where have you been?"

"I found him with the horses," Josie said.

Knowles gave a little tut-tut sound. "Sorry for the trouble."

"It was no trouble." Josie smiled. "Walter and I have just been having a nice chat."

"Good-bye, Josie," Walter said. Cheerfully he put his hand in Knowles' and let himself be led away.

"Good-bye, Walter."

Josie stood for a while on the crescent drive, thinking. Then she headed down the long drive to the entrance of the asylum. She was ready to go home now, but she still had one more thing to see: Ruben Ashford's cabin. She found it exactly where he'd said it would be, in the woods by the gate. Once it must have been a gatekeeper's lodge. It was a small, one-room log building with a stone chimney emerging from the roof. The door was ajar. Josie went in, even though she suspected she would find nothing there. Ruben Ashford would have done his vanishing act there as thoroughly as everywhere else. The cabin looked abandoned. Inside was an iron cot, a moth-eaten blanket, a table and chair, a dry sink. A metal pot and plate stood on a shelf. No personal possessions at all, no clothes or books or journals. Foyle must have ordered everything removed. Cobwebs hung from the ceiling; mouse droppings littered the floor. It had a musty, rodent smell.

Josie left the cabin then hurried through the gate to the road, leaving Rosewood behind. She walked quickly, anxious to reach the train station before dark. She was anxious to get home too. She knew what she would tell Nell when she got there. Abram Sledge and Ida Crofter couldn't possibly have seen Ruben Ashford kill Constance Prentiss. They were coming from the outside and would have been blinded by the sun. But someone else had. Josie put her hand in her pocket, still feeling the warmth of the Walter Thursday's hand in hers. And that someone had seen a horse.

Twenty-two

It was late when Josie returned from Rosewood, the sun down, the temperatures dropping. She was full of excitement, bursting with news. She'd finally gotten some insight into Ruben Ashford's case, she told Nell. Nell smiled. She was delighted to hear it.

They were in the kitchen, eating dinner. It was too dark and cold in the dining room upstairs, where no one had built a fire. Nell had been too busy all day, and with Margaret gone, there was no one else to tend to it. They hadn't replaced her yet; Nell, Josie knew, was still too overcome by Margaret's death to even think about it.

But it was warm in the kitchen, where sconces threw golden pools of light onto the floor while the stove delivered a steady heat. Esme, wearing her best dress, made a brief appearance as the two women sat down. Nell asked her to join them, but the cook shook her head mysteriously. She was, she said, on her way out. No doubt meeting a gentleman caller, Nell confided to Josie after Esme had gone; Esme, maintaining her famous reserve, had said nothing about it.

"Now," Nell said. "Tell."

Over grilled lamb chops and potatoes, Josie told Nell what she'd learned at Rosewood that day, beginning with Aubrey Foyle and ending with Walter Thursday.

When Josie finished, Nell looked at her incredulously. "Are you saying Ruben Ashford is innocent?"

"Innocent?" Josie said. "That I don't know. But I do know one thing. Neither Ida Crofter nor Abram Sledge could have seen what happened to Constance Prentiss. They were outside the stable in the sunshine. They would have been blinded by the light."

Nell stood up and carried her plate to the sink. "Do you mean they lied about it?"

"Perhaps." Josie collected her own dishes and took them to the counter. "Ida Crofter despised Ruben Ashford. She never thought Foyle should have hired him to begin with. As far as she was concerned, Ashford upset the natural order of things. She has nothing against colored people—as long as they stay in their place. She had no compunction at all about asking Ashford for favors, like driving her to the train station. But she couldn't abide seeing him working side by side on an equal basis with white people in the Great House. It offended her sensibility. She might very well have been glad to be rid of him."

"And Sledge? Did he despise Ashford too?" Nell turned on the hot water tap.

"He certainly resented him." Josie picked up a towel so she could dry while Nell washed. "Ruben Ashford would have nothing to do with him, and Sledge took it as a slight. He didn't know Foyle had forbidden Ashford from associating with the farm hands. Given a chance, Ashford would have much rather worked with horses and cows than ledger books."

Josie put the dried plates away in the cupboard. "On the other hand, Crofter is quite religious. It's hard to imagine her telling a deliberate lie. It would go against her ethic. And Sledge did seem to feel genuine pity for Ashford."

"Then why not tell the truth and admit they didn't know what happened?"

"Because they thought they did."

Nell shook her head, smiling. "Josefa Berenson. I can't say you're making much sense right now." She rinsed the sink and hung the scrub brush up to dry.

"Agreed." Josie said. "It's just that the more I learn about this murder, the less I know."

It was late. Time for bed. Josie took Nell's hand and led her up the stairs.

"Tell me more," Nell said, as they went into the bedroom.

"I keep thinking back to my Harvard days," Josie. "One of the experiments we ran was on perception and expectation. We put rats into a cage with two paddles. If the rats pushed on one of the paddles, it gave them food. The other one gave them nothing. They learned this system quite easily, and happily fed themselves by pushing the proper paddle. Then we switched the paddles, so that the second provided food while the first did nothing."

Josie unbuttoned her jacket as she undressed. "It took the rats a surprisingly long time to adjust to the change." She hung her skirt in the wardrobe. "They pushed the first paddle over and over again, even after it had stopped working. Eventually, usually by accident, they realized the second paddle was the source of food. After that they focused quite happily on it and ignored the first."

"Interesting." Nell sat down at her dressing table and drew a shawl over her nightdress. It was cold in the bedroom, too. Then she pulled the pins from her hair, allowing it to cascade down her back. "But I don't see how that applies to Ruben Ashford's case." She frowned at Josie in the mirror. "You yourself said rats are nothing like people."

"True, except when they are." Josie picked up a brush and began brushing out Nell's hair with smooth, long strokes. It was a ritual she looked forward to each night, and it never failed to remind her of the first time she'd unpinned Nell's hair and kissed her on the Cape. She bent over now, pushed the hair aside, and kissed the nape of Nell's neck. Nell closed her eyes, relaxed, and sighed with pleasure.

"It's a question of perception and expectation," Josie said, straightening up and returning to the task at hand. "Or rather a question of how expectation influences perception."

"Meaning—?"

"Meaning that what we see is influenced by what we *expect* to see. As long as the rats expected the first paddle to give them food, they kept going back to it, even after it had stopped."

"So are you saying Crofter and Sledge expected Ashford to be a murderer?"

"Not exactly," Josie said. "I'm saying they had enough natural antipathy towards him, that when they saw him beside the body of Constance Prentiss, it was easy to assume he'd killed her. Later they became convinced they'd actually seen it happen."

If you already believed black people were no good—and Jim Crow would certainly reinforce that belief—then it was just one small step farther to believe they were capable of no good, too. Even Abram Sledge could have internalized that mindset. Maybe, Josie thought, this was what Norbert Richards meant when he said race played a role in Ruben Ashford's case.

"But what about the horse?" Nell said. "You said Ashford claimed a horse killed Prentiss—until he confessed. But neither Sledge nor Crofter saw one, even after they'd run into the stable. That can't be a question of expectation. Horses can't vanish into thin air."

"No, I suppose not." Josie put down the brush and climbed into bed.

Nell turned out the lamp, leaving the room in darkness, except for an amber glow that sifted through the windows from the streetlight outside. She got into bed, shivering in the cold bedclothes, and drew closer to Josie. Josie put her arms around her, glad for the warmth.

"Don't forget Walter Thursday," Josie said. "He said he saw a horse, and he was in the stable. The only one in a position to see."

"You mean the boy who saw a horse dancing with Miss Prentiss," Nell murmured, her face buried in Josie's neck.

"Yes."

Nell pulled back and looked at her directly. "That hardly makes sense, does it?"

"I suppose not." Josie shrugged helplessly. "I just don't know what to think."

Nell rolled over on her back, put her arms behind her head, and looked up at the ceiling. "Let's think it through. Ruben Ashford said a horse was there, but he also said he was shoeing it. The boy said nothing about that. He said the horse was dancing. Maybe he just imagined it. After all, horses and people hardly dance together." Nell tapped a finger against her cheek. "The thing I don't understand the most is why Ruben Ashford would confess if he were innocent. It would hardly further his case. And then there's the question, if he is innocent, of how he got blood on his shirt, or why he had a bloody hammer in his hand."

"All good points, and ones I have no answer for." Josie rolled on her side so that she was facing Nell, just inches apart. "When I first met Norbert Richards, he told me the story of a black man in Annapolis, an ice seller. He was accused of killing a white woman just like Ashford. But the ice seller never confessed. He went to his death insisting he was innocent." She toyed with the ribbon on Nell's nightdress. "Still, if Ruben Ashford is innocent, it changes everything. The question we have to ask then isn't why he killed her, but why he confessed."

"Exactly," Nell said, murmuring. She turned back to Josie and kissed her.

Josie wanted to go on—it was so helpful to talk things out with Nell—but even Josie had to admit they were just going round and round in circles. There were too many things that didn't make sense, too many missing pieces to the puzzle. And now she had other things on her mind. She kissed Nell back and pulled her closer, reaching a hand under her nightdress, gently caressing her, happily feeling her respond to her touch.

Later as Nell was drifting off to sleep, Josie spoke again.

"Yes," Nell said sleepily. "What is it?"

"I keep thinking about Ruben Ashford, about what he looked

like when he recounted the murder to me. It was uncanny. He spoke so strangely, as if he were in a trance, or in a dream. At the time I thought the memory had overwhelmed him, but now I wonder if it wasn't memory at all, but fantasy."

"Ah," Nell said, but nothing else.

"Nell?" Josie said a few minutes later.

"My love. Will you never sleep?"

"I keep thinking about Walter."

Nell sighed, closed her eyes, and rolled over. "The boy who saw the dancing horse?"

"Yes. I think he saw Constance Prentiss die. I think he's the only one who did. But he didn't understand what he saw. He thought it was a dance, or a game. He said, *Ashes, ashes, we all fall down.*"

"Hmm," Nell said.

"I've seen children like him before in the dispensary at Phipps. Sweet, but distant, as if they're living in their own world. The question is, what made him like that? Is it a failure of cognition, or an inability to distinguish imagination from reality? Was he born that way, or did he suffer some kind of illness or trauma? It might be helpful if we knew. We might be able to understand him better—even make sense of what he said. It could mean something for Ashford's case." Josie sighed in frustration. "But there's no way of knowing. Usually at times like these we ask the family to help us, but Walter has no family to ask. Mrs. Crofter said he came from an orphanage in the city."

Nell opened her eyes. "Walter is an orphan?"

"Yes."

Nell sat up. "What did you say his name was?"

Josie looked at her in surprise. "Walter."

"I know that. I mean his last name."

"Thursday. Why?"

"I know of a lot of orphanages in Baltimore." Nell smiled and lay back down, nestling herself against Josie. "But only one that names its children after the days of the week."

Twenty-three

The next day at one o'clock Nell sat at her desk, writing up her notes on her last patient. For once she was glad to work only half-days. She was eager to finish up and leave for the Calvert Orphan Home where, she suspected, Walter Thursday had once resided. She had just slipped the notes into a folder, when James put in his head.

"Ready to close up?" Nell said.

"I was—except…"

"Yes?"

"Bruno Snell to see you, if you will. He just came—that is to say—limped in."

Snell. Not exactly the person she wanted to see under any circumstances, let alone now. "What happened this time?"

"Hard to say." James shrugged. "He's been in a fight from the looks of it."

Nell sniffed. "Wouldn't be the first time."

"Shall I tell him to come back tomorrow?"

She sighed. "Might as well get it over with. Show him in."

She'd known Bruno since he was a child. He was in his early twenties now. An indifferent student, he'd left school early to take a job on the docks as a longshoreman. It suited him. Any place he could push his weight around suited Bruno Snell.

Snell gave her a sheepish grin when he entered the examination room. He must have been coming from the docks when he got injured. He was wearing heavy work clothes, cap, and boots. His pants leg was ripped, and he was limping, just as James had said.

"On the table, please," Nell said.

He winced as he hopped up. She peered at his leg, which had a large contusion on the shin. The knee was beginning to swell. She'd get to that in a minute. First of all she'd see what other damage Snell had managed to do to himself. She started at the top and worked her way down, as was her wont. No sign of skull injury, nothing wrong with the mouth, ears, and eyes. The lungs were strong, the chest and arms intact, but his knuckles were cut and swollen. She manipulated the fingers. Nothing broken. Then she turned to the leg. She manipulated the knee, bending it back and forth.

"Ouch," Snell said.

Nothing broken there either. "You'll survive," Nell said, "although I expect you already knew that. Nothing wrong with you that a little soap and water and iodine can't fix." She fetched supplies from the wall cabinet. "Now," she said as she cleaned his wounds. "Do you want to tell me about it?" She almost hoped he wouldn't. She wasn't sure she wanted to hear.

"Nigger on the streetcar," Snell said with satisfaction. "*White* streetcar. Right there on Fayette. Wearing his army uniform no less. It's been like that all over town ever since those colored boys got home from the war. Sticking their noses where they don't belong, thinking they can get away with things. Ouch," he said again, as she swabbed on the iodine. It stung. Then he grinned. "Nothing I couldn't handle. I made sure he got off. Even if he did catch my knee with his boot on his way out."

He held the knee out for her to see. She put iodine on the cut on his leg, too, feeling extra satisfaction when he grimaced. "That hurts." He frowned at her reproachfully.

She ignored him and finished the bandaging. "Try to keep your weight off it a few days, won't you?"

"Sure will." He made a show of jumping down from the table on both feet. "Thank you, Dr. Nell." Then he winked. "Don't you worry about those colored boys. We know how to keep our women safe."

Our women? Safe? The only person Nell wanted to be kept safe from right now was Bruno Snell. He was infuriating. He stood there smiling at her, waiting for some response, some expression of heartfelt thanks apparently. She opened the door. "James?"

James was there sooner than she would have expected, as if he'd been standing close by, keeping an eye on her.

"Show Mr. Snell out, won't you, please?" She leveled her gaze at Bruno. "He won't be coming back."

Bruno opened his mouth, astounded, but before he could say anything, James had taken him firmly by the elbow—never mind the limp—and had frog-marched him outside. Nell heard the door firmly lock behind him. "Everything all right now, Dr. Winters?" James said when he came back.

"Yes, James." She smiled at him. "Now go along. I'll see you tomorrow."

James would be leaving soon for pharmacy school. She wished him well, but she hardly knew what she would do without him. Well, she'd have to make do, that was all. She didn't know if she would be able to replace him. She still hadn't replaced Margaret. At first she couldn't think of doing it, and then later realized she couldn't afford to do so. The flu epidemic had taken a toll, accelerating the flight of white Baltimoreans to the suburbs, where they looked for cleaner, fresher air. The city was only becoming poorer. She was sorry now she'd told Bruno Snell not to come back. At least he paid his bills. Fewer and fewer of her patients did—especially the ones who came through the back door.

Nell put on her coat and hat, then stopped in the kitchen to tell Esme she was going out. She considered telling her about Bruno Snell's altercation on the streetcar but decided not to. It wouldn't be anything Esme didn't already know. A lot of the colored soldiers had been having trouble since they got back from the war. They'd gotten used to a kind of equality overseas they'd never had at home. Now they thought they deserved better—thought they'd earned it. Nell remembered how cheerfully Theo had gone off to war, thinking to prove his loyalty and earn the respect of white Baltimore. It hadn't worked out that way. Racial antipathy had only worsened since the war ended, with violence breaking out between white thugs who were determined to put colored soldiers in their place, and soldiers who resisted.

She slipped out the back door and made her way to McCulloh Street, suddenly consumed with anger. She was glad after all that she'd shown Snell the door. She had no patience for people like him. On the other hand, she couldn't quite understand the soldier who'd deliberately gotten on the white streetcar either. Why push the limits? She didn't like the rules, but they were there for a reason. They kept the peace. She'd been saying so to Josie ever since she started riding the colored streetcars. They shared the same values, the same desire for a just, equitable world, but to Nell's mind, there was no point in rushing it. It took time.

The Calvert Orphan Home was on the far edge of the Baltimore divide, near the Gwynns Falls. Too far to walk. Nell made her way to Franklin Street then waited for the white streetcar that would take her westwards. As she settled in her seat, she found herself thinking again of Ruben Ashford. Was Josie rushing things as far as Ashford was concerned, too? Was Nell wrong to help her? What if Josie was right, and in the end his life was spared? It would only infuriate people like Bruno Snell. Nell winced, thinking of his knuckles. The reaction in the city could be violent, beyond anyone's ability to control. But if Ashford were innocent, didn't the truth need to be told, no matter what? She was ashamed to realize she had mixed feelings. Josie had taken her far beyond her usual reaction to injustice, which consisted of writing letters to the *Baltimore Sun* or attending an occasional rally. Josie had taken her directly into the realm of action.

Nell straightened her spine. If nothing else, Josie had taught her that actions have consequences—and express our values. Inaction was a kind of choice, too. When had she become so timid? Hadn't she always admired people who went beyond mouthing platitudes to stand up for what was right? She would do the same. She would stand by Josie.

Twenty minutes later she disembarked from the streetcar and walked the rest of the way to the Calvert Orphan Home. Once the land by the Gwynns Falls had been given over to fields, timber, and farms. Nell remembered hiking the unspoiled banks of the river as a child with her father, coveys of ducks bursting into flight as they drew near. Now the city had encroached on the river in long lines of row houses which marched in orderly fashion to the water's edge, each one sporting shining marble steps, and each one looking exactly the same. Nell shook her head. Sometimes she felt as if her city lacked imagination, producing the same kind of rigid architecture, over and over again. Only the orphanage still retained a memory of the wildness that had been. It sat on a plot of greenery, surrounded by trees and sprawling lawns, a grand brick building with a castle-like flair. Nell walked up the front steps and through the front door to a tiled lobby. At the back, behind a desk, sat a young man with a shock of flaming red hair.

"Dr. Winters!" His face broke into a smile that just as quickly vanished. "Goodness. Is someone ill?"

Sometimes Nell felt like a raven, a harbinger of doom, triggering fear and gloom wherever she went. The fact that she was wearing her usual doctoring costume, which was all black—skirt, jacket, hat, boots, and shawl—didn't help. She smiled. "No, Simon, everyone's fine. I'm here to speak to Mrs. Randolph, if she's available."

"Well, that's a relief." He smiled happily back. "I'll check for you."

Simon disappeared down a long hallway to the back of the building. It had been ages since Nell had last been at the orphanage—in the summer, before the flu. Nothing appeared to have changed since then.

The building still held a faded elegance, although it had diminished mostly to shabbiness. The deterioration wasn't Emma Randolph's fault; the director did the best she could with what she had. The patterned rug on the floor, once grand, was stained and threadbare. The walls badly needed a coat of paint, and were soiled from too many toddlers' sticky fingers and the boots of angry little boys. From the dining hall leaked the usual smell of cabbage, greens, and boiled beef. The smell would not be easily forgotten, Nell suspected, invading the dreams of orphaned children even long after they'd left Calvert behind. She heard the distant sound of footsteps, a door opening and closing, muted voices. Somewhere a baby was crying.

The first time she'd met Emma, Nell had been a recently graduated medical student, completing her resident training at Johns Hopkins. Emma had brought in a child from the orphanage who had a bad case of pneumonia. It had been nip and tuck for a while, but in the end Nell's treatments succeeded, and the child had survived. More children followed. A club foot, asthma, rubella. The orphanage had its own nurses on staff, but stubborn cases were sent to the hospital to see the doctors—including Nell. It had seemed natural to keep up the connection once she opened her own practice. From time to time over the years, Emma called Nell in to consult, and in the end they'd become friends.

Simon was back. "Mrs. Randolph will see you now. Shall I take you?"

"No need, Simon. I know the way."

Nell found Emma in her office, a warm space decorated with a polished wood floor and watercolors of pastoral scenes. A cozy fire burned in the grate. In one corner a wooden bin held a bevy of toys. Children's books filled a shelf on the wall. Well into her sixties now, Emma managed to combine the efficiency of the schoolteacher she'd once been with the warmth of the grandmother she'd become. Her face was pleasantly lined, her hair going from grey to white. Despite her age, she was quite stylish, and had a penchant for the latest trends in fashion. Today she was wearing a bright red dress cut daringly above her ankles. Nell felt positively dowdy in comparison.

Emma rose from her desk as Nell came in. "Nell." She took Nell's hands in hers. "It's so good to see you. I heard you were ill."

"Recovered," Nell said with a smile.

"I can't tell you how glad I am to hear it." Emma raised her eyes in a silent prayer of thanks. "Please, sit. Tea?"

"Thank you. No. I don't want to keep you."

They sat in winged chairs by the fire. Emma ran a hand over her eyes. "I'm exhausted today, I'm afraid. So tired, I can't seem to keep up. I never thought I'd be too old for this job but—" She shook her head. "It's the flu. It overwhelmed us. The number of orphans in the city now—" She ran a hand over her face. "We took in eight new children in October, twelve in November. I should have turned the last ones away, but I couldn't bring myself to do it. We've had to double them up in beds. Siblings. Whole families. We lost one of our nurses. One of our aides is still out sick. And no one's adopting. If you know of anyone…"

"Of course." Most of the families Nell knew had lost parents, not children. But she would give it some thought. There was always the possibility that someone might be looking for the consolation a child could bring.

"What brings you to us today?" Emma said.

"A boy you once had—or at least I think you might have had. His name is Walter Thursday."

"Ah, Walter." Emma's face lit up in a fond smile. "Of course. We sent him to Rosewood last summer. How is he?"

"Fine, I believe. Someone I know was just looking in on him. I was wondering if you might be able to tell me a little bit about him."

"Let's see." Emma stood and walked to a filing cabinet, rummaged for a moment through it, and pulled out a folder. "Here it is." She returned to her chair and opened the file on her lap, referring to it as she spoke. "Walter came to us in the fall of 1913. He was just an infant then, around nine or ten months, we guessed. He was left overnight on the front steps."

"On a Thursday?"

"Yes." Emma smiled. "On a Thursday."

"And Walter? How did you decide on that name?"

"One of our nurses has a favorite uncle named Walter. She said the boy reminded her of him. You know what they say about babies looking like old men. She started calling him Walter, and the name stuck."

"Where did he come from?"

"We never did find out. He was left without any identifying information. Whoever left him seemed to have done their best caring for him. He was well fed and dressed in clean, although rather worn, clothes. We made all the usual inquiries, checked with the hospitals and police stations, ran advertisements in the *Sun*. No one claimed him." She sighed. "You always end up wondering what happened in these situations. There's always a story behind an abandonment like that—most often a tragedy."

"What was he like?"

"As a baby? It's hard to say. He was so little. And coming here was a shock to him of course; it always is, especially when they're left like that." She turned a page in the file, ran her finger down it. "He seemed normal enough when we first got him, but he regressed afterwards. He hardly gained any weight at all the first four months. Nurse thought he might not make it. But he was a fighter. I wouldn't say he thrived, but he didn't give up either."

Walter would have had to have been a fighter to survive. As a general rule, as Nell well knew, children weren't suited to institutional life. Even with the best of care, they often withered. The youngest were the most vulnerable. Sending a child to an orphanage before the age of one was all but akin to giving it a death sentence. Even the ones who survived were often sickly. Measles, mumps, whooping cough—all took a toll. Run of the mill colds and ear infections too.

Then there was the emotional toll of institutionalization. Emma's nurses adhered to the most modern methods in childcare; this Nell knew because she'd advised them on the best practices herself. Contact with the children, especially the babies, was kept to a minimum in order to keep germs at bay. The babies' ward had twenty cribs overseen by a single nurse and an aide who wore masks and gloves and touched the children as little as possible. At feeding time, bottles were tied to slats and the babies placed beneath them to suck in a sterile environment. Babies who were upset, cried until they fell exhausted into sleep. Better that, the nurses said, than be touched and risk getting sick. And children needed to learn how to soothe themselves, especially ones without families. Life would be hard for them no matter what. No benefit came from spoiling.

"He was late in learning to walk and talk," Emma said. She read out loud from the record. "'Nurse says he won't look at her. Won't play with others. Spends time sitting by himself at the window looking out. Lacks meaningful speech.' That's a note from when he was three. He liked animals. Especially horses." She laughed. "Apparently by the time he was four he'd developed a talent for disappearing. Luckily the staff knew where to look for him, and they always found him in the stables."

Emma closed the file. "We tried to find a home for him but couldn't. He was adorable in many ways, but he wouldn't engage. We presented him to several promising couples. They always turned him down. They said they felt as if he were in his own world."

She stood and replaced the file in the cabinet. "By the time he turned five—well, I don't have to tell you how difficult it is to find homes for older children. And we don't have the means to keep children indefinitely. Walter wasn't developing. We decided it would be in his best interest to send him to Rosewood. They agreed to take him."

"Do you think he's feeble-minded?"

Emma gave a firm shake of her head. "I never have cared for that

198

word. What does it mean exactly? I'm afraid it's just a basket we throw unwanted children into." She walked back to her chair and placed her hand on the back. "I can't say I ever understood Walter, but I've seen children like him before. Far too many end up with us, I'm afraid. No matter how hard we try—we just can't give them what they need. We did our best for Walter. When I sent him to Rosewood, I thought it was time to let someone else try."

"Of course."

The two women walked arm in arm to the door.

"I hope Walter does well. He deserves better." Emma gave Nell a sad smile. "They all do."

"So you still don't know where he came from?"

"I'm afraid not." Emma paused with her hand on her cheek. "There was one time—I didn't want to mention it, because I didn't want you to think poorly of the boy but…"

"Yes?"

"After he'd been here for a year, a woman came in, claiming she'd left her child with us by mistake and wanted him back. We couldn't be sure, but we thought it might be Walter's mother. By then he'd become a ward of the state. We couldn't just give him back. And she had no proof. No birth record, no certificate, no testimony, no photographs. There are procedures we have to follow in these cases. She could have applied to adopt him, but there are requirements. We can't have the children going into unsuitable homes."

Nell nodded. "Of course not."

"She would have had to demonstrate to us that she had a stable household. Steady income. Mother *and* father."

Nell considered the emphasis on *and*. "I see."

"When we explained this to her, she grew angry. She said we'd stolen her child, that she'd never planned to give him up, and she'd only left him here during a hard patch."

"Her name," Nell said. "Did you get it?"

"We tried, but she wouldn't give it. I had the impression she might be in some kind of trouble." Emma hesitated as if she were reluctant to say more. "I don't believe she was employed in a—reputable way. I only mention it because—"

"Yes?" Nell said.

"If she was Walter's mother—and we had no way of knowing—but if she was, I wonder if, even under the circumstances, he would have been better off with her."

Twenty-four

The best place that Nell knew of to look for women who were employed, as Emma Randolph so delicately put it, in disreputable ways, was at Madame Katya Bulgarov's brothel in Pigtown. It was growing late as Nell left the orphanage, with night already coming on; the December days were so short. She was beginning to feel tired, and she knew Esme and Josie would be worried about her. She should head straight home, but decided to stop by the brothel first. With any luck she would have news about Walter to share with Josie when she got back.

Emma Randolph's description of Walter had given Nell some clues, but hardly solved the puzzle. Emma confirmed that the boy seemed to be lost in a world of his own making, just as Josie had said. It was possible his condition was a function of his abandonment and subsequent institutional life in the orphanage. But it was also possible it had been caused by something congenital or by some kind of trauma. Perhaps his mother—if they could find her—would know more.

Nell rode the Franklin Street streetcar back to the city center, then transferred to the South Carey Street line. Soon she crossed Pratt Street to Mt. Clare Station, the center of the vast Baltimore and Ohio railroad empire, where trains from all over the country disgorged passengers and cargo to feed the warehouses at Camden Yards and the hungry port just to the south. The streetcar rattled across railroad tracks near the roundhouse, past locomotives lined up one after the

---

other like enormous snakes of iron and steel. At the intersection of Washington Boulevard, she dismounted and made her way eastward on foot through Pigtown, the Baltimore neighborhood named for the squealing herds of swine that were herded each day from the trains to nearby slaughterhouses. Some of those pigs, Nell suspected, were either purloined or had escaped to populate her own neighborhood.

Pigtown had a dark and dismal feel, the narrow streets crammed with a jumble of two-story rowhouses that crowded out the last of the fading light. Nell hurried past breweries, bars, saloons, a cigar factory, and—to her surprise—a quite elegant looking stationery shop. Packinghouses and butcher shops populated the area. Streetlights, glowing dimly, only added to the gloom. The air felt thick and wintry, dank with the noisome smell of the harbor along with factory soot and locomotive exhaust. Black clouds billowed from the smokestacks of the coal-fired power plant that generated electricity for the city's streetcars.

Pigtown was where the heart of Baltimore lay, far more than Bolton Hill, Mt. Vernon, Roland Park, and the other moneyed neighborhoods to the north, or even the financial centers to the east. This Nell well knew. For almost a century, the city's fortunes had been tied to the B&O railroad—tied to Nell's fortunes too, since Mary Garrett's railroad money had founded the Johns Hopkins medical school where she earned her degree. The Great War had only made Pigtown more essential to the city's commerce as the neighborhood warehouses provisioned the many military ships and troop transports that plied the harbor. Now that the war was over, the military presence in the city would diminish. While no one was sorry to see the war end, many of Pigtown's merchants, Nell imagined, would be sorry to see the business go.

Now and then a horn from a Chesapeake Bay steamship split the night. The mayor's paving initiative had yet to penetrate here, and the streets were still cobblestone, in a perpetual state of disrepair, piles of cobbles lying in heaps beside stretches of mud and dirt. The promised sewers had not yet arrived either, and the streets doubled as gullies running with dirty bath and kitchen water. Nell picked her way across steppingstones at intersections, dodging the horse-drawn carts, wagons, and motorized trucks that ferried goods from the trains to the warehouses and cargo ships and back again.

Unlike the rest of the city, Pigtown was integrated, a hodgepodge of black, white, native-born, and immigrant households living side by side. The pressing, shifting needs of the labor market required it. This was not to say the communities existed in harmony. White workers resented the competition black workers brought and complained they drove down the price of labor. Labor unrest, with its underlying hint of violence, was a constant threat. Nell remembered hearing stories from her parents about the railroad strike of 1877, when President Hayes sent federal troops to Baltimore to control the riots. Over a dozen strikers were killed and hundreds more injured before the strike was suppressed.

But Pigtown was nothing if not resilient. It had escaped the great Baltimore fire of 1904, which destroyed the center of the city. Nell was in medical school at the time, and remembered hurrying home to help her parents prepare to flee. Together they loaded household goods onto a wagon, all the while keeping an anxious eye on the flames to the south. Luckily the blaze never made it to McCulloh Street, but others in the city weren't so fortunate. Countless lives were ruined, including the mayor's, who committed suicide soon afterwards.

As a doctor, Nell had come to know Pigtown mostly for its many illnesses, the result of squalor and overcrowding. The neighborhood had some of the highest rates of tuberculosis, typhoid, and malaria in the city. And crime. Almost every block, it seemed, housed a gambling den or dance hall, where young women passed from man to man, making commissions on the drinks their dance partners bought. Syphilis and gonorrhea ran rampant, although the advent of Salversan had greatly reduced the former, and was a welcome replacement to the painful and less efficacious mercury injections. A side benefit of the new drug could be seen in the psychiatric asylums, which lost roughly a third of their patients—syphilitics who previously had finished out their lives in paralysis and insanity.

Once Pigtown had been the home of countless brothels too. Baltimore had a long history of tolerating prostitution. Each year madams of the city's brothels—by most accounts more than three hundred—gathered in their finest garb at City Hall to pay the ceremonial fines that ensured their continued operation. But a few years ago the police commissioner, succumbing to complaints about immorality, had closed the brothels down. The purge did nothing to reduce the rates of prostitution, but in many other ways was a scourge. Women who previously had been safely housed in brothels were forced onto the streets, making them vulnerable to violence and exploitation. Katya Bulgarov's establishment was one of the few to survive the purge. No doubt bribes to the police helped as did her famous little red book; Nell often wondered how many of the city's most prominent men had their names inscribed inside. But mostly Madame Bulgarov was a shrewd and effective businesswoman. Her workers kept a low profile and stayed out of trouble. She forbade alcohol or drugs. Illnesses were promptly treated—occasionally by Nell. And Nell was happy to help supply condoms to the brothel, which Madame always gratefully accepted.

As Nell hurried to Madame's house, it occurred to her that the purge might well explain Walter's abandonment at the orphanage, too. The timing was right, given his age. If Emma Randolph was correct, and Walter's mother was a prostitute, she might well have been able to keep him as long as she was housed in a brothel. The other women would have pitched in to look after him while she was at work. But care of a child would have become impossible once she was on the streets. From the point of view of his mother, the closing of the brothels would have resulted in a "hard patch" indeed.

At last Nell came to a small brick row house sitting unobtrusively on a poorly lit block. The curtains on the windows were drawn, although light filtering through at the edges indicated life within. She rang the bell, and a young black woman in a maid's uniform, white cap and apron, answered.

"Good evening, Amelia," Nell said. "Is Madame at home?"

"Yes, miss," Amelia said, curtsying decorously. "Please come in." These words were accompanied by a second curtsy, and then, "I will take you to her," with a third.

Nell followed Amelia into the house, smiling at the curtsies. It was warm inside, and she was grateful for that; the walk through Pigtown had chilled her. She got so easily cold these days; the flu had left her with little reserve. She loosened her shawl and handed her hat to the waiting Amelia, who led her into the parlor. There a stately woman with mahogany hair, dressed in an emerald brocade gown, rose to her feet with a smile and an air of surprise. "Dr. Winters. What an unexpected pleasure."

"Madame Bulgarov. Believe me, the pleasure is mine."

Nell held her hands out and Madame enfolded them in her own. "My dear, you are absolutely freezing. Please, take a seat by the fire. Tea?"

"Yes, thank you." Nell sank with pleasure into the upholstered chair Madame indicated. Katya Bulgarov was nothing if not gracious. The parlor reflected her delicate and exotic sensibilities, from the rich red and gold fabrics on the furniture to the walnut paneling on the walls. On the mantel stood the gilded Romanian icons indicative of her Orthodox faith. Candles emitted a perfumed scent into the air, while tasseled lamps spilled golden pools of light.

"Have you been ill?" Madame said, taking a seat on the sofa opposite Nell. "Or are you just worn out from taking care of those who are?" She shook her head. "You are so pale."

"A little bit of both, I'm afraid." Nell smiled. "I'm supposed to be home resting now."

Madame gave her a motherly tut-tut. "As you should be. What brings you out tonight?"

Nell fell silent as Amelia entered, placed a tray of tea and biscuits at Madame's side, then exited with a curtsy.

"I'm looking for someone," Nell said as Madame poured the tea and handed Nell a cup. "A woman. I'm afraid I don't know her name. I was hoping you might be able to help me find her. She had a child about six years ago, a boy. She managed to keep him for his first year then gave him up to an orphanage. By all accounts she remained attached to him. Later she went looking for him but by then it was too late to get him back."

Madame sipped her tea, a thoughtful look on her face. Before she could answer, Amelia returned. "Pardon, Madame. Your attention is required." She presented Madame a calling card, who studied it with a frown. "Tell him he will have to see Mr. Flinters first." As Amelia curtsied and exited, Madame turned back to Nell with a small smile. "My apologies. Business matters, I'm afraid. Even my best customers have to pay their bills."

Nell inclined her head. "Of course."

"I know of many women who've had children," Madame said, returning to Nell's question, "but your story is somewhat unusual. Do you happen to know the name of the orphanage?"

"The Calvert Home."

Madame nodded. "I see. I can make inquiries if you like."

"Thank you," Nell said. "I won't keep you any longer."

As Nell stood, Madame lifted a bell to summon Amelia, then paused and put it down again. "I'm glad to see you are recovered from the flu, Dr. Winters—that you are recovering. Influenza was here like everywhere else. So many of my ladies were ill. And they are fragile. They don't take care of themselves. They don't eat well or get enough sleep. I tell them, but they don't listen to me. They work too hard." She gave Nell an apologetic smile. "And there is always the danger of complications. Like the woman you mentioned. I tell my girls to protect themselves, but it's difficult for them. The men don't like to comply." She raised her hands helplessly. "And my supplies are running

206

low. Perhaps you can help?"

She meant condoms. "Of course," Nell said.

Madame nodded her thanks and rang the bell. Amelia arrived with Nell's hat and shawl. Once more Madame took Nell's hands in her warm embrace, bidding her good-bye, and then Nell was out on the streets of Pigtown again, finally heading home.

That night Nell told Josie the results of her amateur detective work. Josie was encouraged, but like Nell, knew there was nothing to do but wait. Two days later Amelia came to their door. Nell handed her a box of condoms, and in return, with a flurry of curtsies, Amelia handed Nell an envelope. Inside was a note written on beautiful ivory linen stationery—perhaps from the Pigtown shop Nell had passed on her way to the brothel. As she read it, it exhaled a perfumed scent, recalling Madame's parlor. Only a few words in an elegant hand adorned its surface. *Libby Villard. Try Fell's Point.*

Twenty-five

Choices, choices. Josie sat at her desk in her office at Phipps, contemplating the complex, fascinating—and often vexing—research question that consumed her. Why on earth did people do the things they did, especially when, seen rationally, so much of what they did made no sense? Each decision, each choice, was informed by a set of values. That she believed. The challenge lay in finding out what the underlying values were.

What did Dr. Meyer think about the choices people made? What did he make of her choice to come to Baltimore and take this job? He'd never said. He was as good at concealing his own thoughts as he was at divining those of others. She'd yet to tell him about Nell—yet to tell him, that is, about the true nature of their relationship. It shouldn't matter as long as she did her job and did it well. But she had to be careful. Homosexuality was illegal in Baltimore; according to Nell, the city had passed laws to that effect just a few years earlier. True they were enforced primarily on men or on prostitutes, but even so, they gave her pause. Furthermore, Josie was well aware of the bugaboo that homosexuality represented in some corners of the psychiatric world, where talk of "deviants" and "inverts" reigned. A fair number of those so classified ended up as patients at Phipps, although in Josie's opinion they suffered more from general prejudice and an inability to freely and openly satisfy their desires than from any kind of mental disease.

She just didn't see how choosing a different way to love constituted an illness. She had to admit her decision to take up life with Nell had been based to some extent on impulse. No one had been more surprised than she when she fell in love with Nell—and when Nell fell in love with her. But there was no denying how natural their relationship had turned out to be. In terms of the things that mattered most in life—dedication, affection, loyalty, care—their relationship couldn't be more normal, and indeed was better than many conventionally married couples. They even bickered at times like husbands and wives.

She sat back in her chair, her hands behind her head, her eyes trained thoughtfully on the ceiling. The choice that vexed her most right now was the one Ruben Ashford had made to confess to the murder of Constance Prentiss. Why on earth would he do that if, as she suspected, he was innocent? And if he were innocent, could she prove it? This was one situation, she knew, where her father's admonition to ground her beliefs in objective evidence, held true. The judge considering Ashford's case would hardly consider the testimony of a six-year-old boy who saw a "dancing horse" as definitive. She was beginning to feel a growing sense of urgency. The clock was ticking. They were well into the middle of December, with only two weeks left for Norbert Richards to file the appeal. If she failed, Ashford would hang in the new year.

She stood and paced back and forth in her narrow office, three steps to the window, three steps to the door. At least Nell had made some progress and now they had a name to put to Walter's mother. Or at least a candidate for Walter's mother. But Libby Villard was proving to be quite elusive. Twice already Josie and Nell had looked for her in Fell's Point, a neighborhood which stretched along the waterfront a mile or so to the south of the hospital, without success. They planned to go out again tonight. They would meet at six in Josie's office.

Josie sighed and sat back down. Lately her preoccupation with Ruben Ashford had made it all but impossible to focus on the rest of her work, and there was much to be done. She opened an unfinished case report on Harrison Maltese, one of Dr. Meyer's patients, a thirty-three-year-old Baltimore businessman with an import-export concern, mostly olive oil, olives, sardines and other types of tinned fish, as far as she could tell. Was Maltese from Malta? she wondered idly. And what would that have to do with anything if he was? She forced her attention back to her notes. The olive-oil importer was newly married, and by all accounts had been quite happily so—until his wife became pregnant. Soon after he deteriorated. He lost weight, complained of vague abdominal pains, and became increasingly irritable. He snapped at his wife for no reason and was too distracted at work to complete even the simplest of tasks. At night he roamed the hallways, groaning and clutching at his belly. Warm compresses, seltzer and bismuth remedies, a change in diet—nothing his wife tried soothed her husband. A visit to his physician revealed nothing wrong, and so Maltese landed at Phipps, as did so many others who suffered complaints that defied explanation. He'd been with them over two weeks now, undergoing hydrotherapy and occupational therapy. All without result. Finally Dr. Meyer had asked Josie to see if she could find out more.

Just yesterday Josie had traveled to the Harrison Maltese's home to speak to his bride. Was it possible, she asked her gently, that your husband fears becoming a father? Many men do, she'd added with a smile. The wife insisted the opposite was the case, that the baby was very much desired and planned for. Maltese's parents confirmed the same. But from Maltese's sister Adelaide came a different story. Josie spoke to her in the back room of her notions' shop. When she and Harrison were children, Adelaide related, she around eight years old, Harrison a toddler of two, their mother had given birth at home to a stillborn. In the heat of the moment, the door to the bedroom had been left ajar, and the two children, huddled just outside, saw everything: the doctor hunched over the bed, their mother twisted in pain, their father standing by helplessly, groaning in fear, as the dead baby was delivered. Eventually the doctor emerged with a bloody bundle in his hands, and shocked to find the children there, chased them away.

No one ever spoke of it. Their parents hushed up the death, thinking it the best way to overcome their grief and spare their children. In due time they had two more healthy children, and the stillborn was forgotten. Or so Adelaide said, but Josie wondered. Could Harrison have forced the memory into his unconscious mind, where it festered, like an infection, emerging when his wife became pregnant?

She pulled Dr. Freud's *Studies on Hysteria* from her bookshelf. To her thinking, no one did a better job explaining the power of the unconscious mind than the Viennese psychoanalyst and his associate Dr. Josef Breuer. According to Breuer and Freud, hidden conflicts in the mind could give rise to a host of unexplained symptoms—a disorder called hysteria in women and neurasthenia in men. Josie leafed through the doctors' 1895 volume, revisiting their reports, treatment methods, and results. In a seminal case, a young woman identified as Anna O experienced a variety of symptoms, including paralysis and mutism, that had no discernible cause. Breuer treated her with a course of hypnosis that gradually gave way to a more free-wheeling "talking cure." As Anna O spoke of her father's illness and subsequent death—the psychic injury causing her complaints—she improved. Illuminate what is hidden, as Dr. Meyer liked to say, and the patient will benefit. Josie had seen many of Dr. Meyer's patients improve under this dictum, including one woman who had lost her sight for no organic reason, then recovered it after Meyer helped her uncover the root of her blindness. Nell had her own patient stories to tell about the power of the unconscious mind to wreak havoc on the body, including Wilma Gantry, whose hives disappeared once she received birth control and no longer feared an unwanted pregnancy.

Josie closed the book. Could Harrison Maltese's distress be the result of a repressed memory? She would leave it up to Dr. Meyer to decide. For now it would be enough to let him know of the existence of the childhood trauma.

She was just finishing up her notes—glad for a spate of concentration that made the work go quickly for once—when she heard a knock on the door, and Nicholas Sweeney, Meyer's secretary, stuck in his head. "Someone to see you."

"Nell, already?" Josie smiled and looked at the clock. It was only five o'clock. "She's early."

"No, not Dr. Winters. Someone else. She said it was urgent. You gave her one of your cards. She wrote her name on the back."

Sweeney held out the card and Josie took it, flipping it over to read *Abigail Knowles*.

Abigail Knowles sat on the chair Josie had pulled out for her, twisting her gloves in her hands. She looked utterly miserable, as if she could barely stand to be in her own skin. It didn't help that she was wearing an uncomfortable looking traveling suit that accentuated her plainness and awkwardness, the unpleasant green color lending a sallowness to her complexion. She had yet to look Josie in the eye, even though they sat quite close together in her narrow office, their knees almost touching.

Knowles had told Sweeney it was urgent, but now that she was here, she seemed in no rush to say what *it* was. Josie knew there was no use pressing her; she would come out with it when she was ready.

"A pleasure to see you again, Miss Knowles," Josie said with a smile, attempting to set her at ease. The teacher looked as nervous as a young horse and as likely to bolt. When this was met with silence, she asked the most innocuous question she could think of. "How was your trip in?"

To her surprise, the question unleashed a torrent. The train was late, Knowles said, so very late, she almost changed her mind and didn't come at all, and now she was sorry, so terribly sorry, to be intruding on Miss Berenson like this, and at such a late hour. She would have come sooner, but Mrs. Crofter was very strict, and they only had Sundays and Thursday afternoons off. Sundays were for church, and if Mrs. Crofter knew she was here, on a Thursday, it could cost her her job—

"She most certainly won't know," Josie said firmly. Then, just to put an end to the incessant rambling, added, "Would you like a cup of tea?"

Knowles gulped gratefully and nodded. Josie stepped quickly into the hallway and hunted down Mr. Sweeney. "Two cups of tea, please, if you don't mind."

She returned to her office where they sat in blessed silence until the tea came.

"I don't know if I should be here," Knowles said finally, taking small sips. The tea at least seemed to have a calming effect. "I don't even know if it's my place."

"Please, don't worry about that."

"Yes, miss." She put her cup down. "It was after I saw you at Rosewood. I kept thinking about what you'd said, that you'd come about Connie."

Josie waited.

"But it wasn't just that. It was what you said about Ruben Ashford. You said you wanted to find out why he killed her. Were you able to?"

"No," Josie said carefully. Her breath was quickening, and she was having trouble controlling it. "Why do you ask?"

Knowles raised her eyes and looked at her directly. "Because I know."

Josie sat quietly, her hands folded in her lap, the tea growing cold in her cup, as Knowles told her story. The wind had picked up since Knowles came in—a snowstorm brewing—and the cord to the blinds rattled against the window. But Josie hardly heard it. As Knowles spoke, the sound of the wind retreated until it was as if it wasn't even there.

"You shouldn't speak badly of the dead," Knowles said. "My mother always told me that." She smiled in an apologetic way. "I think it has something to do with ghosts haunting you."

"Your mother would also no doubt want you to speak the truth."

"Yes." The smile faded. "I don't mean to say Connie was bad, not like that. She was a good teacher, and I wasn't lying when I said the children loved her. But she was"—Knowles raised her hands, sculpting the air as if she could better show what she meant than say it—"stubborn. And opinionated. Willful. She knew what she wanted, and she wasn't afraid to take it."

Knowles could use a little more of that quality herself. Timidity was slowing her down, and more than anything, Josie wanted her to get on with it. "What did Miss Prentiss want specifically?"

"I can tell you what she *didn't* want. She didn't want to be at Rosewood. She said it was boring. She said nothing ever happened there. The place—the people—the work. None of it interested her. She came from a little town near Albany. She said she only took the job because she wanted to get away from home, and Maryland was about as far away as she could get."

"When did she tell you these things?"

"At night, mostly. She didn't sleep well, and we bunked together. Two teachers to a room. They assigned her to me. She'd lie in her bed, smoking, and talk. We weren't supposed to smoke, but she did it anyway. I told her not to. I was afraid they would find out, but she didn't care. I think she wished they would. It was like she was looking for something."

"Trouble?"

"Excitement. She lived for Thursdays—for our afternoons off. She'd take the train to Baltimore. I went with her once, but I didn't like it. She went to all kinds of places, the ones where women dance with—" She reddened and grew silent.

"Please, go on."

"—with men they don't know. And she always stayed out too late. We came back long after curfew. I was terrified we'd get caught, but not Connie. It was all part of the fun for her. Sneaking in, sneaking out. After that I didn't go to Baltimore with her anymore. But that was how she met him, going to Owings Mills to take the train."

"Ruben Ashford?"

"No, not Ruben. Bailey Smith."

214

"Bailey?"

"He works for Seiler's. He drives their truck."

"Ah," Josie said. "I know him. I mean, I think I saw him at Rosewood." A vision came to Josie of a young man standing outside the cow barn with striking pale blue eyes and an insolent grin, a cool, appraising glance. "Early twenties, blue eyes. He wears a white uniform." Good looking, she might have added, but didn't.

Knowles nodded. "That's him. They got on together, Connie and him."

"Got on—you mean they saw each other?"

"Not just saw each other. They—" The teacher's voice dropped. "They started up last spring, before Ruben came to Rosewood. They used the cabin by the gate."

"The one Dr. Foyle gave to Ruben Ashford."

"Yes. After that they couldn't use it anymore."

She would have hated that, a girl like Connie, having her desires thwarted. It would have made her furious. No, not just furious: she would have seen it as a challenge. "How did she take it?"

"She laughed. She said she would take care of it. She said she knew how."

Taking care of it meant taking care first and foremost of Ruben Ashford. "She started flirting with him, telling him how handsome he was, things like that. I saw her do it once. I told her not to. I said it was mean. He didn't know she didn't care for him. But she said that didn't matter. She would make him fall in love with her."

He would have been an easy mark, inexperienced around women, especially white women, and he was crippled by loneliness. Ashford had said Prentiss was "kind" to him. Josie was beginning to understand what he meant by that.

"She made him do things for her—drive her to the station, fetch her things, clean her boots. Sometimes I think she just wanted to humiliate him. But he never said no." The gloves twisted back and forth. "I told her to stop. I said he had feelings for her, and it wasn't right to abuse him like that. But she said the feelings of people like Ruben didn't matter, and the sooner I realized that, the sooner I would get what I wanted in life, too."

Snow was starting to fall. Josie watched the flakes drift down in the last of the day's light. It brought a hush to the room, to Abigail Knowles, too. When she began speaking again, Josie had to lean forward to catch her words.

"Eventually she told him to leave his cabin in the evenings so that she could use it. Bailey would come by to pick up the milk and then act as if he was leaving, but instead he'd park his truck down the road and walk back. I was coming home from the village one evening and saw him do it myself. That's how I knew they were in there. Ruben didn't have any place to go. I think he just sat in the woods."

Josie was beginning to feel ill. She thought of Ruben crouched outside the cabin in the woods waiting for Prentiss and that man to finish. It sickened her.

Knowles spoke with a fury. "I thought it was horrible. But she was proud of it—proud that she had that kind of power over him. She enjoyed it."

"Did anyone else know?"

Knowles shook her head. "I never told anyone." Her eyes dropped to her hands. "I wish I had. Maybe then Connie would still be alive."

"Don't blame yourself." It would have been impossible for someone like Knowles to talk about these things—it was all but impossible now. And she would have felt duty bound to remain silent out of loyalty to a fellow teacher—just like the medical students Josie had experimented with in the fall who had felt it was their duty to protect their own. Only the choice Josie gave the students—cheating on an exam—was fairly innocuous. The one facing Knowles was far worse and had led inescapably, Josie was beginning to see now, to murder.

"I think Mrs. Crofter knew. Not about Ruben and the cabin. But I think she suspected Connie of seeing someone in the village. If Connie hadn't died, I think Mrs. Crofter would have fired her. But that wouldn't have bothered Connie. She was planning to leave Rosewood anyway. She said she was destined for better things. She certainly didn't see herself spending her life with a truck driver from Owings Mills. Just before Ruben—before Connie died—she told Bailey so."

"The truck driver? She broke off with him?"

Knowles nodded. "She said she didn't want to see him anymore. She was going back to Albany at the end of the summer to look for another position." Knowles rubbed a hand over her eyes. "I didn't know if I should tell you all this. I know it can't help Ruben, and I feel sorry for him. I always did. I just thought you should know—what he did to Connie—it wasn't entirely his fault."

Knowles put down her cup. She stood and without a word of good-bye saw herself out, creeping away in shame. Josie should have gone after her, should have tried again to convince her she was not to blame herself, but she was too stunned to move. Her thoughts and emotions were in a turmoil. Idly her hands moved across her desk, her fingers falling on the book by Freud and Breuer.

The answer had been there all along, staring her in the face, only she'd been too blind to see it. Freud would have made quick work of Ruben Ashford. Ashford didn't know why he killed Constance Prentiss because he'd repressed the motive in his unconscious mind. The feelings and thoughts Constance Prentiss engendered in him were too painful—and shameful—to bear. He was like a soldier emerging from a battlefield with no memory of what had happened or what he'd done. He had acted in a rage, out of a mix of jealousy and revenge. No wonder he'd retold the murder to Josie as if he were in a dream: it must have felt to him like that.

Forget Walter Thursday and forget the horse. Ashford wasn't innocent. He'd killed Constance Prentiss just like he'd always said. Josie finally had the answer to the question Norbert Richards had asked her so many months ago. She knew why Ruben Ashford killed Constance Prentiss. She'd found the perfect solution, the one that comported exactly with both the evidence and with scientific theory.

Every single piece of the puzzle had fallen into place.

She pushed Freud's book aside. There was only one problem with her solution. She didn't believe it.

"So are you saying he's guilty after all?" Nell said.

"No, not exactly. I'm just saying I finally have a reasonable reason to believe he could be."

It was late, past seven. Josie and Nell had left the diner on Fayette where they'd had dinner and were walking arm in arm down Broadway to Fell's Point. Snow was falling, lending a sharpness to the air, dusting the grassy median that ran through the center of the avenue. Carriages rattled past with a white coating on their roofs, the breath of the horses steaming, while streetlamps cast orbs of light into the night like a glimmering fog.

"What I can't believe," Josie said, holding tighter to Nell while she shivered in the cold, "is that a person like Ruben Ashford would lash out in such a violent rage and kill someone, whether he was unconsciously motivated by sexual rage or not. He's just too passive. It's his most prominent, defining personality trait. Everything I've learned about him tells me so. I even saw it myself when I met him. He was raised to be submissive, especially around women—and above all around white women. He was taught to fear them. If he had felt threatened by Constance Prentiss, he would have run away."

"Unless he was bound to her in some way and felt himself unable to escape."

"Perhaps, but remember, he submitted himself to her entirely. He gave his cabin over to her so that she could have assignations with her boyfriend." Josie shuddered in a way that was more than just from the cold. "If ever there was a time to become enraged, to act against her, it would have been then."

"Yes," Nell said slowly. "The truck driver does complicate things."

Josie nodded. "Knowles said Prentiss broke off with Bailey Smith just before she died. Maybe he was furious with her. He might have come to the stable to argue with her. The whole thing could have been a lover's quarrel that went awry. He's someone I could easily see resorting to violence."

"But if Smith killed her, why wouldn't Ashford just say so?"

"Maybe he didn't see it happen. He could have come on the body afterwards."

"Then why on earth would he say she was killed by a horse?"

Josie shrugged helplessly.

"Or, for that matter, why confess to the crime?"

Josie threw up her hands. "It doesn't make any sense. None of it does."

They walked for a few minutes in silence until Nell spoke again. "Is it possible," she said gently, "that you've come to care too much about this case—to care too much about Ruben Ashford? You're twisting things into knots, looking for alternatives, when it seems to me you've found your answer."

Yes, Josie thought miserably, she'd thought that too. The easiest thing to do would be to go to Norbert Richards, tell him what Knowles said, and put an end to the appeal. It would only be right, and was what Ruben Ashford wanted her to do from the beginning. But she couldn't bring herself to do it. Not yet.

"I can't help it. I know I should go with the evidence, but how can I, when my gut feeling tells me it's wrong?"

The last time she'd faced such a conflict between her head and her heart was when she was contemplating marrying Freddie. Then her head had said yes while her heart said no. What if she had gone against her feelings and said yes to him? It wouldn't have made a difference in his fate—he'd already enlisted—but it would have made every difference in her life. She never would have been with Nell.

Nell tightened her hand on Josie's arm. "So what will you do now?" she said.

"I don't know." Josie quickened her step. "But let's do what we set out to do tonight. Let's look for Walter's mother."

Fell's Point occupied a spit of land that jutted into the harbor at the bottom of Broadway. Once, Josie had heard, it was the home of the famous Baltimore clipper, the fastest sailing ship on the water. It still had the look of a maritime center, with wharves, docks, warehouses, and shipyards. One of those shipyards, she'd been told, had employed Frederick Douglass as a caulker when he was still enslaved. Fell's Point was also one of the oldest neighborhoods in the city, a jumble of streets and alleyways, lined with cramped houses that leaned into one another like disorderly drunks. Smokestacks of freighters and masts of sailing vessels clogged the skyline. Sailors disembarked on the jetties from all over the world, giving the neighborhood an international flavor. They filled the point's many bars and saloons, standing shoulder to shoulder with longshoremen, soldiers returned from the war—and the women who serviced their needs. Tonight the snow gave the point a dismal, wintry gloom, knots of sailors appearing and disappearing in the shadows, the sounds of their voices lingering in the icy atmosphere. The air carried the faint tang of whiskey, urine, and stale beer.

Previously Nell and Josie had searched the east side of the point, and now they turned their attention to the west. Working methodically, they inquired at boarding houses and rooming houses, approaching lone women who lingered on street corners or in darkened alleyways. To everyone they posed the same question: Do you know a woman named Libby Villard? She had a child once. We know where he is. We can help her find him. To the women, Nell handed out her card and packets of condoms, adding, "If you're sick, come see me. I can help you. I promise you'll be safe."

Finally they found their answer. It was at a rooming house on Durham Street. "Libby Villard?" said the proprietress, a frizzy-haired woman with a yellowed face, in answer to Josie's query. "Sure, I knew her." She slouched in the doorway, pulling her soiled dress closer against the cold. "I knew about her child too. She liked to talk about him, didn't she? Said they took him from her and wouldn't give him back. She used to live here."

"Used to?" Josie said, her heart beating suddenly in her throat. "Where is she now?"

The woman jerked her head down the road. "Over there I'd say."

"There? Where?"

"I don't know." She shrugged. "Potter's field. Wherever they put them."

"Put them—put who?"

"You know." She gave them a ghastly grin, revealing blackened teeth, as if she couldn't be more satisfied with the answer. "The ones that died of the flu."

Twenty-Six

That night, when they returned home from Fell's Point, Nell went straight to bed, but Josie disappeared into the office she kept on the other side of the landing. She was still there when Nell fell asleep. Hours later she awoke as Josie came in. Outside snow was still falling, and in the light of the streetlamps, which cast a ghostly glow into the room, Josie looked worried and pale.

"My love," Nell said, sitting up. "What is it?"

"I've been thinking more about what Abigail Knowles told me today. I think I need to go back to Owings Mills."

The fire had long gone out, and it was cold in the bedroom, especially without Josie in bed beside her. Nell pulled the bedclothes up around her. "Whatever for?"

"To speak to Bailey Smith."

"The man you think might have killed Constance Prentiss?" Nell felt a stab of fear. "Is that wise? Is it even safe?"

"He played some kind of role in her death," Josie said firmly. "I'm sure of it. I need to find out exactly what."

"Then contact the authorities. You said yourself Smith might be capable of violence. Let them talk to him."

"The authorities? Like Sheriff Hopper?" Josie shook her head. "I need to talk to him, too."

"Why on earth?"

Josie didn't answer. Instead she crossed the hall to her office and returned with a sheaf of papers. "I've been going over the documents Norbert Richards sent me. There's more there—more than I saw before. Take a look." She turned on the lamp and handed one of the pages to Nell.

Nell glanced at it. It was Sheriff Hopper's report. "What am I looking for?"

"The date."

She found it on the top of the page. "It says right here: September second."

"No, not the date he wrote the report. The date he arrested Ashford."

Nell looked again. "August thirty-first." She read out loud from the page: "'The call came to the Owings Mills Station at 2:20 in the afternoon on Saturday, the thirty-first of August.'"

Josie nodded. "Now look at this." She handed over a second page.

This one was Ashford's confession. "The date again?"

"Yes."

She found it at the bottom. "September fifth." She pointed to the page. "He confessed on the fifth. Here's the signature of the clerk of the county court, certifying it."

"Exactly," Josie said.

"Exactly—what?" Nell put the papers down. "I don't see what you mean."

"*Five days.* Five days elapsed between the time of Ashford's arrest and his confession."

"Yes, and so—?"

"And so, the question is: what happened during that time?" Josie walked to the window and stood watching the snow come down. Then she turned around. "When Ruben Ashford was arrested—on the thirty-first of August—he told Sheriff Hopper that a horse killed Constance Prentiss. We know that from Norbert Richards. Five days later he confessed. What happened during those five days? What made him change his mind?"

"Are you thinking he might have been threatened or coerced in some way?"

"It has come to my mind as a possibility, yes."

Nell frowned. She looked at the confession again. "It doesn't seem likely. Ashford says so himself. At the very beginning he writes, 'I give this confession willingly and under no duress.'"

"True," Josie said, "but isn't that exactly what someone who had been coerced would be required to say?" She left the window to pace back and forth across the room. "Five days. I can't believe I didn't see it before. He all but shouts it out." She took the confession back. "He says, 'Since my arrest *5 days ago.*' And time matters to him. Remember, he's the one who counts the minutes, the hours, the days."

The pacing was unsettling Nell. "Please, sit." She patted the bed, and after a moment Josie came and sat down beside her. "Think reasonably. It can't be all of these things. It can't be that Bailey Smith killed her, and that a horse killed her, and that Ruben Ashford did. And don't forget the blood on his shirt and the murder weapon. How do you account for those?"

Josie looked at her miserably. "I don't know."

"You don't have to do this. You could talk to Dr. Meyer. Talk to Norbert Richards. Tell them what you know. Let them figure out what to do next."

Josie shook her head. "I'm so close to knowing what happened. I just need a little more time."

"Please, think this through. Don't go to Owings Mills."

"You know I have to."

Nell raised her eyes with an air of frustration. Then she took Josie's hand. "Then I'm going with you."

Early the next morning, Nell sat at her desk, preparing a pharmacy order. She was due to meet Josie at the Mt. Clare station in a few hours. Worry over their upcoming plans to go to Owings Mills had plagued her all night, and she'd hardly slept. Now she felt the effects of her lack of sleep, a light headache pulsing at her temple. She'd been hoping for an easy morning, but there was no chance of that. Already she'd seen twins with sore throat and a dry-goods salesman with a fever she sincerely hoped wasn't flu. She finished the pharmacy order and was about to take it to James when a knock came on the door, and Esme marched in, leading a very chagrined-looking Edward St. Cecile.

"I found him by the garden gate," Esme said, eying St. Cecile the way she might a wayward child much in need of a scolding. "He'd been there all night."

"Not all night," Edward protested. "Only since the clubs closed."

That would be two in the morning. Might as well have been all night. Nell would have to examine him for frostbite on top of whatever else had brought him in, some kind of fight, by the looks of it. His eye was blackened, he had a split lip, and from the way he was standing, hunched over with an arm protecting his chest, she suspected broken ribs.

"Oh, Edward." Nell put down her pen. St. Cecile was one of her favorite—and most exasperating—patients. "Why didn't you ring when you got here?"

He hung his head. "I didn't want to wake you."

She had nothing to say to that. "Come on, then. Let's take a look."

Esme left with a huff, her back rigid, thinking, no doubt, that St. Cecile hadn't received half the scolding he deserved. Meanwhile Nell escorted him to her examination room. It occurred to her that late last night, while she and Josie were going over Ashford's confession, St. Cecile was mostly likely already outside, huddled in the cold.

At least her examination revealed he'd managed to escape frostbite, a miracle in itself, given his thin clothing: a sharp, if threadbare, navy suit. Leave it to St. Cecile to focus on fashion over warmth; he was well known throughout the neighborhood for his stylish dressing. The eye would get better on its own, and the lip didn't need sutures, but the ribs were more worrisome. Two felt broken. Nothing she could do about that. They would have to heal on their own. "Do you want to tell me what happened?"

St. Cecile smiled shyly. "Guess you could say some folks didn't like my hat."

"Your hat?" Incredulous, she looked at him. "Edward, were you on stage last night?"

"Yes, Dr. Nell. I was."

St. Cecile was an entertainer, famous for his female impressions. He presented his act in colored clubs downtown—sometimes in white clubs too. Nell had never seen it, but had heard it was wildly popular.

"They loved me," he added proudly. "I got a standing ovation and made over two dollars in tips."

"But the hat?"

"You would have loved it." St. Cecile's face grew dreamy. "Ostrich feathers from here to here." With a wince of pain he sculpted the air high above his head. "I know I should have taken it off before I left the club last night but…" He broke into a grin then touched his lip with a grimace when it hurt. "It just looked so damn good."

"Are you telling me you walked home with that"—*ridiculous* hat, Nell wanted to say, but in deference to his feelings did not—"with an ostrich-feathered hat on your head?"

St. Cecile smiled. "I sure did."

Nell didn't have to ask what happened next. She could well see it: Edward assaulted late at night by thugs on the streets of Baltimore on his way home. They could have been white or black; wearing that hat, he would have been fair game for homophobes of any kind. "Did you tell the police?"

St. Cecile shook his head sadly. "You know I wouldn't do that. They wouldn't do anything."

Except very possibly arrest him, as Nell very well knew.

"Besides, it was just some boys from the neighborhood. They didn't mean anything by it."

"Didn't mean anything by it?" When they beat you to within an inch of your life? Nell wanted to say but didn't. It would only make St. Cecile feel worse. "Please tell me you'll be more careful next time," she said instead as she finished bandaging his ribs. "No hat is worth your health."

"No, I suppose not," St. Cecile said, although she had a feeling he didn't mean it. "Thank you for the help, Dr. Nell. Sorry for the trouble." He stood up, reached gravely into his pocket, and held out a dollar.

It was half his night's earnings. She didn't want to take it, but for his sake she did. She didn't want to shame him either. He left the room and turned automatically towards the back door. All at once she was furious. After everything he'd suffered, did he really have to experience this indignity too? "Go out the front door for once, Edward, won't you, please?"

He shook his head with a smile. "Oh, Dr. Nell, you know I would never do that to you."

To her? To her practice, he meant, which would dwindle even more than it already had if white patients had to interact with colored on their way in or out. Briefly her anger surged and she almost wished her white patients would stop coming if that was how they felt. Almost. She couldn't afford to let them go, and she wouldn't give up on them either. But why did so many of her patients feel like they needed to take care of her, the black ones most of all? When it was she who should be taking care of them.

Nell sighed as she watched St. Cecile walk stiffly towards the kitchen. At least Esme would give him a warm plate of food before he left. What kind of world did she live in, where violence lurked around every corner, and there was no clear path to safety, especially for people like Edward St. Cecile, who defied the usual categories, black and white, man and woman too? Was it better to obey the rules or not? Wear a hat or not? Josie would say it was a matter of value, and a matter of choice. But how did that explain the fog of confusion that swirled around the choices Ruben Ashford had made? People were complicated, and no amount of research, Nell feared, could explain Ashford, or St. Cecile. Or Josie. Or for that matter, in more ways than she cared to think of, herself.

Twenty-Seven

That morning the Mt. Clare train station was crowded with porters pushing luggage carts, smartly-dressed travelers, businessmen clutching cases, and a gaggle of schoolchildren shepherded by a harried-looking teacher. The children were on an outing, if the delighted looks on their faces were any indication. Nell and Josie threaded their way through the grand central hall to the Owings Mills train, dodging a man with his nose in a newspaper and only half an eye on where he was going. Josie marched defiantly past any number of perfectly acceptable white coaches before entering the lone car for colored riders at the rear. Inside a man with a clerical collar was already seated, reading a book, while an elderly woman clutched a straw bag on her lap, and a farmer dozed in the corner. They took seats in the middle, Nell suppressing a sigh over the hard benches so as not to offend Josie. As the train started with a hiss and a lurch, the conductor came through to take their tickets. He stopped at their bench, eyed them over his glasses, opened his mouth then closed it. "You ladies might be more comfortable up front," he said finally, rather mildly.

"No, thank you," Josie said, her head held high. "We are quite comfortable *right here.*"

Nell reddened. Josie was being frankly ridiculous, and Nell would say so, but Josie would never forgive her if she did. Nell wasn't the only one who felt that way. As the conductor moved on, the woman with the straw bag tipped down her face, hiding a smile.

They rode in silence as the train steamed out of the city. Overnight the weather had changed, delivering the kind of mild winter day that sometimes took Baltimore by surprise. The sky had cleared and the sun shone brilliantly from a clear sky, melting the snow and warming the air. Soon the tightly-knit Baltimore rowhouses gave way to farms and woods, with patches of dark earth emerging beneath fields of snow. The train made stops at a few small towns, where passengers boarded and departed. Some glanced curiously at Nell and Josie, but most paid them no mind. The conductor didn't speak to them again on his subsequent forays through the car, but Nell knew, from the way Josie was holding herself rigidly upright in her seat, her lips pursed tight, that she wished he would, just so she could make a scene. How hard it must be to be so principled—and so brave! Nell took Josie's hand, and Josie returned the gesture with a faint smile. How Nell loved her then. Be patient, my love, she wanted to say. One day, your time will come.

As the train steamed northwards, Nell's anxiety over their plans to speak to Smith and Hopper intensified. She picked restlessly at a loose thread on the cuff of her jacket until it all but unraveled. If Josie was nervous, she did a better job of hiding it. Only the slightest tapping of a finger on her knee hinted at tension.

"Have you thought," Nell said, "about what you will say to Smith?"

"No," Josie said, "or rather, yes, but I haven't come up with anything good." The tapping increased in tempo until with an apologetic smile she tucked her hand in her pocket. "I don't know what to say to the sheriff either." The brave façade cracked for a moment, and she gave Nell a worried look. "I'm not making a mistake in this, am I?"

"No, of course not," Nell said, although she very much feared she was. Or rather, they both were. She gave Josie a wan smile and squeezed her hand.

"I'm thinking we might stop by Rosewood afterwards," Josie said. "I'd like to tell Dr. Foyle about Walter Thursday's mother."

"Of course."

"I worry about him."

"Walter? How so?"

"He's so small, and vulnerable. They'll want him to work on the farm when he gets older. It's what all the boys do—what they have to do. Only I can't see it for him." Her face took on a wistful air. "I know I only met him briefly, but he made such an impression on me. He's so trusting, and so sweet, but fragile too. Even if he manages the work physically, I don't know how he'll tolerate it emotionally. I'm afraid it will change him. It will make him into something he's not."

Her finger resumed the tapping on her knee. "I owe a lot to Walter, you know. He's the one who opened the door to the possibility that Ruben Ashford might be innocent, when he said he saw Miss Prentiss dancing with a horse. Strange, isn't it, where things take us?"

Yes, Nell thought, it was. Like the kiss Josie gave her on the Cape that changed both of their lives forever. Nell still remembered how surprised she'd been by it—surprised mostly by how wonderful it had felt. As if she'd spent her entire life until that moment in a darkened room, and Josie had suddenly thrown open the curtains, letting in the light. Everything Nell had ever known or felt was illuminated anew.

Still, choices had consequences, as Josie herself like to say, and sometimes Nell wondered if Josie had ever fully comprehended what her move to Baltimore meant. It wasn't just the friends and family she'd left behind—including her mother who, Nell feared, might never come to terms with Josie's choice. She'd given up the things a more conventional marriage might have given her: the social ease of being a wife, the joy of becoming a mother.

Nell had never wanted children; even as a young girl she'd known that. She'd been far more interested in trying to heal her dolls' ailments than in mothering them. But Josie would have made a wonderful mother. Nell knew that, even if Josie didn't. Even now it was evident in the way she talked about Walter Thursday. Nell could give Josie many things—love, companionship, support—but she couldn't give her children. She only hoped Josie wouldn't end up regretting what she'd never had.

When the train came to a stop at the Owings Mills station, Nell and Josie were the only ones to disembark. Icicles hung from the station eaves, dripping into puddles with a metallic sheen. The platform was bare, creaking with the unexpected thaw. Nell breathed in the thick country air, heavy with the moist breath of earth and animals. Memories of the farm her grandfather had once had in Mount Airy surfaced in her mind: a horse with feathered pasterns pulling a wooden plow shaped like the bow of a ship; biscuits heavy with grease cooling on a windowsill; her grandfather's calloused hands with yellowed, cracked nails. Her grandmother had died before Nell was born and her grandfather had followed when she was eight, leaving her with only faint recollections of the farm, like the apples she used to love to bite into in her grandfather's orchard. In recollection the memories took on a hazy, golden glow. Still she'd never regretted living in the city, had never longed for country life, idealizing it as simpler or more virtuous. She knew how her grandparents had struggled, knew the beauties of their life, but the harshness, too.

The engine steamed and spit cinders as a stationmaster came out, handed a sack of mail up to the conductor, then disappeared back inside. Meanwhile Josie stood on the platform, frowning. Nell feared she was faltering, but she was only gaining her bearings. She gave Nell a steady look and said, "The sheriff's quarters are in the village, but I'd like to visit the dairy first. It's this way."

Josie led her down a muddy village lane past shops, a market, cottages nestled in shrubbery. Snow lay melting on roofs and in dark shadows beneath bushes and trees. The mid-day sun was warm but Nell still felt chilled and pulled her jacket closer around her. Other than a workman in muddy boots, who soldiered past with a a shovel on his shoulder, they saw no one. In time the houses gave way to fields with etched plough lines, water gathering in the grooves, a line of black-limbed trees in the distance. A scarecrow lifted empty arms to heaven. In a paddock a horse with a cocked fetlock stood sleeping while a dog ran barking at them along the fence. Soon they came to a sign for Seiler's Dairy, pointing up a rutted dirt track towards a collection of outbuildings, barns, and pastures. At the end, two men were at work in an open shed, heating milk in a steel vat. Smoke from the fire spilled out, bringing the smell of manure and soot and sour milk into the air. Secretly Nell was hoping Smith wouldn't be there, and the confrontation could be avoided, but of course, he was. She recognized him from Josie's description, an uncommonly good-looking man with fair skin and strikingly pale blue eyes. He was on a step ladder, pouring cans of milk into the vat, while the second man, with chapped hands and a fleshy face, stood below, handing the cans up.

Smith gave them an appraising look as they walked up. "G'day, ladies," he said, with a greasy smile and mock salute.

He made Nell's blood run cold. She despised men like him, the kind who admired women as if they were pieces of merchandise yet nevertheless expected to be admired in return. He hadn't counted on Josie. Her mouth set in a thin line, she went straight to him, tipped back her head, and spoke to him directly. "A word if you please, Mr. Smith."

He seemed surprised she knew him. The smile faded, replaced by an air of suspicion. His eyes traveled to her then to Nell then back again with an air of dawning recognition. "I know you. You were at Rosewood."

"Yes, and now I've come back to speak to you."

"Can't see why." He'd become distinctly guarded. He turned back to the vat. "Hup, Johnny." Johnny heaved up a can, and Smith poured the milk out in a steady stream.

"It's about Constance Prentiss."

Smith slowed as he handed the empty can down.

"I believe you knew her." Josie lifted her chin. "As a matter of fact, you knew her quite well."

Smith stopped moving. Then he came down the ladder. "Give us a minute, Johnny, will you?"

Johnny shrugged, shoved his hands into his pockets, and strolled off.

"And who might you be?" Smith had become insolent. He lounged against the ladder, eying Josie in a vaguely menacing manner.

"Josefa Berenson of the Johns Hopkins Hospital." Josie held out her card, but Smith grimaced and waved it off. She was making a great show of not backing down, but Nell noticed her lip trembling.

"And I'm Dr. Cornelia Winters," Nell said, stepping up beside her. She put a deliberate emphasis on the doctor. Smith struck her as a hollow man, the kind of bully who liked to project strength but would be easily cowed by authority. Sure enough, he seemed to retreat, turning his head to the side.

"I've come here," Josie said, then with a glance at Nell, steadier now, "that is, *we've* come here on Ruben Ashford's behalf."

Smith grew sullen. "What's that got to do with me?"

"I know you were seeing Miss Prentiss. She put an end to it just before she died."

"So what if she did?"

Josie kept her eyes on him. "That might have mattered to you."

Smith gave a twisted grin. "Spurned lover and all that?"

"Well, were you?"

He laughed. "Look. Connie was nice. She was a lot of fun. I liked her. I admit, I liked her a lot. But I never expected it to last. It never does with girls like her. She wasn't about to settle down in Owings Mills—or anywhere, if you ask me. Girls like Connie always see something bigger on the horizon, until there's nothing left." He walked to a wood pile at the back of the shed, picked up some sticks, and threw them on the fire.

"Where were you the day she died?"

"You think I had something to do with that?"

"Did you?" Josie's expression didn't change.

"Is that it?" The insolence was back, along with a sly note of triumph. "That's what brought you here? You figure me for murder?"

He gave her a lazy smile. "I wasn't at Rosewood. I can promise you that."

"Why should we believe you?"

"You don't have to. Ask Johnny. He'll tell you. I broke my arm last summer—an accident with the truck. I went home to get it fixed up. Connie was killed while I was gone. I didn't even hear about it until I got back."

"Home?"

"My mum's place. In Frederick." He pulled up his shirt sleeve, revealing a knobby, reddened scar on his forearm. "Nasty business. The bone came right through."

Josie looked at Nell. She glanced at the scar and inclined her head.

"I wasn't surprised to hear Ashford did her in," Smith said as he rolled down his sleeve. "There was always something off with that boy. He hung around her, making a pest of himself. I can't imagine why you'd want to have anything to do with him." He kicked at the fire until it flared then hollered out of the shed, "Johnny. Back to it."

Johnny shuffled into the shed, and Smith climbed back onto the ladder. "They did the right thing when they arrested that boy. They'll do an even better thing when they hang him." He reached for a milk can, his face perfectly blank as if they'd already gone. "Hup, Johnny. Let's go."

Nell was glad to put Bailey Smith behind her. She supposed he might be lying about his arm—the scar could be from anything—but she doubted it. To men like Smith, women were nothing more than objects to be manipulated for entertainment and pleasure. He would have had no reason to act out against Constance Prentiss. Once she was gone, he would simply move on to someone else. Ashford, on the other hand, had every reason to lash out in a jealous rage. Even Smith affirmed what Knowles had said: that Ruben Ashford was obsessed with Connie Prentiss. Josie didn't say anything as they returned to the village, and Nell kept her thoughts to herself. But she could only imagine how disappointed Josie must be. One by one her theories were falling by the wayside, leaving only one inescapable truth: Ruben Ashford had murdered Constance Prentiss, just as he'd said.

At the sheriff's office, they found a hand-lettered sign reading "At Creedwell's" tacked to the door. The general store sat across the way, a ramshackle, shingled building with a second-floor balcony. They came up the steps through puddling snow into the kind of place where Nell imagined her grandfather might have shopped: sawdust strewn on a wide-planked floor, shelves of goods climbing to the ceiling, stacks of boxes and crates, rows of barrels. Sun streamed through the windows, turning the dusty air into an illuminated cloud smelling sweetly of spices and coffee. A red-headed girl with long braids peered at them from behind a counter while a woman in a cloth coat fingered a bolt of cloth. In the center of the store a cast-iron stove pushed out a steady heat. Near it sat two men in ladder-backed chairs, talking. The one holding forth at the moment was heavy-set, with a beefy face beneath a Western hat. The other was rather slight, wearing a plain black suit like an undertaker. He looked at them idly as they approached.

Josie walked up to the man in the hat. "Sheriff Hopper."

The undertaker seemed amused. He glanced at his companion, smiled, then stood. "At your service."

Josie was taken aback. "I'm"—she swiveled her gaze to him—"I'm here about Constance Prentiss."

"Well, then, Frank." The heavy-set man came to his feet. "I'll leave you to it." He must be Creedwell. With a tip of his hat, he ambled to the back of the store, pushed open a door, and disappeared.

Josie pulled herself together, proffered her card, and introduced Nell. "I'm assisting Ruben Ashford's lawyer, Norbert Richards. I believe you met with him."

"I did." Hopper studied her card and slipped it in his pocket. "Please." With a wave of his hand, he offered them the chairs.

"That won't be necessary," Josie said rather archly, no doubt still suffering under the sting of being made fun of. "We won't be here long.

I just need to ask you a few questions. We can start with the horse."

"Horse?" The sheriff looked at her blankly.

"The one Ruben Ashford said killed Constance Prentiss."

"Ah, that horse," Hopper said, remembering. He still seemed to find her faintly amusing.

"You didn't put it in your report," Josie said, bristling. "I want to know why not."

Hopper studied her. Then his expression changed. "I think we'd better sit." He pulled a crate over, sat down, and looked at them gravely.

The story he told was very much the one Nell remembered from his report: the call that came into the Owings Mills office on a Saturday afternoon, the dash in the buggy to the asylum, the discovery of the murderer held at the Great House under guard. Hopper found Ashford distraught, groaning, pacing, pulling at his hair, saying over and over again, "Oh, Lord, Oh Lord, what have I done?" The sheriff managed to calm him down by saying he would see to things. Then he went to the stable where he found Ida Crofter kneeling beside the body of Constance Prentiss. He returned to the Great House, called the coroner, and with the aid of his deputy, who had since arrived, escorted Ashford to the county jail. Two days later he filed his report. That, he assumed, would be the end of it, and so he was much surprised to hear later on that the prisoner wished to speak to him.

"When was that?" Josie said.

"The next day."

"So, Sunday, the first of September."

"Yes. I went in the afternoon, after church."

"And how did you find him?"

Ashford was harried, drawn, with reddened eyes and dry lips, like a man who hadn't eaten or slept for days. He was tense and agitated, verging on panic, sitting on the edge of his bunk, his hands trembling. "Why am I here?" he said when the sheriff came in.

Hopper was surprised to hear it. Ashford struck him as an intelligent man, yet he seemed to have no idea what had happened.

"You're being held for the murder of Constance Prentiss."

"But I didn't do it! I thought you knew. You told me you would see to it." Ashford then launched into his story—in fits and starts; he could hardly speak—of the horse that struck Constance Prentiss dead.

Hopper listened patiently. Then he said gently, "We have two eyewitnesses, Mr. Ashford. Both said they saw you kill Miss Prentiss with a hammer. Neither mentioned a horse."

"Witnesses?" His hand flew to his mouth. "Who?"

"Abram Sledge and Ida Crofter."

"Oh, Lord, oh, Lord." Ashford dropped his head in his hands. When he looked up, tears were streaming down his face, and something vital seemed to have gone out of him. "What do I do now?" he said, his voice hoarse.

Hopper didn't know what to say. He'd seen men undone by their crimes, who expressed genuine sorrow and regret, and others who rejoiced in their perfidy, remaining defiant and unrepentant. He'd never seen anyone like Ashford before. Something about the prisoner struck him as odd, but he couldn't put his finger on it. "You might think of getting yourself a lawyer," he said finally.

"I don't have money for that." Ashford dragged a hand over his face. The tears stopped, and he made a visible effort to control himself, speaking with a deadened resignation. "And I won't burden my parents."

That, Hopper said, was the end of it. He left and never saw Ashford again.

Josie had been leaning forward as she listened, her elbows on her knees, her chin in her hands. She sat upright. "But you didn't put it in your report."

"What?"

"The horse. Why didn't you report it?"

"There was nothing *to* report. I had no evidence for it. The only conclusion I could make was that Ashford was lying."

"Only he didn't strike you as the kind of man who would lie, did he?"

"No," Hopper said slowly. "He didn't." He ran a finger along his chin. "Later that week I heard he'd confessed. When I met with Norbert Richards, I told him about the horse. It was the best I could do."

Was it? Nell wondered. When a man's life was on the line? When the *truth* was on the line? "Could someone have gotten to Ashford in the meantime?" she said. "Persuaded him—even forced him—to confess?"

Hopper raised his eyes to the ceiling. Then he slowly shook his head. "I can't imagine it. I've known Alfred Sloane—the county clerk—for a long time. He'd never countenance a thing like that."

Josie flushed with anger. "But a few years ago a black man was lynched outside that jail for the rape of a white woman. And there were no witnesses in that case and not a single shred of evidence."

Hopper's face tightened. "Sloane had nothing to do with that, and neither did I."

We've lost him, Nell thought. If we ever had a chance to make a difference here, it's gone.

The sheriff came stiffly to his feet. "Good day, ladies." He turned to go.

Josie placed herself in his path. "You said there was something odd about Ashford. What did you mean?"

Hopper hesitated. "I felt sorry for him, if that means anything to you."

"And?" Josie didn't move.

"And I thought—" He appeared to be at a loss for words. His tie seemed to have become too tight, and he lifted a hand to his throat to loosen it.

"You thought he was the least likely person you could imagine committing murder," Josie supplied.

"Yes," Hopper admitted. "That's exactly what I thought."

Twenty-eight

"He knew Ruben Ashford didn't do it," Josie said. "They all did, Foyle and Sledge and Hopper, yet they let him get arrested anyway—they let him get condemned to death—and they did nothing to stop it."

They were on the road to Rosewood, Josie walking ahead with quick, angry steps, while Nell struggled to keep up with her. She understood Josie's frustration, but at the same time couldn't help thinking she was being unreasonable. "What would you have them do?" she asked.

"Tell the truth."

"What truth would that be?" Nell was becoming exasperated. "They thought Ashford was guilty. Everyone did. Sledge only reported what he saw: Ashford attacking Prentiss with a hammer. Maybe you're right and he was mistaken, but he didn't know that. And Hopper went by the evidence. That was his job." Around and around they went, always ending in the same place. "Don't forget Ashford confessed. He told you so himself. That has to mean something—unless you think he's deluded in some way."

"Dr. Meyer said he isn't."

"And you?"

"I don't think so either." Josie kicked at the road. "That's it. I give up. There's nothing else to say—nowhere else to go. I'll speak to Norbert Richards and tell him to abandon the appeal."

"My love." Nell took her arm. "I'm so sorry. I know this isn't what you wanted."

Josie gave her a small smile. "Am I always this stubborn?"

"Always." Nell smiled broadly in return. "And I wouldn't have it any other way."

They walked ahead silently to a crossroads where a small church sat prettily behind a low stone wall, a grey slate roof emerging beneath melting snow, half-buried gravestones dotting a field. Beyond it were the iron gates for Rosewood. They came up the long drive to the Great House at the top of the hill where Dr. Foyle received them. Over hot coffee and biscuits, which Nell unashamedly tore into—it was well past lunchtime, and she was famished—Josie reported what they'd learned about Walter Thursday's mother. Foyle took it all in gravely, promising to make a note in the boy's file and to tell him one day, when the time was right.

"Any news in Ruben Ashford's case?" Foyle asked.

Josie fell silent, considering, and Nell wondered what she might say. But in the end, she just shook her head. "I'm afraid not."

"I'm sorry to hear it. I'd been hoping there might be a change."

"Yes." Josie gave him a quick smile. "So had we all."

Foyle escorted them to the door.

"Do you think we might see Walter before we go?" Josie said.

He seemed surprised at the request, but acquiesced with a brief nod. "Of course."

He directed them to the boys' classroom building, where they found the classrooms empty, but the sound of voices came up a stairwell from below. The basement was a cavernous room with stone walls and a tiled floor that seemed to function as an all-weather gymnasium. A dozen or so boys—'littles', Nell knew, from Josie's description—stood in orderly lines, passing a ball from one to the other, as a teacher stood by watching, her hair pulled into a severe bun. Nell scanned the boys, wondering which one of them might be Walter, when all at once a boy broke free and ran to them.

Lauren Small

"Miss Josie!"

"Hullo, Walter." She bent down to receive him in her arms.

"Now, Walter, you know better than to leave the group," the teacher said, frowning. She came over to take him by the arm. "So sorry," she said to Josie, as Walter's face fell.

Josie smiled. "It's quite all right. Walter and I are old friends. Dr. Foyle said we might have a visit."

"And that," Walter said, grinning with triumph and wriggling free, "means to the horses."

He scampered ahead, leading them out of the building and down a muddy path that wound down the long hill to the farm: a herd of cows huddled along the banks of an icy creek, the spicy smell of curing meat rising from a smokehouse, pigs lying in pens. In the distance older boys were working, bent over hoes in barren fields. Others chopped wood or loaded it onto a sled pulled by horses. One day, Josie said, Walter would have to work like that. She worried he wouldn't survive it. Nell could well understand why. Walter was engaging and charming, but he was also thin and frail, with pale skin and dark circles under his eyes, the kind of child, Nell knew, who might fall sick easily and had little reserve. She was sorry now they hadn't been able to find better news about his mother. Children like Walter thrived best with special care—the kind of care, she imagined, Rosewood would have difficulty supplying.

At least Walter seemed perfectly happy now, chattering brightly as he led them to the stable, his hand tucked securely in Josie's. Most of what he said sounded like nonsense to Nell—a smattering of lines from nursery rhymes and songs—but Josie listened intently, interjecting, "Is that so?" or "You don't say," from time to time. Nell was struck by how comfortable they looked together, how light and easy. Somehow the two had forged a bond. Maybe it was because Josie had finally given up on Ruben Ashford's case, but it had been a long time since she had looked so free.

In time they came to the stable, a low, timbered building sitting in the farmyard. Nell hesitated before entering, but Walter rushed blithely ahead, full of good cheer. Inside she came to a halt, waiting for her eyes to adjust to the darkness. Gradually she made out a long aisle with stalls on either side, fading away into the gloom. The air felt close and warm, heated by the bodies of the horses, laden with the sweet smell of alfalfa and molasses. Once her grandfather had worked in a stable just like this. She remembered him filing the teeth of a plough horse. The horse had been uncooperative, tossing its heavy head and stamping its broad feet, until finally he had tethered it with cross-ties, chains that stretched on both sides from the horse's halter to the walls. When he pushed back the heavy lips to reach the back teeth, it looked to Nell as if the horse were grinning.

Nell felt uneasy, but Walter was clearly in his element. He seemed to know all the horses, just as they seemed to know him. He skipped ahead, pulling Josie along with him, greeting each one by name, delivering pats to their heads and rubs to their muzzles. They responded by stretching out their necks, lowering their noses to sniff at the top of his head and to lip gently at his hands. As Nell followed behind, she noticed a stable hand, a colored man with grizzled hair in sturdy overalls and boots, at work at the far end of the aisle, grooming a horse, lifting each hoof in turn to clean it. Could this be Sledge? No, Josie had said he was much younger. The horse was wearing a halter with a lead line at his chin dangling loosely to the floor. "Hello, little fellow," the groom said as Walter approached. He bent down to speak to the boy eye to eye. "Would you like to help me out?" Walter nodded eagerly, and the groom handed him a brush. "Gentle but thorough," he said in a serious tone. "Come around here now. We always work from the horse's left side."

Walter applied himself with diligence, vigorously brushing the horse's legs and sides as far up as he could reach, while the groom looked on with approval. As Walter worked, the groom sighed and sat down heavily on an overturned bucket, clearly glad to take a load off his feet. He was chatty too, and seemed to enjoy their company, engaging Josie and Nell in idle talk, asking them what brought them to Rosewood.

Josie smiled at Walter. "We're just here visiting our friend."

"Now, now," the groom said with a smile. "Friends and family. That's what makes living good."

The horse stood quietly, submitting easily to the boy's ministrations. Nell's spirits lifted as she watched him at work. Maybe Walter could have a future with horses. That at least would be something.

All at once the horse swung its head to the side, nipping at its flank. The lead line followed, snapping dangerously in the air. "Whoa, there, Bridger!" the groom called out, leaping to his feet. He grabbed the line and steadied the horse. No harm done; Walter was safely on the horse's other side, nowhere near the rope. But the groom was full of remorse. "You all right there, young fellow?" he said. Then he turned to Nell and Josie. "Sorry about that." He stayed on his feet, holding onto the line, muttering to himself, "Sure do need to fix those cross-ties."

The cross-ties chains were broken, dangling from the walls. Nell walked over and picked one up, weighing it in her hands. "How long have they been like this?"

"A while now," the groom admitted. He seemed reluctant to say more, no doubt embarrassed by his negligence, or afraid they would report him for endangering the boy. "I should have gotten to it. I meant to, I just kept forgetting. And Bridger here doesn't usually cause me any trouble." He scolded the horse affectionately. "Do you now?"

The horse snorted in answer.

Josie had taken a sudden interest in the broken chains. "A while?" she said. "Exactly what do you mean by that?"

The groom shook his head. "I can't tell you how many times I said to myself, fix those cross ties before someone gets hurt."

"Please," Josie said. "I don't mean anything by it. I just need to know."

"Last summer," the groom said finally. "We had a bit of a—a bit of a problem here. The ties got broken then."

Josie let the chain drop. "Thank you." She nodded to herself. "Just as I thought." She reached out to take Walter's hand. "Come along, Walter." Then she turned to Nell. "It's time to go. We need to go home, and I need to talk to Ruben Ashford."

Twenty-nine

Once again Josie sat in the interview room of the Baltimore City Jail across the scarred wooden table from Ruben Ashford. It was late in the day, a gloomy evening coming on. Since her trip to Rosewood three days earlier, the weather had changed, settling back into winter, and a viciously cold one at that. The last of the snow had congealed into grimy patches of ice throughout the city, making travel treacherous. Steam laced with soot rose from chimneys, slithered across rooftops, and dropped to the ground in noxious clouds. Inside the jail it felt even colder than outside. Damp from the Jones Falls River, smelling of sewage, seeped through the walls and froze on the bare, unforgiving stone. The lone tree visible through the window shivered in the wind.

Josie shivered too, despite her warm hat and woolen coat. Ashford was wearing the same prison uniform he'd had on when she met him the first time, the coarse gray cotton jacket and trousers. It wasn't at all fitting to this kind of weather. Either the jail had no winter clothing for its inmates or didn't care to provide it. It had been three months since she saw him last, and the passage of time and the onset of the cold had left its mark. He was even thinner than before, the uniform hanging loosely on his frame. His face was gaunt, the cheekbones pronounced, the eyes sunken into dark shadows. His hair had grown out and fell in uneven hunks over his ears. His skin was ashy, his lips cracked, his eyes bloodshot, his fingers swollen with chilblains. As before, the guard led him into the room, shackled at the ankles and wrists, seated him at the table, then exited. Ashford had yet to meet her eye. But something different hovered in the air between them. Ruben Ashford had grown wary of her. He didn't know why she had come back.

There was no time to waste. His hanging, scheduled for the first of the year, was only ten days away; he would know exactly how many hours and minutes. She came directly to the point. "I know what happened. I know you didn't kill Constance Prentiss. It was the horse, just like you said."

For a moment he sat silently, studying his hands, which rested on his thighs. Then he looked up, and a note of defiance came into his face. "You can't possibly prove that."

"Actually, Mr. Ashford, I can." Speaking slowly now, and deliberately, gaining confidence as she went, she told him what she'd known ever since she stood in the stable beside Nell and Walter, holding the broken cross-tie in her hand—the scene unfolding in her mind like the reel of a moving picture show, replaying over and over again until she became convinced of its rightness.

She saw the stable hunkered low to the ground beneath the oppressive August sun; saw Ashford at work in the gloom and darkness inside, shoeing Dr. Foyle's mare. He had set a coal fire in an iron bin to heat the shoes, and as it burned, he held each shoe in turn over the flames until it was glowing hot, then shaped it with sharp blows of his hammer on the cast iron anvil. The clang of metal on metal reverberated in the air, along with the smoky smell of the burnt hoof trimmings. It was hot, and sweat dripped into his eyes as he worked, so that from time to time he lifted the back of his hand to wipe it away, and it ran in rivulets down his chest, wetting his shirt.

Even under the best of circumstances Foyle's mare was nervous and skittish, but today she was particularly so, bothered by a horsefly, a nasty beast that buzzed at her persistently. She shook her head at it, stamped her feet, and swung her head around to nip at it when it was in danger of alighting on her flanks. It was impossible for Ashford to work in circumstances like that, and finally he secured her to the stable walls with the heavy chains of the cross-ties. Even so she tried to rear, shifting her weight to her hind end, her hooves skittering on the ground, until he gentled her and settled her back down.

He was shaping the mare's last shoe when Constance Prentiss appeared in the gloom at the end of the aisle, coming gaily towards him. This was where Josie's imagination failed her, because she had no idea what he felt when he saw her. Excitement, dread, a mixture of both? Resentment? Anger? Humiliation? Despair? Any or all of these were possibilities. All she knew was that he couldn't have been indifferent. He'd been made vulnerable to her manipulations by months of living and working at the asylum, by the soul-wrenching isolation and back-breaking loneliness that had been imposed on him there solely because of the color of his skin.

Prentiss, on the other hand, had not a care in the world. She walked towards him light and easy and full of good cheer. She had escaped Mrs. Crofton's grasp for the afternoon and was going into Baltimore, she said. Would he drive her to the train station, please? It was too hot for walking, the breeze in the buggy would be so delightful, and he didn't want her to sully her dress in the dust on the road, did he? This last was delivered with a coquettish swirl of her skirt and a tip of her chin, followed by a pretty pout when he asked her to wait while he finished with the mare. But he assured her he was almost done, and she agreed.

"Pretty girl," Prentiss said to the mare, or maybe she meant herself. "Pretty, pretty girl." Bored, forced to wait, she came closer, seeking to amuse herself with the horse.

She was unsettling the mare. "Wait," Ashford said, alarmed, "don't do that, stand back."

But Prentiss wouldn't listen. She laughed and said, "What are you afraid of, Ruben, you're not afraid of me, are you?"

Then the fly bit and the horse screamed and reared up, breaking the chains. For a moment Prentiss looked at the mare complacently as if all this was happening to some one else. Then she realized she was wrong and it was happening to her. As the mare balanced on her hind legs, her hooves pawing at the air, Prentiss's eyes widened in fear, her skin blanched, and she threw up her arms.

It looked as if they were dancing, the pretty white girl and the horse, and for a fraction of a second Ashford thought maybe that was all they were doing, that it would be all right, and they would dance that way forever. But gravity would have its way, just like all the other actions and ideas and beliefs and attitudes that had led up to this moment—actions of cruelty, indifference, and neglect, which dictated that those with darker skins were less human than their whiter counterparts, were objects to be manipulated for use or pleasure—all of those things had their way, and the horse's hoof came down with a sickening thud on the girl's skull.

Ashes, ashes we all fall down.

"Oh Lord, oh Lord, no, no, no, what have I done."

He fell to his knees beside her as the horse spooked and ran to its stall, the place where it would feel the safest, and where a little boy was hiding, witness to it all. The hammer fell from Ashford's hand into the blood that had already begun to pool on the ground as he lifted her up, cradling her in his arms, her blood mingling with his sweat, while Abram Sledge came running.

Josie had finished speaking. Ashford said nothing as she delivered her tale, neither confirming nor denying it, but from the way he looked at her, she knew it was true, or if not exactly true, then true enough.

"What I don't understand," she said softly, "is why you said 'what have I done'? It wasn't your fault. You'd done nothing."

"I should have kept her away." He spoke quietly, but she could hear the strain in his voice as he endeavored to control himself. "I let her come too close."

"You mustn't blame yourself. She wouldn't have listened to you." Josie stood up and walked to the window, contemplating the bare, black limbs of the tree, caught in the desolation of winter. Then she turned to face him. "You didn't kill her. You're innocent. You know it. *I know it*. It's time to let the rest of the world know it too."

He didn't speak.

"You have to stop this—this charade. Recant your confession. I'll speak to Norbert Richards. I'll tell him what I know. He'll file the appeal. It will give us time and then—"

"No."

It was such an unexpected—such an impossible response—she was sure she hadn't heard him right. "No? What do you mean, 'no'? It's the only chance we have to save your life."

"No." The word was spoken more firmly now. "Don't you see? It won't matter."

"It will if I tell them. They'll see the truth." Even as she said it, she knew he was right, and they wouldn't. But she wasn't willing to admit it. She wouldn't give up. "I'll *make* them see it."

"With what evidence? A broken chain? Anything could have broken that chain. *Anything*." He looked at her meaningfully. "They don't have to believe it." Ashford smiled sadly at her, and Josie's heart broke. He was comforting her. In the midst of it all, with death facing him, he was worried about her feelings.

She sat back down and leaned towards him across the table. "Tell me why you confessed. Tell me why you changed your story."

"They were going to hang me no matter what I said." He lifted his chin. "I decided to let them get on with it."

"That can't possibly be," she said desperately. "You can't let them destroy you like this. You deserve to live. You haven't done anything wrong. You must recant. I'll tell Mr. Richards what happened." She was scrambling now, trying to keep the tears from coming. She didn't want to embarrass herself—or him. "I'll tell Dr. Meyer. He'll know what to do."

"They were going to hang me from the beginning. They were going to hang me before they even knew me. It's all they know to do." He held his empty, shackled hands out to her. "I have two hundred and thirty-two hours left." He closed his eyes for a moment, calculating. "One thousand three hundred eighty minutes. I've been here long enough. I told you from the beginning not to do this. I told you I'd made up my mind." His voice had grown hoarse, whether from anguish or anger she couldn't tell. "I'm asking you to let me be. You and Norbert Richards too."

Her tears were falling freely now, blinding her, so that when she reached out and took his hands, she couldn't even see what she was doing. All she knew was the warmth of his skin against hers. She held on tightly, clinging to him so desperately, he had to struggle to free himself. But at last he did.

He stood and called out, "Guard!" Then the door opened, and he was gone.

Josie was still shaking when she left the jail, clutching her handkerchief. She was too overcome to think and broke her own rule, taking the streetcar for white riders home. She didn't mean to do it; her feet took her like an automaton to the North Avenue stop, and when the streetcar came, like an automaton she boarded.

Night had come on while she sat with Ruben Ashford in the jail, a dreary fog with sleet falling. Outside black people waited in the biting cold, shivering with their backs turned to the wind as the white streetcar came and left. But inside the car it was warm and cheery, the atmosphere filled with good fellowship. After years of war and epidemic, years of sickness, turmoil, and death, peace and health had finally returned to the city. The holidays were upon them, and the new year was only days away. Joy suffused the faces of the white riders, imbuing them with a happy camaraderie, the kind that came to people who congratulated themselves on being warm inside while others of darker skin were shut outside in the cold. Josie was surprised to find herself succumbing to the feeling. How easy, how seductive it was to slip into that warm, peaceful, comfortable white world! And she was tired of fighting; she was so, so tired. Did she really want to spend the rest of her life waiting in the cold for colored streetcars? For what?

It was time to admit she would never make a difference, not in this world. If nothing else, Ruben Ashford had taught her that.

A man sitting across from her tipped his hat to a young woman with a smile, then stood and offered her his seat. She responded with a flirtatious flip of her hair as she sat. Beside her a grandmother cooed as she played patty-cake with a baby on her lap. Two girls put their heads together, laughing and whispering about the kind of things young girls laugh and whisper about. Not a single person looked outside the car as it rattled steady westwards in the cold night; not a single person noticed the colored people standing outside in the wind and in the sleet.

Enough, Josie thought, and then, whispering, "Enough." Then without thinking—without even knowing what she was doing—she leapt to her feet, and as the people in the car opened their mouths in shock and surprise, she shouted at the top of her lungs, "Enough, enough, enough!"

Thirty

"I've been thinking," Josie said.

"Yes, my love?" Nell was glad to hear it. Ever since the evening two days before, when Josie had returned from seeing Ruben Ashford, she'd been uncharacteristically quiet, leaving Nell in the dark. All she'd said was that she'd confirmed Ashford's innocence but had been unable to convince him to recant his confession. Something seemed to have broken in her; Nell could see it in her eyes, in the slump in her shoulders, in the helpless way her hands hung by her sides, empty and limp. Josie hadn't gone into work, and had sat for hours in her upstairs office, staring into nothingness. She'd hardly eaten and Nell knew for a fact that she hadn't slept. Nell had never seen her like this before. Now, as they drove down Roland Avenue in a horse-drawn carriage, on their way to Nell's parents for a holiday dinner, Nell hoped Josie would say more, unburdening herself, giving Nell an inkling of what was wrong with her—an inkling of how she might help restore her to herself.

"I was remembering the last time I took this road," Josie said. She spoke quietly, and distantly, as if from a dream. "I was going to the Bryces' house, to investigate Evangeline's illness. That was only three months ago, but it feels like a lifetime. Look how much has changed since then. The war has ended; influenza has come and gone. Look how much I have changed! I was so happy then—so excited to be in a motorcar—and so confident I would make the difference I wanted in the world. Then I met Norbert Richards." She gave Nell a sad smile. "Now I hardly recognize the person I was then."

The streetlights lining the avenue glittered in the wintry air, casting a silvery light on trees and bushes, porches and rooftops. The warmth of the woolen blanket on their laps, coupled with the steady beat of the horses' hooves and the huffing of their breath, brought a feeling of intimacy to the night. Nell took Josie's hand. "You are still the person I love."

Josie gave her a wan smile. "I've come to a decision. I've decided that I will speak to Mr. Richards. I need to tell him the truth, that Ashford is innocent. By all rights, Richards should drop the appeal. Ashford is correct. We have no definitive proof of his innocence. And on the small chance that it succeeds—and he receives a life sentence—we will only increase his suffering. But I'm going to do my best to persuade Richards to pursue it anyway. Even if he fails, he will have made the attempt, and that has to count for something." She turned her head. "Someone once said to me something about sacrificing foot soldiers for the greater good of the war. I didn't understand him then, but I do now. Experience has hardened me."

Josie was trying to project an air of confidence, but Nell had a feeling she wasn't at all sure. "And yet?"

Josie sighed. "And yet this is precisely the fight Ashford won't have." She ran her fingers along the edge of the blanket. "For the first time in his life, he has stood up and said 'no.' He has wrested his life from the hands of his accusers and become the agent of his own destiny. He has found his voice. Who am I to deny him that?"

"Even if it means his death?"

"Even so," Josie said softly. "Ruben Ashford has made his choice and now I must make mine. How strange to find myself in this place. After all I've said about the choices people make—after all the research I've done—it turns out the final choice comes down to me, and I have no idea what—or even how—to decide. There is value on either side, the pursuit of justice against the wishes of one solitary man."

"Take heart." Nell touched her cheek. "When the time comes, you will know what to do."

They arrived at Nell's parents' house, descended from the carriage, and instructed the driver to return for them later. It had been over three years since her parents had moved to Roland Park, but Nell still had trouble imagining them here. She had no idea how her mother satisfied her love for the social stage in the comparative quiet of the suburbs, or how her father coped with the free time brought by his retirement. Yet she had to admit they seemed happy here. The house was pretty in its own way, a brown-shingled cottage surrounded by boxwood gardens, a wisp of smoke emerging from the chimney. The roses and irises in her mother's garden were hidden now in the snowy soil, but would emerge in the spring with glorious color.

She led Josie up the flagstone path to the broad front porch, which had ample room for sitting in the warmer months, and rang the bell. She didn't recognize the colored woman who came to the door; Martha, her parents' usual maid, must have been out. Nell tried to introduce herself, but the woman just dropped her eyes shyly, took their coats, and showed them to the parlor where Letitia and Mercer were sharing drinks with another couple.

"Francine and Fordham Elliott," Mercer said, making the introductions. "The Elliotts are new to the neighborhood. My daughter, Nell."

"And this is Miss Berenson, Nell's boarder," Letitia added hastily, with a glance at Mercer as if confirming something that had been previously decided upon. The Elliotts seemed a bit nonplussed to hear it; people didn't usually invite their boarders to family dinners. But they covered their surprise nicely and shook Josie's hand.

Nell glanced anxiously at Josie; she knew how impetuous—and quick to anger—Josie could be. But Josie said nothing, accepted a glass of sherry from the maid, and took the chair Mercer directed her to, even though—in keeping with her presumed status as a boarder—it was a bit outside the circle of family and friends. She even maintained her silence when Letitia opened the conversation by addressing Nell as if Josie weren't even there. Josie must be too preoccupied with Ruben Ashford to notice how the Winters were slighting her. Or perhaps she'd decided to keep the peace on Nell's behalf. Either way, Nell was grateful. The last thing she wanted was an argument with her parents, especially in front of their neighbors.

The Winters' parlor was conducive to intimate gatherings, chairs and sofas drawn in a cozy circle around a lively fire. For a time the conversation centered on the usual things, the end of the epidemic and the war. Francine, a portly woman with a powdered face and long strand of pearls, was quite chatty, her husband, less so; he sat silently with a severe expression on his face as if he found such gatherings tiresome and much preferred a quiet evening at home. Nell was glad to see her parents looking well. Letitia looked attractive as always, wearing a cream silk dress with turquoise beads, her auburn hair coiffed to perfection. She was quite animated, gesturing broadly with manicured hands, enjoying this opportunity to command a social setting. Mercer, in a dapper tweed sport coat, looked on admiringly at his wife, punctuating her conversation with a ready laugh. But Letitia tut-tutted over her daughter, saying she still looked pale and thin after her bout of illness.

"Yes," Nell said. "Josie says the same thing." Then, turning to her, "I don't know how I would have made it through if you hadn't taken care of me."

Mercer cleared his throat. "Miss Berenson is from Boston," he said to the Elliotts.

"Is that so?" Fordham said with the air of someone who felt compelled to say something.

"Any relation to the Winfield Berensons?" Francine said. She turned to her husband. "The Winfield Berensons are from New England, aren't they, dear?"

"Philadelphia," Fordham said with a frown as if he often faced the onerous burden of correcting his wife's mistakes.

"Of course, silly me," Francine said, giving a little laugh. Then, to Josie, "Boston must be so interesting."

But apparently it wasn't so interesting after all, because no one said anything more about it, and the talk swirled once again among Nell, the Elliotts, and the Winters, leaving Josie out.

The Elliotts were quite interested in Nell's work as a doctor. That formed the nexus of the conversation as the group sat down to dinner. The maid returned to serve and clear the courses, summoned by a little bell Letitia kept at her elbow. Nell found herself next to Francine, with Josie once again seated a bit apart. "Josie works at the Johns Hopkins Hospital," Nell said at one point, trying to draw her in.

"How unusual," Francine said, but what she meant by that was never explained. Instead the conversation returned to the war, with Fordham venturing a rare comment to say their son, Randall, who was a major in the army, would be coming home soon. "And about time, too," Francine said. "Randall's boys have practically been orphans ever since he went overseas."

"Orphans?" Nell said.

"Randall's wife died in childbirth just before he deployed."

"Oh, dear," Nell said. "I'm sorry to hear it."

"But you must come over after Randall returns," Francine said with a brave smile, reaching over to press Nell's hand. "He would be so glad to meet you."

Nell colored and dropped her eyes but Letitia spoke up. "Of course, she will. She will be glad to. We will both come together."

Coffee was taken at the table, served by the maid, although Letitia had to call her back twice, first for the spoons and then for the cream and sugar. "I just can't seem to manage without Martha," she said, with the sigh of one undergoing extreme deprivation. "Why she had to go to North Carolina just now to visit her mother, I can't imagine."

"Servants," Francine said with a sympathetic look. "I know how difficult they can be. Just when you get one trained properly, they leave and you have to start all over again."

Fordham must have found this talk of servants tiresome, because he spoke up and changed the topic back to Nell. "Are all your patients in Baltimore, Dr. Winters?"

"Yes," Nell said with a smile. "I'm afraid I haven't wandered far from my roots. I still live in the house I grew up in, and I see my patients there too, in a clinic I run on the first floor."

"And you haven't thought of leaving the city?" Francine said. She gave a light laugh. "Fordham and I held out longer than most, then became refugees like the rest." She and Letitia exchanged meaningful looks.

"I can't tell you how many times I've asked Nell the same thing," Letitia said. Then to her daughter, "Honestly, dear, I can't understand why you won't move. You would be such a success here. So many people in Roland Park have said they would love to have you as their doctor, if only it were more convenient."

"Indeed, Dr. Winters," Francine said, "I wonder how you manage in Baltimore at all. It's become so unpleasant lately. The water, the air, that awful smell from the harbor." She wrinkled her nose. "Every time I go into the city, I can't seem to escape it. And look at how many people died there in the epidemic. Surely, as a physician, you must agree life is much healthier in the country."

Before Nell could answer, Mercer spoke up. "The fact of the matter is, Baltimore isn't safe anymore. People used to get along with one another. They don't anymore." He gave Nell a meaningful look. "I'm not ashamed to say I don't like you living alone like you do. I don't like it at all."

Josie kept her eyes on her coffee cup and said nothing, but Nell was becoming increasingly angry. "I'm not alone," she said pointedly.

But no one acknowledged that. Instead Francine turned to Mercer. "If I had a single daughter in the city, I would worry, too." Then she turned back to Nell. "I'm sure it isn't easy to think of leaving the home you grew up in. No doubt you have many happy memories there. But you would be closer to your parents if you moved north.

And I can only imagine how hard it must be to work there, especially if you have to take in boarders to make ends meet."

Everyone seemed surprised to have Josie mentioned—as if they'd forgotten she was there. As they turned to her, she opened her mouth, but before she could speak, Nell rushed ahead. "I—" she said.

Mercer didn't let her finish. "The problem with Baltimore is its Negro population," he said, forging ahead on a topic he clearly had strong opinions on. "Everyone knows it, even if they won't say so. Colored people used to know where they belonged. They don't anymore. The rules have changed, and it's no good for anyone. Mark my words. If this, this—integration—keeps up, the city will break down entirely."

Once again Nell tried to speak, but all at once Josie spoke up. "Perhaps," she said evenly to Nell's father, "if people like you and your friends weren't so averse to living in mixed neighborhoods, the city would hold together quite nicely."

Francine's hand flew to her mouth. Letitia reddened. Mercer looked furious. But Fordham lowered his eyes with a small smile as if the evening had suddenly become quite bearable after all.

"How dare you," Mercer said furiously, "in my house—"

Nell leapt to her feet. "That will be all," she said, holding up her hand and silencing him. She turned to the Elliotts. "I'm afraid my parents have misinformed you. Miss Berenson isn't my boarder. She's my companion, the woman I love and plan to spend the rest of my life with." To her parents, she said, "As far as Baltimore is concerned—we won't discuss it again. I won't be leaving the city, but if I did, it's a decision Josie and I would make together."

There was a moment of shocked silence. Josie had lowered her eyes, but Nell saw a small smile playing at the corner of her lips. Then Fordham spoke up. "Bravo, Dr. Winters." He eyed Nell with approval. "You are exactly the kind of doctor anyone with an intelligent thought in their head would want for themselves." He turned to Francine. "Unfortunately that excludes my wife."

Francine looked as if she would say something—if only she could think of something to say. She was spared when the maid came in to clear the table. "Thank you," Nell said to the maid. Then, "I'm sorry. I didn't get your name when I came in."

The maid looked at her in surprise. "Rosemary."

"Rosemary…?" Nell said.

"Rosemary Brigham."

"So nice to meet you, Miss Brigham," Nell said. She shook the maid's hand. "Thank you for a most lovely evening. I'm afraid Miss Berenson and I have to go now, but please don't bother yourself. We'll show ourselves out."

Nell and Josie stood on the side of the road in front of the Winters's home, shivering in the cold. They had left earlier than planned and now had to wait for the carriage. Nell was miserable. "How could I have done—" she said. Then, "I'm sorry. This is all my fault." Then, reddening with anger. "But how I sat there so long and let them humiliate you like that—I will never—"

"Shh," Josie said. She took Nell's face in her hands. "Don't blame yourself. The evening was quite enlightening. And Fordham Elliott—he was rather nice. I wouldn't mind seeing him again."

Nell smiled. "Nor I." Then she laughed. "But his wife!"

Josie laughed, too. Then she grew serious. "How brave you are, to tell your parents the truth about us. I've never spoken to my parents that way." She gave Nell a rueful smile. Nell saw a renewed spark of life in her eyes—a flame of determination. "Telling the truth ought to be the easiest thing in the world, so why is it so difficult? I've been thinking about that—not just about us—but about Ruben Ashford, too. You taught me something tonight, dear heart. Tomorrow I will see Norbert Richards, and I will need to be brave, too."

Thirty-one

"I've come to tell you I've finished my investigation," Josie said to Norbert Richards early the next morning. "I'm afraid I don't have the answer we were hoping for. I was unable to find any reason for Ruben Ashford to kill Constance Prentiss."

The lawyer eyed her gravely from across his desk. His office was in even more disarray than usual, if that were possible. Boxes and crates, some sealed and others half-packed, stood in heaps around the room. The bookshelves had been emptied; piles of papers and folders littered the floor. It looked as if the occupant were on the verge of fleeing. The chair Josie had sat in the previous time she visited Richards had disappeared, leaving her to perch on the edge of a crate for the duration of their conversation. One thing had remained unchanged: it was just as cold inside as outside, and she shivered as she drew her coat closer around her.

"I read all the documents you sent me," she said, "and spoke to Mr. Ashford twice, once last October and again just recently. I went to Rosewood, interviewed both eyewitnesses, spoke with Aubrey Foyle, and surveyed the stable where Miss Prentiss died. I even heard from Mr. Ashford's parents through a"—she hesitated—"an intermediary. No one said anything to me that might indicate a motive for the crime."

"That is indeed a disappointment."

"Yes, I agree. I know you had high hopes for Mr. Ashford's case."

Richards shuffled a paper from one pile to another. "You said you saw Ashford recently. How did you find him?"

"He's suffering. But I believe he's reconciled to his fate. Everett Crane told me so when I met him last fall. There's some comfort in that."

"Perhaps," Richards said, although he seemed unconvinced.

Josie gestured at the boxes. "Are you leaving us?"

The lawyer's face creased in his particular grimace-smile. "If by us you mean Baltimore, then no. But I will be leaving this office. I've been asked to work for the National Association for the Advancement of Colored People."

"The National—what?"

"An organization devoted to achieving justice for black people. They opened an office in Baltimore not too long ago. Perhaps you might consider joining us. We could use someone with your investigative skills, your insight into human psychology." He studied her. "Not to say your ability to speak truthfully even while guarding the truth."

Josie colored.

"So you were unable to convince Mr. Ashford to change his mind," Richards said.

"I'm afraid so." She looked down at her hands then raised her eyes to him directly. "Am I to understand you knew he was innocent all along?"

"Knew?" Richards shook his head. "I wouldn't go so far as that. But suspected? Yes, most surely." He ran a hand along his chin. "Most men who commit violent murder have a reason for doing so. It seemed odd to me Mr. Ashford didn't. In any case, I was unable to budge him from his position. I thought it was worth letting someone else have a try. Dr. Meyers agreed. It's a shame that in the end…" His voice trailed off. "Well. Failure, I'm afraid, is something one must always be prepared for in this line of work."

"It was an accident," Josie said. "Just like Mr. Ashford said. A horse struck Miss Prentiss and she died. But no one believed him. No one would ever believe him. He came to understand that. In the end he decided to take his destiny into his own hands."

"Ah." Richards nodded with a heavy sadness.

"Under the circumstances, I know it's difficult, but I'd like you to file the appeal anyway. I can share with you Mr. Ashford's story, the evidence such as I have."

"Even though he's against it."

She lifted her chin. "Yes, even so. Ruben Ashford will hang, no matter what we do. He's right about that. He knew it from the beginning. Filing the appeal won't change his fate. But if nothing else, it will strike a blow for the truth, maybe even for the justice you so ardently seek, and that has to be worth something."

Richards nodded. Then he stood. "Thank you, Miss Berenson. I hope this will not be the last time we meet."

"As do I." Josie stood and took his hand. She had become transformed. For the first time in her life she understood what it was like to be a material in her father's laboratory, changing from one thing to another, revealing an entirely new state of being. She was like a liquid hardening into gel, a powder bursting into flame. "Good-bye, Mr. Richards, and Godspeed."

Thirty-two

Two days after Ruben Ashford's appeal was denied, his hanging day came. That morning a cold rain fell. It sluiced down roof tops, collected in gutters, melted the last of the snow and ice on sidewalks and streets, and turned the alleyways where the colored people lived into sloughs of mud and grime. The locomotives on the B & O railroad line crept through the city, slick and gleaming, emerging and disappearing in the mist. Foghorns sounded on ships in the harbor; around them the dark waters steamed. The lower reaches of Fell's Point flooded, causing damage and inconvenience to hundreds of residents and commercial establishments alike. In saloons and bars and rooming houses the floorboards warped and groaned; dirt washed free from the cobblestones, leaving the streets naked and rutted. In later years most people, if they remembered this sixth day of January 1919 at all, remembered it for the unusual winter rains that caused widespread flooding. Hardly anyone remembered it for the death of one more innocent black man at the hands of the justice system, which was not unusual at all.

With the advent of the new year, Nell's practice saw a slight uptick in influenza cases. Fortunately the virus seemed to have moderated since the fall into a less deadly version of itself, and all of her patients recovered. Nevertheless, the resurgence was worrisome. She wasn't concerned about herself, as no doubt she was immune, but she worried a great deal about Josie and Esme and James. She had the feeling flu would never completely leave them, and in one form or another, would be something they would have to live with forever.

In other respects her clinical practice remained the same, although she instituted one important change. She closed the kitchen door to patients. From now on everyone, black or white, would come and go through the front door equally, and those who didn't like it could find themselves another doctor. A few did, but to her surprise, the change in policy garnered her new patients as well. One of these was Fordham Elliott, who came to see her for headaches. Living with Francine, Nell imagined as she prescribed aspirin powders, would be a strain on anyone. Esme Dubois smiled when Nell told her about the new policy in a way that made her feel as if the change were long overdue. "You could have said something to me earlier," Nell grumbled, but Esme didn't answer, preferring to keep her thoughts to herself. The only thing she insisted on was that her kitchen remain open to anyone who needed a hot meal, and on this, they agreed.

The night before the hanging, Nell slept fitfully. Josie slept not at all, remaining sequestered in her office, emerging before dawn, pale and drawn but resolute. Nell had wondered if Josie might waver in her determination to witness Ruben Ashford's death, but there was no wavering for Josie. The two women dressed silently in the half-dark then crept downstairs so as not to wake Esme, only to find her already awake and waiting for them in the kitchen with hot coffee on the stove. She pressed steaming cups into their hands and insisted they drink, then accompanied them to the front door and stood watching on the steps, a sentinel figure, as they walked away. There would be no riding streetcars today; Nell and Josie would approach the jail on foot, like penitents. Without saying a word about it, both agreed.

McCulloh Street was quiet and asleep at this time of the morning, although a lone pony cart, the driver's face obscured by the mist, clattered by. Josie and Nell walked south, their hats and cloaks dripping with rain. At Preston Street they turned east and headed across the Jones Falls, whose muddy, overburdened waters churned and swirled. Nell found herself thinking once again of the school lesson she'd learned years ago about the Baltimore divide, the land that stretched between the Jones Falls and Gwynn Falls rivers. No doubt her teacher wanted the idea to be a positive one, bringing a sense of belonging to the children: we are all in this together. But experience had taught Nell something else entirely, about how deeply riven her hometown was and no doubt would remain. The Baltimore divide, she understood now, was a wound that never fully healed. Living with it left her feeling vulnerable and tender and tough all at once.

Now and then, as they walked, she stole a glance at Josie, whose eyes were fixed firmly forward, her lips pressed together in a grim line. Josie was right; she had changed. Nell hardly recognized her from the giddy, reckless, impulsive woman she'd met a year and a half ago on the Cape. Josie no longer talked of changing the world; instead she approached life as the arduous practice, despite the odds, of setting one foot in front of the other. That, Nell had come to believe, was the true meaning of hope.

A few days after her meeting with Norbert Richards, Josie had gone to see Dr. Meyer. She didn't tell Nell everything they spoke of, but Nell had the feeling the conversation ranged far from Ruben Ashford. Afterwards Josie had closed herself in her office and had written a long letter to her mother. And then, most surprising of all, she'd informed Nell she was leaving the Phipps Clinic for a new position at the National Association for the Advancement of Colored People. Nell had heard of the NAACP before; one of her patients, a young boy from the neighborhood named Thoroughgood Marshall, often spoke of it. He was bright and engaging with a penetrating intellect, and Nell had no doubt he would go far. At first Nell found Josie's decision surprising, but ultimately decided it wasn't surprising at all. Given the new person Josie had become, the NAACP was the sensible choice. Josie seemed to have finally solved the research question that had bedeviled her ever since Nell had met her—or at least, if not solved it, come to an understanding. So many of the choices we make, she said to Nell, and above all the most important ones—including the people we choose to love—defy all attempts at explanation, and remain at their heart, like the fraught human beings we are, forever elusive and imbued with mystery.

By the time they reached the east side, the city had come awake. Despite the cold and wet and early hours, a crowd had already gathered outside the jail. Most were men, white working class from the looks of them, although some had brought wives and children too, making the hanging a family affair. In the shelter of the walls, a group of colored women, their arms around one another's waists, swayed softly and sang hymns. Nell feared Violet Ashford might be among them, but she wasn't. It was just as well. No doubt the Ashfords had left Baltimore by now and if not, Nell sincerely hoped they would stay away. The idea of the parents witnessing their son's death was too excruciating to contemplate.

As Nell and Josie shouldered their way through the crowd, the rain lightened somewhat, although the sky remained heavy and grey, and a cold wind blew. Water ran in runnels down the street, swirling into storm sewers. Someone had set a fire in a steel drum, and several men stood around it, holding their hands out to the smoldering heat. Meanwhile vendors moved through the crowd, hawking food and drink, their voices lending a festive air to the gathering. Beer and spirits flowed freely, and many in the crowd looked drunk already, their faces broadened into sloppy grins, their steps reeling. Some laughed and sniggered and told jokes; two men brawled in a good-natured way, fell down in a heap then helped each other up in a clumsy embrace. What was the hanging of a black man if not a cause for celebration? But others in the crowd were more sullen and surly. "It's about time," someone said, and someone else answered, "The nigger had it coming."

Nell and Josie approached the iron door to the jail, handed the document granting them access to the jailer on the other side, and slipped inside. Silently they followed him through the dank jail corridors to the inner courtyard where a pair of prisoners were putting the finishing touches on a gallows. Hammer blows thudded hollowly against the stone walls as the wooden steps creaked in the wind, and the scaffold rose straight towards the sky, the yardarm with the rope stretching outwards like a deadened limb. From the river wafted the sour smell of sewage and moldering leaves. Their work finished, the prisoners disappeared inside, leaving a dozen or so people standing outside. All of these, except for Josie and Nell, were men, the warden and other judicial functionaries, Nell assumed. To her surprise Dr. Meyer was among them, standing quietly apart in a somber coat and hat, his collar turned up against the rain. Beside him, as weighty and imposing as a block of granite, was a man she took to be Norbert Richards. Both men turned briefly towards Josie and with silent nods acknowledged her presence. Was it Nell's imagination, or did a faint smile cross Meyer's lips when he saw her? As if Josie had finally confessed to him the true nature of their relationship, and he approved.

Josie was shaking. Nell wrapped her arm around her and pulled her close. Then the door to the courtyard opened and the prisoner emerged in shackles, escorted by two jailers. It was the first time Nell had seen Ruben Ashford since he was nine years old. Even at this moment—the moment of his death—she recognized the boy he once was, the one who had stood at the back of the room, overcome with fear and shyness, as she tended to his ailing mother. He stood for a moment in the open air, blinking, looking around in wonderment. Then he raised his eyes to the sky, and as rain washed over his face, his lips worked silently. She had the feeling he was counting in his mind, figuring something out, as if he'd reached the end of a complex calculation and were finally satisfied with the result.

Slowly the jailers escorted him, an unholy trinity with Ruben Ashford at the center, to the gallows. One bent down to unlock the chains at his ankles while the other removed the shackles on his wrists. Then they accompanied him to the top of the platform. Behind them came a man in a clerical collar, who conferred quietly with Ashford then retreated. Next came a man in a sheriff's uniform, so intoxicated he could hardly stand unassisted, who stumbled up the steps and fixed the rope around Ashford's neck. The two jailers descended, leaving Ashford alone with his executioner, who swayed drunkenly on his feet beside the lever to the trap door. A third man, in a bureaucrat's black coat and hat, ascended to the platform and read Ashford's death sentence out loud. A stir came to the witnesses.

Over the years, Nell had seen many people die. She'd dissected corpses, watched people with influenza drown in their own secretions, seen people riddled with cancer contort with agony in their death throes, and watched others grow cold and rigid with the stopping of their hearts. She'd come to believe death held no more mystery for her. But she was wrong. In the end death defeated her. She couldn't watch. But Josie, sweet, brave, uncompromising Josie kept her gaze fixed ahead throughout the execution. Nell had the feeling she was absorbing something, taking it in, setting a cold fire in herself that would never stop burning. Ashford looked down, surveying the onlookers, and as his eyes rested on Josie, a look of recognition crossed his face. A small gasp, like a whimper, escaped Josie's lips. And then the executioner raised his arm, and Nell looked away.

Thirty-Three

Mrs. Charles Forester
226 Commonwealth Avenue
Boston, Massachusetts

March 19, 1919

Dear Adele,

Someone once asked me, "Are you blinded by hope?" At the time I was taken aback by the question, and frankly offended. As a scientist, I always prided myself on my ability to see the world objectively, as it truly was. But the events of the past year have taught me otherwise. To be blinded by hope, I understand now, may very well be a blessing— perhaps the most important one we can have. Without it we have nothing to hold onto, and risk wavering in our resolution to keep moving forward.

I am writing to tell you that I have left the Phipps Clinic for a new position at the National Association for the Advancement of Colored People. The work there is challenging, exhilarating, and exasperating all at once. Also unending. I admit I no longer believe I will make the changes in the world I once so ardently desired. But I am equally unwilling to give up trying.

Last winter I witnessed the hanging of a black man in the courtyard of the Baltimore City Jail. I won't go into details; the image is seared into my memory, and I don't want to burden you with it. I knew the victim—yes, Adele, victim is the right word, because he was innocent. How I came to know him is a story for another day, perhaps when we are together, and have time to spin tales of things that have changed us and given direction to our lives. Since his hanging, two more black men have met their deaths in that same courtyard. The temptation is to let them all blend in together, to fade into the background, to throw up one's hands and say: Such is the world, and what am I to do about it? Perhaps, some would say, a sensible attitude to take. But I have never claimed to be sensible, as you well know. And so I go forward, step by step, day by day.

Spring has finally come to Baltimore. It's such a pretty time of year here. The crocuses and daffodils are blooming, and the azaleas are budding out. After briefly surging again over the winter, the flu epidemic finally seems to be sputtering out. Nowadays Nell sees few patients who are affected, and most of these have mild cases. With the war behind us, we have every reason to be optimistic the future will bring us better things. So, in any case, Nell reminds me daily.

I have some good news to share. In the summer Nell and I will be coming to Boston for a visit. My mother—yes, Adele, she of proper ladyhood—has invited us. Last winter I wrote to her and told her the truth of my relationship with Nell. To my surprise, she accepted it. What wounded her, I see now, was not who I am, but that I felt the need to hide it from her. How delighted I will be to see her and my father, and all of you, Calvin, and Eleanor too. Perhaps when we're together we will raise a glass to Freddie. I miss him still.

When Nell and I come for our visit you will meet the newest member of our family, a sweet tow-headed six-year-old boy named Walter Thursday. Walter has been with us for over a month now, and has brought us such joy, already neither Nell nor I can imagine how we ever managed without him. Of course, we must vie with Esme for his attention, for she is quite taken with him, as he is with her. Despite everything, Adele, I never stopped believing that one day, like you, I would be a mother. Quite selfishly, I admit. That, at least, and my endless vanity, are two traits I admit to holding on to.

Until we see each other again, I remain, with great affection,
Your Josie

Acknowledgments

I would like to thank the Alan Mason Chesney Medical Archives of the Johns Hopkins Medical Institutions for permitting me to consult certain Archives collections when conducting background research concerning Adolf Meyer and the Phipps Psychiatric Clinic. As per Archives policy, no individually identifiable health information from Archives material is published in this work of fiction or forms the basis of any event or encounter described in the book.

In particular I am grateful to Andrew Harrison and Phoebe Evans Letocha for their help in accessing the Chesney Archives. I am also grateful to the Maryland State Archives for their aid in researching this novel.

This novel is a work of fiction, and all of the places, characters, and incidents mentioned in it are either the products of my imagination or are used fictitiously. However, a few have basis in history, such as the Johns Hopkins Hospital and the Rosewood State Training School. Rosewood opened in 1888 as the Maryland Asylum and Training School for the Feeble-Minded and remained in operation for over a century, until it was finally closed in 2009. Adolf Meyer was the head of the Phipps Psychiatric Clinic from its inception until his retirement in 1941. Through her philanthropy and strength of will, Mary Garrett, the B&O Railroad heiress, ensured that the Johns Hopkins Medical School admitted women on an equal basis with men. As city health commissioner, John Blake coordinated Baltimore's response to the influenza epidemic. Thurgood (originally Thoroughgood) Marshall grew up in West Baltimore and would have been a young boy when this book takes place. I like to think of him as one of Nell's patients.

At least forty-three lynchings (the number is continuously revised upwards as more historical information comes to light) took place in the state of Maryland between the 1860's and the 1930's, including two just outside the Baltimore City limits. The Towson lynching represented in this novel is fictional, although some of the details come from the lynching of Howard Cooper in Towson in 1885. In May of 2021, Cooper's murder was finally memorialized with a marker. John Snowden, an Annapolis ice seller, was granted a posthumous pardon in 2001 by Maryland Governor Parris Glendening "to correct a past iniquity," and Governor Larry Hogan issued full pardons to thirty-four other lynching victims in May of 2021.

I am grateful to Mariana Damon, M.K. Graff, Melissa Westemeier, Dawne Allette, Maureen David, Nancy Civin, and Sara Small for their thoughtful readings of this novel in early drafts. Mark Reutter and Antero Pietelo generously shared their deep knowledge of West Baltimore with me. Lynn Taylor guided me into the world of Walter Thursday, and Mary Ellen Kaplan took me on a revealing tour of Bolton Hill. Madeleine Mysko provided essential, and well appreciated, editing. Lynn Jones brought careful attention to proofreading the book.

My gratitude goes to Clarinda Harriss and J.C. Rammelkamp of BrickHouse Books for their enthusiastic embrace of my novel. The talented Ace Kieffer did the beautiful design work. I am also thankful to Mel Berger of William Morris Endeavor for his support of my work.

My deepest thanks go to my family and above all to my husband, Don, for the unwavering confidence and love that sustain me in this and all my writing endeavors.

About the Author

Lauren Small is a writer with a PhD in Comparative Literature. She is an assistant professor in pediatrics at the Johns Hopkins University School of Medicine, where she conducts AfterWards, a program in narrative medicine, teaches in the health humanities, and runs a creative writing group for teens hospitalized on the psychiatry ward.

Small has published fiction, essays, and articles in numerous literary and professional journals. She has also published two novels of historical fiction, has contributed to the On Being blog, and is a Pushcart Prize nominee. She has lectured internationally and presented at numerous regional and national conferences.

The Hanging of Ruben Ashford grew out of her deep love for Baltimore, where she has lived and worked her entire adult life, her passion for social justice, and the extensive research she did into the history of Baltimore, including at the Maryland State Archives and the Alan Mason Chesney Medical Archives at the Johns Hopkins University.